Rebecca blinked. "You want me to take off my clothes?"

Austin opened the armoire beside the big, black satin-covered bed and pulled out a fluffy towel. "You *are* dripping on my floor."

Rebecca glanced down at the puddle her rain-soaked sundress was creating beneath her.

Naked. She was going to be naked in Austin Lucas's house. Her. Little Miss Ordinary, naked with the devil. No one would believe it.

She glanced up—and stared. Austin had stripped off his wet shirt, baring his gleaming chest, and was now unbuttoning his jeans. From where she was standing, it didn't look as if he was wearing anything underneath them.

Rebecca swallowed hard and tried to speak. Nothing.

She urged herself to run for the door. Her feet wouldn't budge.

It would have taken an act of God to move her.

And everyone knew Austin Lucas was the devil....

Dear Reader,

Welcome to Silhouette **Special Edition**...welcome to romance.

Bestselling author Debbie Macomber gets February off to an exciting start with her title for THAT SPECIAL WOMAN! An unforgettable New Year's Eve encounter isn't enough for one couple...and a year later they decide to marry in *Same Time, Next Year*. Don't miss this extraspecial love story!

At the center of Celeste Hamilton's *A Family Home* beats the heart of true love waiting to be discovered. Adam Cutler's son knows that he's found the perfect mom in Lainey Bates— now it's up to his dad to realize it. Then it's back to Glenwood for another of Susan Mallery's HOMETOWN HEARTBREAKERS. Bad boy Austin Lucas tempts his way into the heart of bashful Rebecca Chambers. Find out if he makes an honest woman of her in *Marriage on Demand*. Trisha Alexander has you wondering who *The Real Elizabeth Hollister* is as a woman searches for her true identity—and finds love like she's never known.

Two authors join the **Special Edition** family this month. Veteran Silhouette Romance author Brittany Young brings us the adorable efforts of two young, intrepid matchmakers in *Jenni Finds a Father*. Finally, when old lovers once again cross paths, not even a secret will keep them apart in Kaitlyn Gorton's *Hearth, Home and Hope*.

Look for more excitement, emotion and romance in the coming months from Silhouette **Special Edition.** We hope you enjoy these stories!

Sincerely,

Tara Gavin
Senior Editor

Please address questions and book requests to:
Silhouette Reader Service
U.S.: 3010 Walden Ave., P.O. Box 1325, Buffalo, NY 14269
Canadian: P.O. Box 609, Fort Erie, Ont. L2A 5X3

SUSAN MALLERY

MARRIAGE ON DEMAND

Published by Silhouette Books
America's Publisher of Contemporary Romance

To my stepson, Larry. After a somewhat rocky start, we seem to have found something wonderful together, and I'm grateful for that. I wanted to give you some sage advice about life and living, but hey, I'm still figuring out this journey, as well. I'll always be here for you. Much love.

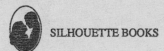 SILHOUETTE BOOKS

ISBN 0-373-09939-8

MARRIAGE ON DEMAND

Copyright © 1995 by Susan W. Macias

Printed in U.S.A.

Books by Susan Mallery

Silhouette Special Edition

SUSAN MALLERY

has always been an incurable romantic. Growing up, she spent long hours weaving complicated fantasies about dashing heroes and witty heroines. She was shocked to discover not everyone carried around this sort of magical world. Taking a chance, she gave up a promising career in accounting to devote herself to writing romances full-time. She lives in Texas with her husband—"the most wonderful man in the world. You can ask my critique group." Susan also writes historical romances under the name Susan Macias. She loves to hear from readers, and you can write to her at P.O. Box 1828, Sugar Land, TX 77487.

AUSTIN'S DECADENT BLACK RUSSIAN CAKE

Cake:
1 package yellow cake mix
1 4 oz package instant chocolate pudding mix
1 cup oil
4 eggs
¼ cup vodka
¼ cup Kahlúa*
¾ cup water

Glaze:
½ cup powdered sugar
2 tbsp Kahlúa*

Cake:
Mix ingredients together and pour into greased and
floured Bundt cake pan. Bake at 350° F for 50 minutes.
Cool for 30 minutes, then take cake out of pan and
glaze.

Glaze:
Moisten powdered sugar with Kahlúa. Add additional
Kahlúa if necessary for correct consistency to drizzle
over cake.

*Sweetened cold coffee may be substituted for Kahlúa.

Chapter One

She'd forgotten how good the devil looked in blue jeans.

Rebecca Chambers stood just inside the garage door, soaking wet. The sound of the storm outside blocked the steady drip-drip from her dress and hair, but she could feel the individual drops collecting on her arms and legs, then falling to the ground. No doubt her mascara had formed perfect half circles under her eyes. She didn't normally wear much makeup, but today she'd taken special pains with her appearance. Her white T-top was silk, and washable, thank goodness. But her loose floral-print jumper was a silk blend that wouldn't survive the drenching. Mud caked her new black flats. She probably looked like something the cat dragged in. Or worse.

She didn't know if God was punishing her for all her ridiculous fantasies, or if the Fates were having a good laugh at her expense. She sighed softly and brushed her wet hair out of her face. Did it matter? For whatever reason, every time she was in the presence of the man in front of her, she made a complete and total fool of herself. She couldn't stop thinking wicked and inappropriate thoughts. They muddled her brain and left her gasping for air and complete sentences. It had been going on for two years. She glanced down at her dripping self and bit back a groan.

Her gaze was drawn away from her bedraggled appearance to the man bent over a car engine and the way he filled his jeans. It wasn't fair, she told herself, staring at the worn denim and the tight rear end that led to illegally long, lean legs. He was going to stand up, turn around and see her. She was going to look like a dripping, homeless rat, and he was going to be gorgeous. He would stare at her with his killer gray eyes and wait for her to speak. If her tongue didn't get tied up in knots, her knees would start shaking. It didn't matter that she was almost thirty years old and a responsible adult.

In the past two years she'd been in the same room with Austin Lucas exactly eleven times. She'd made a fool out of herself twelve times. Once she'd not only knocked over a small table containing the refreshments for the local meeting, but she'd been in such a hurry to escape from his presence that she'd turned without watching where she was going and ran smack into a wall.

She tried not to think about that. Despite the slight chill from her wet clothing and hair, her cheeks were hot with embarrassment. She pressed her hands to her face and wished she had somewhere else to go. But she didn't. He was her only hope. What on earth was he going to say when he saw her?

She glanced frantically around the garage, hoping to find a source of courage. A radio sat on the workbench lining one wall. Soft rock music filled the room. Next to the front left bumper of the car stood a red toolbox on a dingy cart. Nothing very inspiring, although the maleness of the equipment made her feel even more out of place. She was one of three girls and had little experience with guy stuff.

She drew in a deep breath, inhaling the odors of machine oil, wet cement and something that could only be the heady scent of Austin himself. She fought the urge to back up a step. Inside her belly, nerves and expectations joined hands in an uneven dance of hyperawareness. Please, God, why did it have to be him? Around town, women whispered he was as tempting as the devil himself. Heaven knows he tempted her.

She cleared her throat. "Mr. Lucas?"

He chose that moment to drop a wrench and swear loudly. The curses drowned out her words. She opened her mouth to speak again, but he bent down to pick up the tool and his jeans stretched tight across his rear.

Fourteen years ago, Rod Dowell had walked into her sophomore algebra class wearing tennis whites. She'd melted into her school-issue wooden chair and had wondered if she would ever be able to breathe normally again. She finally had, but it had taken almost three years. She'd carried the secret of that crush with her all the way until graduation when she finally found the courage to wish him luck. His brief, "Yeah, you, too," had sent her reeling with excitement.

Now, staring at Austin Lucas, or rather at his long legs and tight, rounded rear end, she could feel her tongue twisting itself into knots and her hands getting sweaty on top of already being damp. It didn't matter that she was far too old for adolescent crushes. It didn't matter that he wouldn't be interested in a woman like her. It didn't matter that she was completely out of her league with him—a peewee ball player trying to compete with a pro. She couldn't resist him, and she couldn't walk away. He was her only hope.

Rebecca squared her shoulders and told herself she had to say something before she shivered to death. She opened her mouth. He spoke before she could.

"How long are you gonna stand there dripping?"

"Not long," she said, her voice shaky. "Another ten minutes or so." She clamped her hand over her mouth, not able to believe she'd actually said that. Her eyes fluttered shut. She wanted to die. She prayed for the cement floor to crack and swallow her whole. The floor didn't budge.

"You can look now," he said, a hint of teasing deepening his already low voice.

Rebecca opened one eye, then the other. Austin stood in front of her, wiping his hands on a dirty rag. He wasn't especially good-looking, she told herself, then wondered why she bothered to lie. It didn't do any good. He wore a faded denim shirt tucked into even more faded jeans. The slashed fabric by his left knee had nothing to do with fashion and everything to do with his life-style. His sleeves had been rolled up to his elbows. The top three buttons of the shirt were undone, exposing just enough chest to threaten her sanity.

Her gaze rose higher past the square jaw and firm mouth—not smiling, of course, for Austin rarely smiled— to hollow cheekbones and a straight nose. His cold gray eyes carefully shuttered all emotions. Thick dark hair had been brushed away from his face. It hung down long enough to scrape the bottom of his collar.

He was handsome as sin. Her gaze flickered to the small gold hoop earring he wore. The delicate circle of gold looked out of place on his totally masculine form. She'd never known a man who wore an earring. The small hoop looked perfect, she thought in defeat. It made her think of pirates and women stolen away for secret pleasures. It made her wonder about his flaunting of convention. It made her think about being in his bed. No doubt she would die of pleasure, but what a way to go. She stiffened her spine and told herself to get a grip. He was just a guy, and the gold hoop was just an earring. Of course Glenwood was a small town and slightly right of the rest of the nation. Men didn't wear earrings here.

But Austin made up his own rules. That was, she acknowledged, part of his appeal. He was the bad boy, the devil in disguise. How could a woman like her be expected to resist that?

"Rebecca?" he said.

The sound of her name on his lips made her toes curl inside her damp, muddy shoes. "Huh?" Eloquent to the last, she thought, fighting back a groan.

"Why are you here?"

She opened her mouth to speak. Nothing came out. She closed it and thought carefully, then tried again. "My car's stuck."

He frowned, his dark eyebrows drawing together. "Okay. Where is your car?"

He was speaking slowly, as if to a half-witted child. She wanted to get indignant and tell him she was perfectly capable of carrying on a conversation. Unfortunately she wasn't. With him she'd never managed more than a sentence or two without some sort of disaster striking. She glanced around the open garage. At least there wasn't anything to break or spill here.

"It's in the driveway," she said, moving out of the room and into the rain. The drenching downpour had slowed somewhat, settling into a steady sprinkle. She felt the drops on her head and shoulders.

He hesitated before stepping out into the open. "Do you want an umbrella?" he asked.

She glanced down at her floral-print dress. It hung loosely, albeit damply, around her body. The long, calf-length skirt was heavy and probably stretching. "I think it's a little late for that, don't you?"

His gaze slipped over her, heating her chilled flesh and sending electric bolts zooming through her blood. When their eyes met, he smiled slowly. "I guess so."

He stepped past her, his worn black cowboy boots squishing in the mud. She stood rooted in place. It wasn't the thick muck that held her so firmly. It was his smile. She'd never seen Austin smile before. Lines had collected by his gray eyes; his teeth had flashed white. The smile had made him look teasingly dangerous, like a wolf pretending to be a lapdog. It had reminded her she was completely out of her element. He was all black leather and five different kinds of sin. She was a babe in the woods, uncomfortable and unwilling to play in the fast lane. He would find her as interesting as flat beer.

She turned on her heel, almost losing her shoe in the process, and started after him. He stood next to her old station wagon. Most of the fake wood paneling had long since cracked and peeled. The side of the car was two-tone, from an accident several years before. The engine had been rebuilt twice, and the vehicle needed new tires.

"You drive this thing?" he asked, staring at it as if he'd never seen anything so pathetic in his life.

"The home owns it," she said. "I don't have a car of my own. There's a bench seat in the back, allowing us to seat five more kids, six if they're small. It's practical."

He glanced at her and raised one eyebrow. She'd never actually seen someone do that. She wanted to see him do it again, but she didn't ask him to. He might not understand.

"Practical or not, it's sure as hell stuck." He walked around the wagon. Each footstep squished in the mud.

His property stood at the far end of Glenwood. He had about ten acres. There was a three-car garage, an oversize, two-story barn and a huge empty house. The house was the reason she'd come calling in the rain.

According to rumors, which she couldn't help but overhear, he was richer than God, had never married and was determined to keep his private life private. Glenwood was too small for him to achieve that. His long-term affairs were well documented by most of the women in town. A stunning redhead driving a white sports car had made biweekly trips through town and down his dusty, unpaved driveway for almost six months. Several times Rebecca had seen her and felt a stab of jealousy. Austin's collection of ladies made men envious and women dream. Rebecca had dreamed, too, even as she'd known it was useless. Austin's women had two things in common: curves and attitude. She glanced down at the wet clothing clinging to her straight, girlish body. She had neither.

He bent over the hood and rocked the car. She watched the muscles bunch in his arms. His shirt was already soaked and clinging to his back and chest. Rain fell on her face and dripped off the end of her nose. In the distance, she heard the rumble of thunder.

"Where are your keys?" he asked.

"In the ignition."

He opened the door and slid into the seat. Within seconds the car started. Dependable as always, she thought, realizing she had a lot in common with the old car. Not very exciting, but they both got the job done.

Austin put it in drive. The wagon rocked forward. He eased on the gas. The wheels spun wildly in the mud. Rebecca jumped back to avoid being sprayed. Her right shoe stuck. She waved her arms in the air to try to maintain her balance. The car engine shut off. She heard squishing footsteps moving toward her but she didn't dare look. She didn't want to see the disgusted or amused expression in his eyes.

She started to go down and was forced to lower her stocking-clad foot into the mud to save herself. The thick cold earth swallowed her up to her ankle.

"Perfect," she muttered.

A warm, strong hand gripped her arm. "You okay?" Austin asked.

She looked up at him. Her dark hair was in the way, so she moved it off of her face. She stared at him, dumbfounded.

Water rolled off his face and onto his chest. Drops slipped down into the open V of his shirt. The cotton clung to him, hugging his tanned skin, outlining his muscles, leaving nothing to her imagination.

She swallowed hard. Where his fingers touched her, she felt individual jolts, as if she'd been hooked up to an electric current. Her breasts swelled inside her damp shirt.

"Rebecca?"

"What? Oh, I'm fine." She glanced down at herself. One foot was in the mud, the other almost as dirty. Her wet and stretched dress flapped in the cold wind. The color from the fabric was bleeding into her white silk T-top. The damp material clung to her chest, outlining her rather pitiful curves. So much for swelling. No one would notice, much less be impressed, she thought, remembering the generous curves of Austin's redhead.

"I think I lost my shoe," she said, pointing to a lump in the mud.

In the distance there was a flash of lightning. "The storm is getting worse," he said. "I can't get the car loose. Kyle's borrowed my truck, and I don't think my car is going to have any better luck in this mud. Come on up to my place and we'll call a tow truck."

"I don't want to be any trouble."

He smiled again. Her heart beat faster inside her chest. "It's a little too late for that."

He released her and bent over to dig through the mud for her shoe. When he'd retrieved the ruined flat, he handed it to her. She took it and stared at the coated leather. It would never be the same again. The fitting end to a lousy week.

He started walking toward an enormous barnlike structure partially concealed by a grove of Chinese maple trees. He didn't bother to look back to see if she followed. She limped along with one shoe on and one shoe off. Thank goodness they were flats. The rain increased its intensity, turning from a steady sprinkle into a downpour again. The temperature seemed to drop considerably, too.

When they reached the brick-bordered cement path, it was easier to keep up with his long-legged stride. Her lone shoe made a squishy noise with each step. Her wet hair flapped in her face. She pulled off her velvet headband and saw it was ruined along with everything else she was wearing. Why hadn't she grabbed an umbrella before she left? No, she thought, shaking her head. That would have required a brain—something she didn't seem to have when it came to Austin.

She glanced at the clipped grass stretching out on both sides of the path, then at the slabs of cement. At anything but the tall, dark and very appealing male specimen right in front of her. It didn't work. Again and again her gaze was drawn back to him.

He walked with an easy loose-hipped grace. His arms swung with each stride. Despite her bedraggled appearance, she couldn't help thinking that if she hurried and caught up with him, their arms might brush and then she—

Stop it! she commanded herself. This was insane. And embarrassing. She was here on a mission and she couldn't forget that. Still, his scent drifted to her and made her think about tangled sheets and bare skin and—

"Oh, my," she whispered, trying to ignore the heat suddenly blossoming in her belly.

"What's wrong?" he asked, stopping and turning toward her.

She almost plowed into him. As it was, she skidded to a stop, the big toe of her one bare foot jabbing painfully into the concrete. "Nothing," she said through gritted teeth, fighting the urge to grab her toe and hop on one foot until the pain faded.

He glanced down at her. She stood five feet eight inches in her stockinged feet. The low shoe gave her a half inch more. She stood eye to eye with a lot of men. Austin topped her by a good seven inches.

"You are the most peculiar woman," he said, then turned away and crossed the last few feet to the door of the barn.

Great, she thought, grumbling. Peculiar. That was romantic. Peculiar. When she wanted to be beautiful, witty, curvaceous, intoxicating. She shrugged. She was never going to be any of those things. Her destiny was to be ordinary. That was the reason Rod Dowell had never noticed her and Austin wouldn't, either. She was the girl next door. Wholesome, innocent, ordinary. Like milk. People took it and her for granted. She wanted to be the dash of cognac at the end of a perfect evening. Instead, she was reserved for pouring over breakfast cereal. It wasn't fair.

Austin cleared his throat. She looked up and saw he was holding open the door, obviously waiting for her to step inside. She ducked in, careful not to slap his legs with the hem of her soggy dress.

The foyer was a small room with no furniture. A big metal door with a window in the top half led to what looked like a large machine shop and laboratory. To the left, stairs curved up to the second floor.

"Up there," he said, pointing to the stairs.

"Up there?" She swallowed.

"Only if you want to get dry."

"Oh. Sure. Thanks."

He lived up there. Alone. Except for the occasional female visitor. Like the redhead.

It wasn't that Rebecca went out of her way to learn things about Austin. She might have a crush on him, but she wasn't completely nuts. Still, people talked, especially about him. No matter how much she tried to slip away or tell herself not to listen, she always heard things, and remembered them.

She gripped the metal railing and started to climb. She could feel the moisture rolling off her and dripping on the stairs. Her footsteps sounded uneven, the clunk of her shoe, the silence of her bare foot.

He was right behind her. She could feel his gaze on her back, heating her. Was he staring at her the way she'd stared at him? Foolish to think he might. He probably barely realized she was female.

At the top of the stairs, she stepped onto a hardwood floor. Her first impression was of space, light and warmth. The living quarters covered the entire loft of the barn. There were no separate rooms; areas flowed into each other.

Eight-foot-high windows added to the feeling of openness in the cavernous room. Two overstuffed couches cordoned off an area to form a living room. Entertainment equipment provided a divider between that room and the kitchen. A king-size bed with—she gulped—a black satin comforter lined up against the opposite wall.

She stared at it, stunned, then grinned. Now she had a new element to add to her fantasies. Black satin. Who would have guessed?

The only walled room was at the far end of the loft. Through the open door she saw the sink and tub of the bathroom. The temperature in the loft was pleasant after the chill of the rain.

A brilliant flash of light cut through the late afternoon. On its heels, thunder boomed, shaking the building. Rebecca jumped and grabbed for the railing. Instead of cold metal, her fingers encountered warm skin.

Before she could pull back, he caught her hand in his. "Are you afraid of the storm?" he asked, his voice quiet after the thunder.

She started shaking. It had very little to do with her body temperature and her damp clothes, and everything to do with his closeness. "A little," she murmured.

Their gazes locked. Gray irises darkened like the coming of night. He gave away nothing, no emotions, no thoughts. It was like staring into the storm itself and only being able to imagine the destruction. His fingers slipped between hers and he tugged her closer to him. Her bare foot rested against the edge of his cowboy boots.

"Don't be afraid." He reached up. With his free hand he brushed the moisture from one cheek.

The tender gesture, so incongruous when compared to his reputation, made her want to snuggle against him.

"I have a lightning rod on the other side of the house. We're perfectly safe."

She blinked. So much for a romantic moment. "Gee, thanks."

"You're welcome. Stay right there, and I'll go get some towels."

"Towels?" she echoed.

He was already walking toward a large armoire on the far side of the bed.

"To dry off. You'll probably want to get out of those wet things. I'll call for a tow truck, but it may take a while."

"You want me to take off my clothes?"

He opened the armoire and pulled out an armful of fluffy towels. "You *are* dripping on my floor."

She glanced down, but the puddle beneath her made little sense. Naked. She was going to be naked in Austin Lucas's house. Her. Little Miss Ordinary was going to spend the afternoon naked with the devil. She didn't know whether to laugh out loud or run for the door.

"Rebecca?"

She stared at him, trying to focus. "Yes?"

"Are you sure you're okay? You didn't fall and hit your head or anything, did you?"

No, I'm just naturally stupid around you, she thought, knowing she could never admit that aloud. "I'm a little tired," she said, then realized it was the truth. This had been the longest and worst week of her life.

He moved from the armoire to a closet concealed in the wall. With a push of his hand, a hidden door swung open. He reached inside and pulled out a white terry-cloth robe, then started walking toward her.

She held her breath. When he was standing in front of her, he handed her everything. She glanced at the robe. It looked new. As if to confirm her guess, he reached for a sleeve and pulled off a tag dangling from one end.

"A gift from a friend," he said by way of explanation.

A woman friend, who else? She found it hard to believe a guy would give another guy a bathrobe. No, some foolish female had bought this for Austin expecting him to wear it and think of her.

"The bathroom is through there," he said, pointing to the half-open door at the end of the loft. "You look cold. Maybe you should take a hot shower to warm up."

Maybe you could kiss me and warm me up.

Rebecca felt her eyes widen in panic. Oh, please, God, let me not have spoken that thought aloud. She held her breath and waited.

Austin's eyes gave nothing away, and the expression on his face didn't change at all. Slowly she let her breath out. She'd only thought it. Danger. The man was pure danger.

"Thanks for everything," she said. "I didn't mean to be such a bother."

His gaze flickered over her face. "No problem. While you're taking a shower, I'll call for a tow. Then you can tell me what brought you out here in the first place."

She nodded and continued to stare at his face. She wanted to see him smile again, but she couldn't think of anything funny to say.

She felt a little push on her back, as if he was urging her to get on her way. She took one step, then another, heading for the bathroom. This was really happening to her. She was actually in his house. Austin's house. No one would believe this. Of course she wasn't going to tell anyone. Okay, maybe Travis and Elizabeth. She sighed and hugged the towels close to her chest. Maybe not even them. It was all too wonderful, too precious. A dream come true.

As she reached the bathroom door, her memory kicked in. Austin had said he didn't know why she'd come by. In her stupor, she'd forgotten to tell him the reason for her visit. She shook her head.

"I can't believe I didn't tell you why I stopped by," she said, turning back toward the center of the room. "I'm sure you heard that—"

She stopped in midsentence and stared. Austin stood beside the large bed. He'd already stripped off his shirt and was in the process of unbuttoning his wet jeans. As she looked at him, his hands slowed. His chest was bare, gleaming in the dim afternoon light. Her gaze followed the sprinkling of hair on his chest as it arrowed down to the open waistband of his worn jeans. From where she was standing, it didn't look as if he was wearing anything underneath them.

She swallowed hard and tried to speak. Nothing. She urged herself to turn and keep walking toward the bathroom, but her feet wouldn't budge. It would have taken an act of God to move her, and everyone knew Austin Lucas was only the devil.

Chapter Two

Rebecca looked as stunned as a doe caught in headlights and as wet as a drowned rat. Her long dark hair hung in wet curls, draping over her shoulders and dripping onto the floor. She opened her mouth to speak. No sound came out. She tried again, made a squeaking noise, then fled into the bathroom. The door slammed shut behind her.

Austin chuckled. He finished stripping off his wet jeans and tossed them onto the floor. He reached into the closet and pulled out another pair. He'd barely stepped into the first leg when he heard a loud shriek from the bathroom. After dropping his jeans, he sprinted to the door and knocked.

"Rebecca? What happened?"

There was a low moan from the other side of the door.

"Rebecca? Damn it, open up. Did you hurt yourself?"

"No. I just..."

He heard footsteps and the door opened a crack. He could see part of her face and one brown eye. Mascara collected under her lower lashes. Any color on her face had long been washed away. Her dress hung damply from her shoulders. She was a mess. The one eye he could see closed briefly.

"I just saw myself in the mirror. Now I know why you were smiling so much."

The tension left his body. "Oh, that."

Her eye opened. "Yeah, that. I'll just be a minute here, while I try to repair the damage."

"Take your time."

"I'm going to need it," she mumbled.

Her gaze drifted down from his face to his chest, then lower. She blinked and her eye got bigger. At that moment he realized he'd dropped the dry jeans he'd been pulling on. Her gasp was audible.

"I... I... Oh, heaven help me!" The door slammed shut.

Austin shook his head and headed back across the room. He couldn't have been the first naked man she'd ever seen, but she'd been staring as if he was. He slipped into his jeans and buttoned the fly, then grabbed a shirt and shrugged it on. He didn't bother fastening it.

His bare feet slapped against the hardwood floor as he made his way to the kitchen and started coffee. He rummaged around in a bottom cupboard until he found a bottle of whiskey, then poured a half inch into both coffee cups. If nothing else, the liquor would chase away the rest of her chill.

The sound of the storm increased. Bolts of lightning arced across the darkening sky. Rumbles of thunder shook the building. He stared out the window at the rain and the flashes of light. Behind him he could hear the gurgle of the coffeepot and the faint sound of the shower. He tried not to picture the woman standing under the warm spray or the way she would slowly lather her slender body.

He rubbed his hand over his face, but the action did nothing to chase away the tiredness. He'd been tired for days now, but he knew it had nothing to do with the hours he was putting in. Everything was changing and he didn't know how to make it stop.

The coffeepot gave a last hiss and then was silent. Pipes rattled as the shower was turned off. He stepped back and leaned against the kitchen counter, watching the door. He knew she would come out eventually. He also knew exactly how she would look, swimming in his oversize bathrobe. Her skin would be pale, her eyes large and questioning, her hair a damp mantle of silk. She would look at him and blush, then stare at the ground. He would be torn between telling her she was in no mortal danger and wanting to make every one of her ridiculous fantasies come true.

Rebecca Chambers had a crush on him. It had been obvious from their second meeting when she'd managed to spill an entire pitcher of water at dinner one evening. He'd just dropped by to give Travis a message. Rebecca had been there, wearing one of her flowing floral-print dresses. With her loose clothing and headbands holding her curly dark hair off her face, she reminded him of a schoolgirl out of uniform for the day.

He knew she wasn't a girl, but it was easier to think of her that way. Safer. She wasn't for him.

It took another ten minutes, but at last the bathroom door opened a crack. He thought about calling out that he wasn't naked anymore but didn't. She had enough backbone for three warriors; she just hadn't figured it out yet. Besides, he liked teasing her and watching her blush. It was about the only innocent pleasure he had in his life.

One bare foot eased out of the open door. He glanced at the pale skin and trim ankle. His muscles tensed as a familiar heaviness filled his groin. The dim light would make his condition harder for her to discern. Just as well—for both of them. If she kept on blushing around him, her face would be permanently red. If she didn't blush, he would be tempted to do exactly what she'd been thinking about.

She took another step and this time cleared the bathroom door. She looked exactly as he had pictured, all soft and pale, overwhelmed by his robe. She'd rolled up the sleeves a couple of times so they only hung to her knuckles. The knotted belt trailed almost to her knees.

"Do you want some coffee?" he asked, raising a mug.

Her head jerked toward him. She'd washed away the rest of her makeup, and without cosmetics, she looked about seventeen. Her mouth was well shaped, slightly wide and normally tilting up at the corners. Now it twisted down on one side as she nibbled her lower lip.

Her hair fanned out over her shoulders just as he'd pictured it. A flash of heat seared through his belly. For that second he wished she was like the widow in the next town. Jasmine visited him a couple of times a week. She was rich, lonely and bored. They made hot and fast love, seeking mutual release and no commitment. It had been easy to be with her, and easy to let her go. Three months before, they'd decided to end the affair. He didn't miss her, but parts of him missed her body. It would be a mistake to start something like that with Rebecca, even if her slender shape, so different from Jasmine's lushness, taunted him. Rebecca would be long and lean, a wildcat, he suspected. It was the innocence in her eyes that kept him from finding out.

"Coffee would be nice," she said, her voice low and steady. She took a step toward him, then paused.

He turned his back to her and poured the steaming liquid into both mugs. "Cream, sugar?"

"Cream," she said, sounding a little closer.

He grabbed a small carton from the fridge, added a splash then picked up the mug and held it out. She crossed the hardwood floor and took it.

"Thanks. I'm sorry to be such a bother. Dripping all over everything. Thanks for the robe. I'm sure my clothes will dry quickly and then I can be on my way. Except for the car. But you said you'd call for a tow truck. I guess that'll take a little while, what with the weather and all. I really appreciate—"

"Rebecca?" Slowly, so as not to alarm her, he turned toward her and leaned against the counter.

She stopped chattering and glanced at him. Her eyes were dark and wide, her face flushed with embarrassment. "Yes?"

"You're babbling."

The flush deepened. "I know. I'm nervous."

"Don't be." He reached over past her to the phone mounted on the wall. He drew the receiver to his ear and listened to the silence. Grimacing, he set it back in place, then motioned for her to follow him.

"What is it?" she asked, trailing behind him as he headed for the living area.

"Phone's out. Usually happens during bad weather."

"You can't call the tow truck?"

The panic in her voice almost made him smile. Almost. He didn't necessarily like scaring her, even if it wasn't a bad idea. Maybe if she was scared enough she would stop looking at him as if she'd already imagined them together in bed.

He sat in the single chair opposite the sofa and set his mug of coffee on the upturned crate that served as an end table. She slowly lowered herself to the middle of the couch. The oversize cushions threatened to swallow her whole.

"If I don't lose power, they should get the phone working in a couple of hours," he said, reaching over and clicking on a floor lamp.

She clutched the mug tighter. "And if you do lose power?"

"It means the whole line is down, and you'll be stuck here until tomorrow."

Her mouth opened to form a perfect O but she made no sound.

"I promise I don't bite," he said, leaning back in the chair.

"I know." She sighed, sounding disappointed.

Lightning flashed outside the windows, and thunder filled the room. Rebecca flinched at the loud noise, then took a big gulp of coffee. She sucked in a breath, then coughed. "There's liquor in this!"

"So?"

She raised her eyebrows and looked at him as if he'd just suggested they take a naked stroll through the local church. "What do you think you're doing by serving liquor?"

"My mistake. I could have sworn you were over twenty-one. At least twenty-two."

She straightened in her seat and glared at him. The gold tones of the sofa contrasted with the pristine white of the borrowed robe and the dark brilliance of her curly hair. "I'll have you know I'm twenty-nine, but that isn't the point."

"What is?" he asked mildly, his calm voice a contrast to her shrill tones.

"That I...that you..." She drew a deep breath, then sagged back against the cushions. "You could have warned me."

"I thought it might warm you from the inside."

Like electricity seeking a conductor, her gaze sought his mouth. Oh, no. He knew exactly what she was thinking, damn her innocent little hide. He told himself she was a fool. He told himself to ignore her. It didn't help. He could practically taste her. His heartbeat quickened and his blood flowed hotter.

She sipped her coffee, never taking her gaze from him. Most of the time he found her feelings for him faintly amusing. From a distance she was easy to take. But here, in the close confines of his loft, with the storm cutting them off from the rest of the world, it would be far too simple to take her up on her offer.

He eyed her relaxed posture and the way his robe had slipped off one of her knees, baring her calf and part of her thigh. Her skin looked smooth. He knew it would be warm to the touch, soft and supple.

He forced himself to look away and concentrate on the facts. One, she was a friend of Travis and Elizabeth's. He wouldn't hurt either of them for anything, and dallying with Rebecca was bound to upset them. Two, she wasn't his type. At twenty-nine she'd probably been involved with men before, but not men like him. He knew that. There was something about him. He didn't know if it was his money or his desire to stand outside and observe without always participating, but women seemed to find him attractive. The invitations came fast and furious. He was always careful about which ones he accepted. The rules of the game were simple—no emotional involvement, no promises, no commitment. He glanced back at his guest. Rebecca Chambers and those like her played for keeps.

"Austin, I—"

"Don't worry about it, honey. Just tell me why you're here."

Her eyebrows drew together in a delicate frown. She reminded him of a porcelain doll come to life. He would do well to keep thinking of her as off-limits, he told himself as the collar of her robe parted slightly, allowing him a view of her pale throat.

"Because of the fire."

"Fire?" He jerked his thoughts back from their erotic journey and concentrated on what she was saying.

"The one in town a few days ago. I'm sure you heard about it."

"Just that a couple of old buildings burned down." He shrugged. "I've been working hard this week, and I haven't been to town."

"Oh."

She took another sip of her coffee, then set the mug on the table in front of her. As she bent forward, the robe gaped more, allowing him to see down the front. She had a small build, but the shape of her breasts was perfect. Creamy ivory crested in coral. His mouth grew dry. He clenched his hands into fists and wished to hell she would stay upright.

"The children's home burned down."

"What?" He sprang to his feet. "Is everyone all right?"

"We're fine. We were lucky. It was during the day. The older kids were at school and the younger ones were at the park playing. No one was there, so there weren't any injuries. But we lost the whole building. All our supplies, the kids' toys, everything."

"It's gone?" He stalked over to the large window taking up most of one living room wall. He didn't even have to close his eyes to picture the old two-story building. It had been built sometime in the thirties. Most of the bigger rooms had murals. He'd often stood for hours studying those paintings, wondering who the people in the pictures were and what the artists had been thinking as they'd painstakingly worked their art.

He reached the window and braced his hands on the sill. He could feel the chill of the wind and the dampness from the storm. A large bolt of lightning flashed across the sky and the lights in the room flickered.

"Austin?"

"Yeah?"

"Are you all right?"

"What?" He inhaled sharply, as if he could still smell the odors of stew, old athletic shoes and baby powder. "Yeah. I'm just surprised."

"I didn't know you had a connection with the children's home."

He heard her bare feet on the floor as she walked toward him. He didn't turn around, but continued to stare out in the darkening afternoon and the rain pouring down. "I lived there for a couple of years."

He glanced down at her. She stood next to him, staring up. Her mouth hung open. She closed it slowly and didn't say anything, but he could see the questions in her brown eyes. If he told her the whole story, she'd get all compassionate and misty-eyed. It happened to women all the time. Occasionally he used the story to his advantage, but not today. Not with Rebecca. He didn't want to encourage her. Not because he wasn't interested, but because he was.

"You're an orphan?" she asked, her voice low and sympathetic.

"Not exactly."

"Then why were you in the home?"

He didn't answer. He stared down at her, knowing he was giving her what Jasmine had laughingly called the ice glare. She hadn't been intimidated by it because she hadn't been involved enough to care. Rebecca swallowed hard as his expression became more forbidding. She looked away and folded her hands together in front of her waist.

He felt as if he'd just kicked a kitten and had to fight the urge to apologize. Damn. What was wrong with him? Why was she getting to him? Was it the unexpected desire he felt when he looked at her? Or was it something more ominous? A whisper of envy for the innocence in her face. The knowledge that he had never been that open to the world, not even when he was a child. Life had taught them very different lessons. He'd always known he wasn't like everyone else. He'd accepted that fact, had even been proud of it. Until about a year ago, when he'd awakened to the realization that he would always be alone.

"You don't want to talk about it," she said, brushing a strand of hair off her face and turning away. Her shoulders slumped.

He swore under his breath. Why did she have to be so easy to read?

"I was transferred there from another home. I was a troublemaker when I was a kid."

She looked back at him and gave him a sweet smile. "That I believe."

"I'd hated where I'd been and I'd planned to hate this place. Then at school I met Travis and his brothers. They sort of changed everything for me."

"I've always wondered how the two of you became friends. You seem so different."

He raised his eyebrows. "In what way?"

She leaned against the wall and tucked her hands in the small of her back. "He's so open and friendly. Always good for a laugh. And you're..." She stopped talking and looked up at him. "What I meant to say is that you're..."

"Yes?" He folded his arms.

Her breathing increased, and with it the rise and fall of her chest. The thick robe parted slightly, exposing her neck and the hollow of her throat. It shouldn't have been provocative, but the sight of her bare skin made him want to move close to her and touch and taste every inch of her body. He shifted so the natural reactions to his thoughts would be less obvious.

"You're different," she said at last. "How exactly *did* you meet Travis?"

"I tried to beat him up."

"What?"

He grinned at the memory. "We were both in the eighth grade. I think I'd been in school about two days and I'd already been in four fights. Travis said something about me being a bully. I turned on him. What I didn't know at the time was that if you mess with one Haynes brother, you mess with all of them. The other three came running, ready to take apart my hide."

"What happened?"

"I was ready to get the—" he glanced at her "—living daylights out of me, when Travis did the damnedest thing. He took my side against his brothers. They wouldn't fight him. Then the vice principal showed up and they *all* defended me."

"And you've been friends ever since," she said, staring straight ahead with a dreamy expression in her eyes. "That's a lovely story. Travis must have seen that you were just a scared and lonely little boy."

Austin was torn between a desire to frighten her back into being afraid of him and surprise that she'd figured out the truth. That was exactly what Travis had seen. Funny, he'd never told anyone that before. But his relationship with Travis and his brothers had been the reason he'd returned to Glenwood. This was the only place he'd ever liked well enough to stay for more than a few months at a time.

"Yeah, well, it was a long time ago." He pushed off the windowsill and walked over to a desk in the corner by the stairs. "What's going on with the children's home? Do you need money?" He opened the top drawer and pulled out a checkbook. "Is that why you came to see me?"

"Not exactly."

He'd picked up a pen, but now he put it down. Rebecca crossed the room and stopped behind the wing chair he'd been sitting in. She rested her hands on the high back and gripped the fabric. The lights flickered again; the sounds of the storm increased. He could hear the rumble of thunder and the pounding of the rain on the windows.

He would have given his soul to see her slip the robe off her shoulders and walk into his arms. The corner of his mouth quirked up. He didn't have a snowball's chance in hell of that happening. She might have a crush on him, but she wasn't about to throw herself at him. Just as well. He would have a hard time refusing that kind of invitation.

He studied her face, the high cheekbones, the wide mouth, and tried to figure out what it was about her that made him want to break all his rules. Some of it was her crush. It was tough not to be flattered when a woman like her acted like a fool in his presence. Normally women fawning over him made him uncomfortable enough to start checking for the closest exit. But Rebecca was different. Maybe it was because she watched him with such adoration. Ironically it was her high ideals that would keep her safe from him. There was just enough decency left in him not to want to destroy her false image. If Rebecca Chambers knew the truth about him, she would run screaming in the opposite direction.

He was doing her a favor by keeping the truth a secret. He ignored the voice inside that whispered he might not just be doing it for her. That maybe he had something to gain. Maybe her blushes and stammerings and long glances fed some empty, almost dead part of his useless heart.

She raised her hands and grabbed her hair, pulled it back into a ponytail, then released the long curls. She was a fairy-tale princess, he thought, then scoffed at his own fancy. Get real, Lucas, he told himself.

"I need your house," she said, and drew a deep breath as if preparing to deliver a long speech. "Oh, God, I know what you're thinking. It's too much to ask. I *wouldn't* ask you except I've been everywhere else. I have twenty kids sleeping in the school auditorium, but they can't stay there indefinitely. The state has assured me I'll have money to build a new facility, but in the meantime, I'm on my own. Travis suggested I see you. He said there's an empty house on your property that'd be big enough. We wouldn't be a bother."

"Somehow I doubt that."

She took a step closer. Her hands twisted together, the fingers lacing and unlacing. "Oh, Austin, you're my last hope. I've checked around town. The problem is I don't have any money. I have some, but I need to replace food and clothing and toys. People in town have been great, but it's not enough. We'd only need the house for about three months." She grimaced. "Gosh, that sounds so long. I could split the kids up, but I hate to do that. David is just seven. His parents and older sister were killed in a car crash. He's pretty normal, considering what's happened to him. He talks and still does his schoolwork. But he can't seem to make friends. He stands outside all the games the other children play. He watches them. Even when they invite him, he won't join in. It's been six weeks since the accident."

She rubbed her palms together, then held out her hands pleadingly. "He has relatives, but they're too busy fighting over the estate to care about a seven-year-old boy. The deal they've all worked out is whoever gets control of the money is willing to be stuck with the kid." She shook her head. "*Stuck*. He's sweet and funny and very bright. If I can find a family willing to adopt him, I'll petition the court for custody. In the meantime, we're the only family he has."

He tried not to think about the lost boy, but deep in his chest he felt a familiar ache. "Rebecca, I don't see—"

"Then I have to make you see." Her voice became husky. "Oh, Austin, there are so many children. There are the twins. They've been abandoned by their alcoholic grandmother. And Melanie, she's just f-five." Her voice cracked. "Her uncle... His older brothers had done bad things to him, so he took it out on Melanie. The doctor's aren't sure if she'll ever be able to have children.''

He cursed under his breath and stood up. In three strides he was standing directly in front of her. He placed his hands on her shoulders and shook her gently.

''Hush, Rebecca. It's okay. What I started to say is that I don't think it's going to be a problem. You're welcome to the house. For as long as you need it.''

She blinked several times and he realized she was fighting tears. Through the thick layer of the robe, he could feel her slender shoulders tremble. There were dark circles under her eyes and lines of weariness around her mouth.

''Really?'' she asked.

''Really. Have you been handling all of this alone?''

She nodded. Her head dipped toward her chest. ''I haven't hired a new assistant since Elizabeth went on maternity leave.'' She sniffed, then raised her head. Her smile was a little shaky, but it hit him like a right hook to the jaw. ''I can't tell you what this means to us.''

He released her and stepped back. Great. He'd just gone up three points in her estimation. He didn't need to fuel her case of hero worship.

''It's nothing,'' he said, flicking his hand dismissively. ''The house is empty. You'll have to rent some beds and stuff. I'll pick up the tab for that.''

When her big eyes got bigger, he grimaced. ''I'm not doing this for you, Rebecca,'' he said bluntly. ''I'm doing it for the kids and because the people who ran the home were good to me when I stayed there. This isn't anything but a business deal. I'm paying an old debt. Don't make it more than it is.''

Judging by the light in her eyes, he hadn't made his point well enough.

"This is wonderful!" she said. She tugged on the belt around her waist. "I was so afraid of what would happen if you'd said no." She laughed. "I can't tell you how uncomfortable it is sleeping in a cot in the elementary-school auditorium."

"Why have you been staying there?"

"I lost my night supervisor, and I haven't been able to hire someone to replace her. About a month ago, I moved into the home. It was easier."

"You lost everything in the fire, too." It wasn't a question.

"Not everything, exactly. I had some stuff in storage."

He wanted to pull her into his arms and hold her until all the bad things went away. He wanted to hit the stairs running and never look back. "Saint Rebecca," he muttered.

"What?"

"Nothing." He shook his head. "Let me guess. You've been doing this all by yourself. Coordinating where the kids are going to stay temporarily, finding a new place, collecting clothes."

"You sound as if I've done something wrong. The children are my responsibility."

He felt old and tired, and far too cynical to spend time with someone like her. In his ugly little world, very few people went out of their way to do more than they had to. He was as guilty as the rest of them. It was easier to stay detached that way. Easier to forget why he couldn't get involved.

"Did I say something to offend you?" she asked.

He looked at her, at the long dark hair, at her big eyes and the trembling set of her mouth. From the top of her head down to her unpainted toenails, she was alien to him.

He leaned toward her and slipped his hand over her shoulder to the nape of her neck. She stiffened but didn't move. Despite her recent shower, he could smell the sweet scent of her body. It reminded him of vanilla and sunshine, nothing like the musky Oriental fragrances his lovers normally favored.

Her skin was as smooth and warm as he'd imagined. His thumb traced a pattern on her spine, then he curled his fingers into her hair. Her expression held no fear, only faint anticipation and a trusting calm that made him want to bellow with impatience.

"Who the hell are you, Rebecca Chambers?" he asked. "What are you doing in my life?"

"I don't know how to answer that," she whispered.

His other hand reached for the collar of the robe. It would be so easy to grab the thick material and jerk it open, exposing her to his gaze. Would she fight him or submit willingly?

He touched the terry cloth, moving back and forth, but didn't go near her skin.

"Have you ever gotten a ticket?" he asked.

She nodded. "I forgot to put enough change in the meter."

A parking ticket. He almost groaned. "Ever been really stone-face drunk?"

"No."

"Had sex with a stranger?"

She blushed and shook her head. Her eyes never left his. He saw the flash of fear, but it was gone before he could feed it.

"Have you ever, in your entire life, done anything bad?"

Her gaze dropped to his mouth, then to the floor. "No."

He released her and stalked away. Figures.

"Where are you going?" she asked.

"To call the tow truck and get you the hell out of here."

There was a brilliant flash of lightning, followed by a boom of thunder. The building shook as if God had reached down and bumped it. The lights inside flickered once, twice, then exploded into darkness. He stumbled into an end table and swore. If the power was out, the phone lines were down for the night. He was stuck here. And so was she.

Chapter Three

"Are you all right?" Rebecca asked as Austin stumbled in the darkness.

His answer was a mumbled curse.

She stood where he'd left her, in the middle of his living room. Her heart was still pounding in her chest, and her knees felt weak.

He'd touched her. Even thinking about his brief caress sent the blood racing through her veins. His hand on the back of her neck had been hot and hard. He'd stared at her as if he wanted to devour her for dinner, then dish up the remains for breakfast. She wasn't sure she would have refused him.

Even though it was dark and there was no one to see her blush, she covered her cheeks with her palms. How could she think that about him? A crush was one thing, but casual sex with a man she barely knew was something quite different. Oh sure, she'd thought about making love with

Austin hundreds of times. But thinking and doing were two different things...weren't they?

Have you ever had sex with a stranger?

He would never know the images his question had evoked. She'd already seen Austin naked, so it wasn't difficult to picture him aroused. His body had been all that she'd imagined. Before she'd slammed the bathroom door shut, she'd seen his long, powerful legs, the breadth and definition of his chest. Between his thighs she'd seen dark curls and his...his organ!

In all her twenty-nine years, she'd only ever seen one other man naked. Wayne had been blond and built like a bear, all thick limbs and barrel-chested. He'd been an all-American linebacker at college their senior year. Everything about him was so different from Austin's lean grace, and dark, demonic, good looks.

Wayne had been someone she'd laughed with, someone who had grown up with the same rules and goals as she had. Wayne had understood about values, about the importance of other people's feelings. Wayne had been warm and sensitive.

Austin was none of those things. He was a loner. She'd always wondered about his past, but she'd never thought he would have lived in the Glenwood children's home. She'd heard that he'd been wild as a teenager, breaking rules and the law, getting into trouble. Even now he lived up to his reputation. Between his self-made fortune, his gold earring and his women, he flouted the conventions of their small town. He was nothing like Wayne, nothing like herself. So why couldn't she stop thinking about him?

The sun had set behind the clouds, taking away the last of the light. From another part of the loft, drawers were being opened and slammed shut. After several minutes she heard the scratch of a match, then a weak flicker of light danced off the far wall.

"You might as well come into the kitchen," Austin called out. "I don't have enough candles for the whole place. Can you see your way?"

"I'm fine," she said, and wondered if she had the courage to take him up on his less than gracious invitation. She'd hoped he found her at least slightly attractive. But her answers to his questions had pointed out to both of them that she was far from his type. A man with a reputation of being the devil himself wouldn't be interested in a woman like her.

She walked around the wing chair and toward the light. Austin stood by the phone, staring at the receiver. He banged it once against the wall and listened. Then he slammed it back in place.

"The line's out."

"I figured as much," she said.

He planted his hands on his hips and stared at her. "Looks like you're stuck with me for the night."

I don't mind.

She didn't say the words, but she must have thought them pretty loudly because Austin stiffened, raising his head slightly and staring at her. He reminded her of a wildcat catching scent of its prey.

Squat candles sat in saucers around the kitchen and on the butcher-block table. The flames danced in time to a rhythm she could neither feel nor hear. The storm raged around them, but for once she wasn't afraid of the lightning or the thunder. It was as if the rest of the world had ceased to exist. She was alone with this man. Time had disappeared, along with common sense. She had this night. Ignoring the fact that she was naked under his robe and feeling extremely vulnerable, she balled her hands into fists and promised herself not to waste it.

"Are you hungry—"

"Would you like me to fix—"

They spoke at the same time. Austin recovered first. "Are you hungry?"

"A little. I could fix something, if you'd like. Is the stove gas or electric?"

He turned to glance at the range set into a granite counter. "The starters are electric, but the unit is gas."

"No problem. If you have another match, I can start it manually." She spoke briskly and walked over to the refrigerator. After pulling it open, she glanced at the contents. "What sounds good? There are a couple of steaks, some salad, a—"

Something warm brushed the back of her hand. She gasped and jumped back. The refrigerator door slowly swung shut.

Austin stood close enough for her to see the hairs on his chest and the slow thudding pulse at the base of his neck. She had the most incredible urge to plant her mouth there and taste his skin.

She bit down hard on her lower lip to keep from yelping her embarrassment. What on earth was wrong with her? She hadn't had more than a sip of his doctored coffee, so it couldn't be the alcohol. Maybe standing out in the rain had left her brain waterlogged.

"You don't have to cook for me," he said.

"I don't mind. It's the least I can do after all the trouble I've been."

"Far be it from me to interfere with a woman on a mission of mercy." He stepped back and motioned to the refrigerator. "Help yourself."

She worked quickly and efficiently. He directed her when she needed to find a bowl or a pot, and within twenty minutes they were eating dinner.

While she'd been cooking the steak, Austin had set the table and opened a bottle of red wine. She sipped cautiously, not wanting the wine to loosen her tongue. She was already in too much danger of saying something stupid. Heaven knows what would happen if she got drunk!

They chatted about mutual acquaintances in town and the children. She forced herself to concentrate on his words, rather than on the way the candlelight made his skin glow like burnished gold. He'd pulled on a shirt, but hadn't bothered to fasten it. She didn't want to say anything and have him do up the buttons, but it was hard not to stare.

"What about you?" he asked, pouring her another glass of wine. "Why are you taking care of other people's children, instead of having a half dozen of your own?"

"What makes you think I want children?"

He raised one eyebrow. Gosh, she really wanted to know how he managed to do that. The storm had decreased in fury, but the lights hadn't come back on yet. The candlelight slipped shadows across his face, making his expression impossible to read.

"You're the type," he said. "Are you telling me you don't?"

"I do." She pushed her fork around her plate. "It just hasn't worked out that way."

"Still waiting for Mr. Right?"

For the first time that day, she could meet his gaze without thinking anything improper. She shook her head. "Not exactly. Mr. Right died."

He'd raised the wineglass to his lips, but now he set it down untasted. "I'm sorry."

"Thank you. It's been a while, so I've recovered. I'll never forget him, of course. Wayne was—" she smiled "—nothing like you."

"I'm not surprised." His expression was unreadable.

"I don't mean that in a bad way."

"I never thought you did."

She wasn't sure if he was angry or simply making conversation. It was easier to assume the latter. "Wayne and I met in college. He was bright, funny. He looked like a big blond bear, but he was sweet and gentle. We got engaged, but I wanted to put off the wedding until I had my masters degree. We'd set the date and everything, but three months before the wedding, he was in a bad car accident. A year later he died."

"Must have been hard on you."

A polite remark most people made. Funny, but she had the feeling Austin really meant it. "It was. About a year and a half after I lost him, I moved here. Like I said, I'll never forget him, but it's getting easier."

Most of the time. Without wanting to she remembered the way Wayne had looked in his hospital room and the expression on his face when the doctor had told him he would never walk again, would never do all the physical things he'd so loved. She remembered his pain when the doctor had gently explained he would never be "a man" again. Wayne hadn't been able to meet her eyes. He'd never cried in her presence, but she'd shed enough tears for the both of them.

It was her greatest regret, she acknowledged to herself. She would have married Wayne, anyway, and had that last year together, but he didn't want to. He told her he wouldn't saddle her with someone who was less than a man. He'd sounded so bitter that she'd never brought up the subject again. But it had lingered in that hospital room like an unwelcome third party. He'd never said the words, but she knew he blamed her.

It was her fault. She'd been the one to hold back. While they'd dated and been engaged, they'd played and loved like any young couple, but they'd put off going all the way until they were married. Because she'd asked him to. There had been so many wonderfully sensual things to do together that she hadn't minded not consummating their love. Until it was too late and she'd found out their love would never be expressed in the ultimate act of sharing. She would never marry the man she loved, never carry his child.

All the years they'd spent together, she'd guarded her virginity, ready to give it as the most precious gift a bride could bring her husband. In the end, Wayne had died hating her for keeping herself from him. Her innocence had mocked him, reminding him of what he'd lost, of what he could never have again. It mocked her, as well. She was an anachronism. A twenty-nine-year-old virgin who had saved herself. For what? Her "gift" was a reminder of all she'd lost. It no longer had meaning. She wanted it disposed of and forgotten.

"Rebecca?"

"Hmm?" She glanced up and saw Austin staring at her. She blinked several times. "I'm sorry. I was just thinking."

"About Wayne?"

She sighed. "Yes. It's difficult losing someone like that. There were so many unresolved issues. I wanted to explain it all to him, but he wouldn't listen. I can't blame him. It was my fault."

She stopped talking and realized Austin didn't have a clue what she was going on about. He nodded encouragingly, giving her permission to continue, but she couldn't. What was she supposed to say? *Gee, Austin, I'm really upset because my late fiancé and I never went all the way. I'm a twenty-nine-year-old virgin and I'm sick of it. Want to help me out?*

Her line of thinking should have shocked her. It didn't. Which meant she was in more trouble than she'd thought.

She didn't know how long she'd been quiet, but suddenly she became aware of a tension in the room. It was a subtle vibration that seemed to reach deep inside of her, warming her from the inside out, causing her pulse to quicken and her skin to tingle.

She glanced across the table and saw Austin watching her. His gray eyes glowed in the candlelight. His irises were the color of the storm. Stubble darkened his cheeks and jaw, shadowing the lines of his face, making him look more dangerous. He inhaled deeply. The slight movement caused his earring to catch the light. The gold glinted sharply, once again making her think of pirates and treasure, of captured women and forbidden love.

It was becoming difficult to breathe. She told herself it was just a foolish reaction to being in the same room with the object of her crush. Maybe it was because she'd been thinking about and missing Wayne. Or it could have been the result of her exhaustion. Since the fire, she hadn't had a decent night's sleep or a moment's rest. When she hadn't been scouting for supplies, she'd been figuring out a way to approach Austin about borrowing his house. She still found it hard to believe he'd said yes. He didn't have to. A lot of people would have turned her away, citing problems with noise, potential destruction or insurance.

So many people nicknamed him the devil, but he'd been very nice to her. In fact—

"Stop looking at me like that," he growled.

She stiffened, startled by the anger in his voice. "Like what?"

"Like I'm some damn noble prince riding in on a white horse. I'm not anybody's idea of a hero, and if you think I am, then you're worse than a fool."

He drained the last of the wine into his glass, then slammed down the bottle. "The storm is already almost over," he said, glaring at her. "In the morning the road will be dry enough for you to drive out of here. If not, I'll dig out the damn car myself."

"You swear a lot," she said without thinking.

"You don't swear enough."

"I don't swear at all."

He grimaced. "That's my point. We have nothing in common. I like my women experienced and easy. You're not either."

She was too shocked to blush. She stared at him. "Wh-what are you talking about?"

He leaned over the table far enough to grab a handful of her hair. He wrapped it around his hand twice and then pulled her close, until their mouths were millimeters apart.

"You know exactly what I'm talking about, Rebecca. Believe me, I, of all people, understand the appeal of what's forbidden. But I'm one man you shouldn't try to tame. I'm not interested."

She flinched as if he'd slapped her. Before she could control herself, her eyes filled with tears. Her face grew hot, then cold. She tried to pull away, but he held her firmly in his grasp.

"Damn it all to hell," he muttered. "I'm not trying to hurt you. You're not my type. More important, I'm not yours. I'm no Wayne whatever-his-name-was who helped little old ladies cross the street. I'm a selfish bastard. And I do mean bastard, lady. In every sense of the word."

She studied his mouth as he spoke, feeling the sweet puffs of his breath on her face. He was being cruel in a good way. She was sure in time she would be grateful. For now she just wanted to crawl under the table and die. Or have him kiss her. Despite his taunting words, her body was reacting to his closeness. She wanted to scream in frustration. She was too old to have a crush on a man.

She drew in a deep breath and gathered what little dignity and strength she had left. "Austin, I'm sorry if I offended you. I didn't—"

She never got to finish her sentence. He pulled on her hair, dragging her that last millimeter so that their lips touched. Mouth to mouth, he held her in place, not moving, not breathing, just touching gently, firmly, erotically.

Involuntarily her eyes fluttered shut. Heat poured through her as if someone had doused her with sun-warmed rain. Her toes curled and her fingers gripped the edge of the table. When she thought she would go mad from the bliss, he moved his head slightly, brushing her lips. More heat, fiery heat, flared between them. She gasped for breath. His tongue reached out and touched the tip of hers. Before she could melt in place, he released her and rose to his feet.

She sank back in the chair and listened to the thundering of her heart. Her hands were shaking, her breasts felt inflamed, that secret place between her thighs throbbed painfully. She didn't dare look at him. What if he hadn't felt the same reaction?

She caught her breath. What if he had?

Without saying a word, Austin stood up and stalked across the room. He opened the armoire and pulled out a pale garment, then walked back to her.

"Here," he said, tossing it to her.

She grabbed the item, then stared at it. A man's T-shirt, she thought. But what—

"It should be big enough for you to wear to bed."

She stared at him.

He cursed again. "Alone. Damn it, Rebecca, stop it. It's late. You're tired. You take the bed. I'll sleep on the couch. In the morning you'll be out of here, and we'll pretend this never happened."

She didn't point out that it was still quite early. She was too curious about what the "this" they were to pretend never happened was. What had happened between them? A brief kiss? Or something she hadn't realized? She drew her eyebrows together and wished she were a little more experienced at the whole man-woman thing.

"I don't want to go to bed yet," she finally blurted.

"No one is asking your opinion," he said sharply. "You're reacting to the situation and probably to the trauma of the fire earlier this week. It doesn't have anything to do with me, and I'm not going to be responsible for your regrets come morning. I might be a bastard, but I'm not a complete jerk.''

Now she was really confused. She dropped the T-shirt on the table and rose to her feet. After tightening the belt of her robe, she shoved her hands into the deep pockets and looked at him. "I don't know what you're talking about. One minute we're having a nice conversation about our lives and the next you're kissing me, then sending me to bed.''

He circled around the table until he was standing in front of her. They stood close enough for her to feel the heat of his body. She supposed she should have been nervous or afraid, but she wasn't. Despite what everyone said, deep inside, Austin Lucas was a nice man. Only someone nice would donate his house to needy orphans. How was she supposed to resist him?

"I'm not your damned fiancé," he said, his eyes flashing like the storm.

"I know."

"That's my point. You want me because I'm different, and dangerous. You want me to help you forget. You want me to be the exciting bad thing in your life. You want me in your bed.''

She couldn't have been more shocked if he'd slapped her. How had he guessed? Had she been that obvious?

"I—I don't want you," she stammered, knowing she was blushing and praying the candlelight was faint enough that he wouldn't see the color flaring in her cheeks. All her confidence disappeared like smoke in the wind. She turned to leave, but he grabbed her arm and held her in place.

"Did you hope I wouldn't see what you were thinking?" he asked, his voice low and husky.

She moaned softly, shame joining embarrassment.

"Did you imagine I couldn't read the fantasies, Rebecca, that I didn't notice you staring at me, wanting to touch me, wanting me to touch you?"

It was worse than her dream about showing up naked at church. She felt as if someone had stripped her bare and was now mocking the pitiful being she was inside. Her soul felt raw, scourged by the sharp edge of his words. She had to get out, run away and hide. He was laughing at her. Making fun of her. She wanted to die.

"I'm sorry," she whispered, trying to turn away. Tears threatened. She blinked them back, but it wasn't enough. One rolled onto her cheek. "Just let me go. I'll never bother you again."

He released her arm, but before she could step away, he placed his hands on her shoulders and drew her close.

"Damn you, Rebecca Chambers, don't cry. I warned you I was a bastard. Why couldn't you have listened? I'm not trying to hurt your feelings. I want you to understand that I'm nothing like the man you think I am. There's nothing good in me. Forget me. Find another Wayne and have babies."

His gentle words washed over her, easing some of her exposed rawness inside. His body was warm and hard, offering shelter and comfort. She sniffed back her tears until he touched her hair. The tender stroking of his palm on her head was more than she could stand.

Her sob caught her by surprise. Her whole body shook. "I'm sorry," she said, trying to get control. "I—I'm not usually like this. I think it might be the f-fire and everything."

"I know. It's okay. You cry as much as you want."

She didn't want to cry at all, but she couldn't seem to help herself. His strong arms wrapped around her, holding her safely in his embrace. His heartbeat was steady against her cheek. She cried for all she'd lost, for the children's fears and her own. She whispered her concerns, about lying alone at night and wondering how she was supposed to keep it all together. She confessed that the responsibility scared her sometimes, but she kept on because there was no one else.

When the sobs had faded to sniffles, she became aware of the fact that her mouth rested against the bare skin of his chest. He was damp from her tears, yet still warm and smelling faintly musky. Through the thickness of her robe— his robe—she could feel the length of his legs, but little else save his heat. His hands moved up and down her back with long, comforting strokes. His chin rested on her head and he spoke quietly to soothe her.

"You must think I'm a fool," she said, knowing she should pull away, but not wanting to.

"No. I think you're very special. I'm sorry I said anything. I didn't want to hurt you. I was trying to make you see that I'm not anyone's idea of a fantasy lover."

"I don't want a fantasy."

His hands grew still.

She raised her head until she could stare at him. "You're right, Austin. I do—" she searched for the right word "—think you're attractive, partially because you're nothing like Wayne. But I don't have a romantic fantasy about you. I don't know you well enough to be picturing home and hearth." She swallowed hard. He'd apologized to her, but she was the one who'd started the whole thing. "I'm sorry if I embarrassed you. If I'd known you could tell what I was thinking, I would have thought about something else."

His gray eyes flickered with some emotion she couldn't read. His mouth twisted into a wry smile. "I wasn't complaining," he said. "I was trying to explain why I was turning you down. I won't deal with your regrets."

"And if I promise not to have any?" she asked without thinking.

"Rebecca." His voice was a low growl. She felt it vibrate in her own chest and realized her breasts were plastered against him. She thought about pulling away, but didn't. A wave of courage surprised her. She might never have this chance again.

In a way he was perfect for her. As he'd pointed out, he wasn't interested in a relationship. She'd already figured that one out on her own. He was wild and experienced. She would never choose to fall in love with someone like him. Which was what made him so safe. She was a twenty-nine-year-old virgin, and she needed a man to fix that. She'd recently started dating, but had always broken things off before they got serious. She didn't want to have to explain about her condition. She'd tried twice and both men had stared at her as if she were a two-headed snake. Being a virgin at her age said something about a person, and she didn't like what it said about her. She'd been saving herself for Wayne and then he was gone. Her gift had no meaning, save a painful one. It reminded her of what she'd kept from him. She wanted it done away with.

Who better to help her out than Austin? Heaven knew she'd had enough fantasies that being in bed with him would almost be familiar.

"I'm serious," she said, drawing in a deep breath and sliding her hands up his arms to his shoulders. She could feel the rock-hard strength of his muscles. "Maybe if we make love, I'll get over my crush and leave you alone."

"That doesn't say a whole lot about my skills in bed," he muttered.

She was afraid he would be repulsed by the idea and turn away, but he didn't. His hands resumed their stroking of her back, but this time they moved lower, sliding over the curve of her derriere.

"No regrets," she said. "No dreams about white picket fences. No fantasies about a future together, I promise."

His gaze locked on hers. She couldn't read his emotions. It was like staring into a bottomless pool or jumping off a cliff into a cloud. She didn't know how far down she would go. Would he catch her, or let her fall and shatter?

He brought his hands around to her face and cupped her cheeks, then lowered his head toward hers.

She drew a breath in anticipation of their kiss. His mouth brushed hers, slowly, carefully, as if she were the most fragile of creatures. Back and forth, back and forth. Her fingers curled slightly as she gripped his shoulders. Her knees began to tremble.

He pulled back. Their gazes met and for the first time she could read something in his eyes. Desire. It dilated his pupils so much the gray got lost in a sea of need. Until that moment, she'd wondered if she was setting herself up again. Had he toyed with her, making her confess her wants, knowing he shared none of them?

Now she knew the truth. He shared the trembling, the heat. Her confidence returned and with it the sense of rightness about her decision. Austin Lucas might be the devil, but she trusted him not to hurt her. She smiled slightly. So much for being logical. For the first time in her life, she was going on instinct.

"No regrets? You promise?" he asked.

She knew this was completely insane, but it felt right. Wayne was gone. She needed to get on with her life. Austin was the perfect solution. Plus, she would finally find out if her fantasies had come close to the real thing. She smiled. "Yes."

It was as if her single word gave him the permission he'd been waiting for. Before she knew what was happening, he buried his hands in her hair, holding her head still. His fingers flexed against her scalp, sending tingling sensations down her spine.

His mouth angled over hers, searing her with hot, fast kisses. He devoured her, sucking her bottom lip, nibbling on her top. He touched his tongue to the corners of her mouth, then swept across the closed seam, urging her to part for him.

She opened to admit him, her breath already quickening with anticipation. In and around, over and under. Hot, wet, seeking. He plunged inside like a marauding warrior, ready to take that which he'd won. Then he retreated, playing with her, touching, stroking, tasting, discovering every inch of her tender mouth, making her pant with longing.

His hands moved down from her head to her neck. His thumbs traced a line from her chin to the hollow of her throat. His fingers left small warm brands on her sensitized skin.

She clung to him, her anchor in the storm, her source of strength. Mindless half phrases passed through her consciousness. It had never been like this. Not with those men she'd dated, not with Wayne. Before, the buildup had been slow, gentle kisses, a natural progression from kissing to petting. It had been quiet and lovely.

Not frantic like this. Her body was too hot, quivering with need and heat. Her breasts ached. Her nipples pressed against the terry cloth, throbbing for his touch. Between her legs an answering echo pulsed in time with her thundering heartbeat.

His mouth left hers and moved along her jaw to her ear where he whispered that she was beautiful. His tongue traced the shape of her ear. His teeth nibbled on her lobe. Ribbons of heat and desire rippled down her body, making her legs shake and threaten to buckle.

She slipped her hands down his chest and across to the bare strip of skin exposed by his open shirt. He was warm to her touch, smooth except for the crinkling hair. Muscles bunched under her fingers. She moved to his waist and drew her palms up slowly, then across his broadness. He answered with a quick intake of air.

She felt his hand at the tie of the robe. With one tug, it was free. He grabbed the collar, then drew it apart and down her arms. She was naked before him.

The cool air of the room surprised her. Without thinking, she brought her hands up to cover her breasts. As always, their small size embarrassed her.

Austin stared into her eyes. "Has there been anyone since Wayne?"

The intensity of his gaze made it impossible to lie. Not that she would have, anyway. "Just a few dates."

"So you haven't made love with anyone in the past couple of years?"

She swallowed. "No." She hadn't made love with anyone, ever, but he hadn't asked that.

"Do you want to change your mind? We don't have to do this."

"I want to." She needed to. Not just because it would rid her of her pesky virginity, but because her body was on fire for this man. She had to feel him on her, in her. She had to know what it was like to be with him in the most intimate way possible.

"Then why do you hide yourself from me?"

She glanced down at her hands covering her breasts. "I'm not like her."

He frowned. "Who?"

"I don't know her name. She's pretty, with red hair. She used to come out here a couple of times a week." Rebecca bit down on her lower lip and wondered why she was trying to explain this. "I wasn't spying on you or anything, but people in town talk and it's hard not to listen when they just happen to mention it and—" She clamped her mouth shut.

"You think you're too small," he said bluntly.

She nodded.

His slow grin surprised her.

"What's so funny?"

"Your old boyfriend did a lousy job, Rebecca. You are a beautiful woman, perfect in every way. Long, lean, with just enough curves to drive a man wild."

Her spirits lifted slightly. "Really?"

"Yes."

"Well, that makes me feel better. I've always been worried that, you know, I was too little on top. I— What are you doing?"

He bent over and picked her up in his arms. She squealed and wrapped her arms around his neck. With only the flickering candles to guide him, he walked to the bed and set her in the middle of the black satin comforter. The slick fabric was cool against her heated skin. Before she could slip away to one side, he placed his hands on either side of her waist.

"You're just right on top. Trust me, I know." His smile faded. "I don't have any protection with me, but I had a blood test for my life insurance a couple of months ago," he said. "It came back clean. I haven't been with anyone else since."

She stared at him. What on earth? Oh! That. He waited patiently. "Ah, yeah, me, too. I mean, I'm okay. You know." How could there be a problem? She'd never been intimate before.

"So you're safe then?"

Safe? Of course she was safe. She couldn't possibly have any sexually transmitted disease because she'd never had the sex required to do the transmitting. "Yes."

"Good." He shrugged out of his shirt.

When he stood up and started unfastening his jeans, she told herself to look away. But she didn't. She'd already seen him naked. It had been thrilling, and she wanted to see him again.

But he didn't look exactly the same. When he pushed his jeans past his hips, his arousal sprang free. He was a lot larger than she anticipated, hard and ready. Despite the flicker of fear that raced through her, she was glad. At least she knew he wanted her, too.

Without speaking, he lay down beside her. There wasn't enough light from the candles for her to be able to see his expression, but she felt his warmth. He leaned over her, trapping her arms between them. He raised up, pulled her arms free and drew them around his neck. Then he bent down and kissed her.

The touch of his lips was electric. Hot, sparking sensations shot through her body, clear to her toes. Her fingers curled into his hair and she felt the silky brown strands slipping against her skin.

He moved his mouth slowly, as if he had all the time in the world. As if nothing existed but them and the night and the storm. She supposed she should be nervous and appalled at her own behavior. She would be. Later. For now there was only this man.

He raised his head and smiled at her. She smiled back. Bare legs brushed. Shivers raced from each point of contact and collected in her breasts and between her thighs. Anticipation made her muscles contract.

He moved his chest back and forth. His sprinkling of hair tickled her breasts and made her nipples pucker. Then he bent his head lower and took one hardened tip in his mouth.

She sucked in her breath on a gasp. His lips caressed the taut point. His tongue traced erotic circles over and over again. He reached for her other breast, cupping her small curves, stroking the sensitive skin, tweaking her nipple into a tight bead.

She felt his hardness against her thigh. She longed to touch him but didn't have the courage. Instead, she stroked his back and sides, reaching down to cup his rear, squeezing the firm, muscled flesh.

She touched his shoulders, then his long hair. Warm to cool. His scent invaded her. Her index finger traced his ear and the gold hoop.

He moved his mouth to her other breast, exchanging fingers for tongue and vice versa. Her heart rate increased and the pulse between her thighs grew more insistent. Her arms fell to her sides. She grasped at the satin comforter and held on. It had been too long. Her breasts were too sensitive. Just the feel of his hot breath, his tongue flicking over the nipples, making the tight points higher and tauter, sent her flying toward ecstasy. Her last conscious thought was that her fantasies about making love hadn't even come close to the sensual magic of this moment.

Austin raised his head and looked at Rebecca's face. Her eyelids closed and her mouth parted as she drew in more and more air. He felt her quivering response as he suckled her.

He slipped his hand lower, across the smooth skin of her flat belly to the dark curls below. Heat radiated from her. It would be so easy to bury himself inside her waiting warmth and just explode. However, as hard as he was, that explosion would occur in about three thrusts. Hardly enough to satisfy her. He wanted to feel her body ripple with satisfaction and watch her eyes slowly return to focus. He wanted to learn every inch of her. Only then would he take his own pleasure.

His finger sought and found her tight opening. He traced the entrance to paradise, making his stomach tighten in anticipation as her body thrust toward him.

The night made her pale skin glow as if iridescent. Despite his best intentions, his need throbbed heavily. Just looking at her and thinking about what he wanted to do was enough to send him close to the edge. He forced himself back.

He drew her nipple deeper into his mouth. At the same time, he sought out the tiny point of her pleasure. He touched it with the tip of his finger. She jumped. Slowly, carefully, he caressed that place, over and around, moving faster and lighter.

Her body quivered, her hips shifted beneath his hand, making it easy to find the rhythm that pleased her. He'd planned to bring her close, then take his time tending to every part of her before finally sending her over the edge. But when her breathing suddenly quickened and her muscles tensed, he knew he couldn't stop.

He raised up on one elbow so he could watch her face. Her eyes opened, but she stared at him without seeing. Her pelvis thrust in time with his movements. Soft moans escaped her lips.

He could feel her tension and the promise of her release. His finger moved more quickly now. She spoke his name and was suddenly still. He rubbed her sweet spot once, twice, forcing her into the fiery explosion. He urged her on, touching gently, keeping pace with her, until she relaxed against his touch.

He looked at her. Perspiration coated her chest. She gasped for breath. Slowly her eyes focused on him. Another spasm caught her and her entire body trembled. It was the sexiest thing he'd ever seen in his life. He had to have her now.

He rose to his knees and positioned himself against her slick opening. She smiled welcomingly.

"Finally," she whispered.

He closed his eyes as he eased himself inside. So damn tight and wet. He held on to her legs, struggling for control. He wanted to let go right away, but he didn't. He couldn't.

He was less than halfway in when he felt resistance. His mind tried to focus but his body wouldn't let him. His need was overpowering. He flexed his hips and pressed on. The barrier resisted, then gave way. Against his palms, the muscles in her legs stiffened.

He stared down at her. Realization dawned and, with it, a sense of disbelief. Rebecca Chambers had been a virgin.

Chapter Four

Austin tried to gather enough self-control to pull back. The flash of anger helped. What the hell kind of trick was she pulling, anyway?

Rebecca's eyes opened and their gazes locked. He wasn't sure what he'd expected to see there, but it wasn't contentment and relief.

"Don't stop," she whispered, and flexed her hips.

The unexpected movement sent him farther inside her. Involuntarily he arched into the pleasure.

"Damn you," he muttered, digging his fingers into her thighs. "If you think I..."

She drew her knees back toward her chest, exposing herself to his gaze, making it easier for him to go deeper. Around his engorged organ her muscles rippled with an aftershock of her recent release. He sucked in his breath, fighting for control.

"Please," she whispered. She raised her hands to his arms and gently stroked his skin. "Don't stop."

She moved her hips again. The awkward, inexperienced movement should have sent him running in the opposite direction. Unfortunately the throbbing between his legs had other plans. Pressure built rapidly. He gritted his teeth and sucked in his breath, then exhaled and gave up the war. The damage had already been done. It couldn't get any worse.

He bent over her, placing his hands on either side of her shoulders. After pulling almost all the way out, he thrust in deeply. She arched toward him, her pelvis tilting in an exaggerated movement.

"Not so much," he whispered, kissing her neck and ear. "It's more of a rocking motion."

She changed her rhythm instantly and about sent him over the edge. He knew he was ready to explode inside her.

He reached down and took one of her nipples into his mouth, sucking deeply. Her breath caught in her throat. She breathed his name. He raised his head until their eyes met. A smile curved her mouth. And then he couldn't focus on her anymore. Inside him, the pressure and need built. He straightened, kneeling between her thighs, thrusting quickly, holding her hips. He tried to think about hanging on, giving her the time to catch up with him, then the thought disappeared into the fire that engulfed him. Heat built as the vortex of sensation grew.

In the back of his mind, a voice whispered he might be hurting her, and he tried to hold back. Then she reached forward and cupped his buttocks, pulling him closer.

The explosion ripped him apart from the inside. Pleasure sucked at his breath and turned his muscles into quivering stone. Scattered pieces of his psyche remained suspended for a single heartbeat, before reassembling.

Sanity returned and, with it, the ability to move. Austin stayed where he was but slowly opened his eyes.

Rebecca stared up at him. Her face was flushed, her full mouth smiling faintly. There was nothing mocking about her expression, or predatory. But she'd come to his bed a virgin. What the hell was going on?

"You probably want an explanation," she said, turning away from his gaze.

"Probably," he agreed.

The blush started just above her small, perfect breasts and climbed quickly up her neck to her cheeks.

"I didn't lie to you," she said, her voice soft and laced with embarrassment.

"You left out a pretty big detail." He probed his emotions and was surprised to discover he wasn't angry. Confused, a little panicked perhaps, but not outraged. Unless of course she had planned this.

He drew his eyebrows together and glared down at her. "If you thought you were going to try and trap me—"

"I didn't," she said quickly, turning her head toward him and meeting his gaze. "Far from it. I…" She swallowed and the blush got deeper.

"Yes?" He rested his hands on her knees, liking the feel of her soft, naked skin under his palms. He supposed if he was any kind of a gentleman, he would pull out of her so that she could cover herself with the sheet. Fortunately for him, he wasn't a gentleman, so he didn't have to worry about her embarrassment. He wanted to keep her off guard. After what had just happened, he was damn well going to get the truth out of her, regardless of how low he had to stoop to get it. Besides, being this close to her was exciting him again.

"I didn't tell you I was a virgin because I knew if *you* knew, you wouldn't make love to me." She spoke very quickly, as if forcing the words past a constricted throat. "Don't be mad at me, please? I sort of picked you on purpose. Because of your reputation and all. I thought if anyone could fix my problem, you could. Maybe you should be flattered.''

She ended her speech with a tentative smile. He kept his face stern and her smile died quickly, leaving her mouth trembling and vulnerable. He had to fight the urge to bend down and gather her into his arms. The need to hold her close and comfort her was almost as overwhelming as the need that had pushed him to take her virginity.

"Not good enough, Rebecca," he said, deliberately making his voice cold.

She shivered and crossed her arms over her bare chest. "You're angry at me." It wasn't a question, so he didn't answer. "I suppose I understand why. I guess a man doesn't like to be burdened with a woman's virginity without at least having some kind of warning."

That got him where he lived. He was about to pull back and let her cover herself with the sheet when she reached out one of her slender pale hands and touched his thigh. Instantly heat seared him, going directly from the point of contact on his leg to his groin. Blood flooded him, causing him to fill and stretch her. Her brown eyes widened.

"Austin?"

He muttered a curse and started to shift away.

She grabbed his wrist and held on. "Don't go yet. I have to tell you I'm glad it was you. I know it's silly, but you made me feel safe and wonderful. I want to thank you for that."

He shook his head. "This is the craziest thing that's ever happened to me."

Her smile returned full force. "I doubt that. You must always have women throwing themselves at you. I can't be the first one who's succeeded in seducing you."

Despite his confusion and the anger that could flare to life at anytime, he grinned at her. "You did *not* seduce me."

Her hips flexed, drawing him closer. "Sure I did."

"Rebecca," he growled, "don't toy with me."

"Then don't be angry. Oh, Austin, I know this isn't what you planned, but it was perfect for me. You made my first time wonderful. I'll treasure this always. I didn't come here to trap you, and I didn't mean to lie. If you knew what it's been like being a twenty-nine-year-old virgin... I told a couple of men I'd been dating and they stared at me like I was crazy. They couldn't get away from me fast enough."

"Then they were fools."

Her blush had faded, but now it returned. "Thank you."

He stared down at her, at her naked, slender body, so pale against the black satin comforter, at her hair fanning out around her shoulders. Her mouth was slightly swollen from his kisses, her skin flushed with faint embarrassment. Despite the warmth of the room, or perhaps because of their intriguingly intimate position, her nipples were hard, two coral-colored, tempting peaks.

He ran his hands down her bare thighs toward her center, then drew back before touching her soft, protective curls. "I'm not the answer to your prayers, Rebecca. I'm no hero."

"You're wrong about that, but I know what you mean. I'm not looking for a commitment. I just want to forget about my past, and my virginity was the last reminder. I'd saved it for Wayne and he's been gone a long time. I wanted *it* gone, too. Please don't make a big deal out of this. I won't."

"I want to believe that."

She raised herself up on one elbow and drew an X over her left breast. "Cross my heart. I'm not involved. I know you're not, either. You've had so many women that in two weeks you won't even remember my name."

Her smile was too much to resist. He bent forward and pressed his mouth to hers. She still tasted sweet. That surprised him. He pulled back and studied her face. The air of innocence continued to cling to her, as if it had nothing to do with the loss of her maidenhead. He grimaced at the old-fashioned phrase. What was wrong with him? So she'd been a virgin. So he'd been the one to change that. So what? It didn't *mean* anything.

"I'll probably remember you for at least a month," he said, trying to match her light tone.

"I'm not going to get all weird on you, Austin." She traced his face, her touch warm and soft against his skin. "I know you're completely out of my league."

He was only five years older than she was, but suddenly he felt like a debauched old man. Her sweetness mocked his black soul, her quick, easy smiles hurt his tired eyes. He'd seen too much, done too much, lived too long in the dark. She was right—he was out of her league, but not in the way she imagined.

He felt her hand slip from his jaw to his neck and then lower. She rocked her hips slightly, urging him to take advantage of their position and his aroused state.

He couldn't. He swallowed and tasted the bitterness of regret on his tongue. When he started to pull out, she murmured a protest. He silenced her with a quick kiss. "You'll be sore enough in the morning," he said quietly.

He went into the kitchen. Candlelight danced against the walls and ceiling, weaving erotic patterns that made him want to forget what he'd just done. But he couldn't.

Deep inside the darkest, blackest part of him, a primal rage swelled. It wasn't directed at Rebecca, but at the cosmos and fates that had drawn them together. His muscles tensed. Sound vibrated in his throat, but he swallowed the words because they had no meaning. He fought the sexual thoughts that flooded him and the urge to claim this woman again.

The primitive reaction, the desire to proclaim her as his own, shocked him. He'd spent most of his adult life fighting against his primal nature and the sudden confrontation with that animalistic side of him was unexpected. Was it about bedding a virgin or bedding Rebecca? A shudder racked his body. He didn't want to know.

"Austin, are you okay?" she called from across the room.

He cleared his throat. "I'm fine." He banished those thoughts to a small place in his mind and turned his back on them.

He returned to the bed, knelt beside her and brushed the hair from her face. "How do you feel?"

"Wonderful."

"Sore?"

She shifted, then grimaced. "Maybe a little."

Her pale body looked so slender and fragile on his big mattress. He wanted to take back all they'd done together and forever erase it from both their memories. At the same time, he wanted to take her again. He didn't. Instead, he slipped under the covers beside her. The storm had passed, but the electricity stayed off. She snuggled against him, her body feminine and warm. He thought about pushing her away, then told himself it was a little too much like closing the barn door after the horse was long gone. So when she rested her arm on his chest, he pulled her close, slipping one leg between hers.

"Thank you again," she said, resting her head on his shoulder. "Now I'm just like everyone else. Normal."

"What are you going to do with your newfound freedom? Start seducing unsuspecting men?"

She giggled softly. Her breasts gently brushed his side and her breath fanned his face. He tightened his arm around her back and rested his cheek against her hair.

"No. I'm not the seducing type. I would like to find someone and get married. Have a few kids."

"Maybe you'll meet another Wayne."

She stiffened slightly, then relaxed. "I don't want another Wayne. I could never love anyone the way I loved him."

He hadn't expected her words to affect him, but they did. Occasionally he was reminded of his solitary existence. Most of the time it didn't bother him; he even preferred life that way. But sometimes, like tonight, the words crept past his barriers and entered his soul. Sometimes he felt regrets for what he'd lost and a sense of longing for what he would never have. If only things had been different.

Austin grimaced, then called himself a fool. It hadn't been different, and he'd given up on wishes a long time ago. They didn't make any difference, anyway.

Rebecca snuggled closer and sighed. "Are you still mad at me?"

"I was never mad."

"Good." She leaned over and kissed his cheek, then settled down with her head on his shoulder. "Night, Austin."

"Good night, Rebecca."

Within seconds she was asleep. He listened to the sound of her breathing. He would like to think his expert lovemaking had worn her out, but he had a feeling her exhaustion was more about the stress caused by the fire than anything else.

He tried to turn away from her, but even in her sleep she clung to him, seeking out his warmth, holding on to him with her arms and legs. He fought against the desire her presence evoked. His body betrayed him, hardening into throbbing need. It would be easy to roll her over and take her again. She probably wouldn't mind. But he couldn't.

Rebecca Chambers had been a virgin. He shook his head, unable to believe it even now. She'd been right. He wouldn't have made love with her if he'd known the truth. Not because he was afraid of hurting her, but because it implied a gift he didn't want to have. She'd promised to walk away from him and not look back. Was that possible? She'd sworn she had no emotional connection to him.

He shifted slightly, pulling her closer and gently rubbing her back with his hand. She slept on.

He couldn't argue with her logic. He wasn't relationship material. He didn't want a wife and didn't know the first thing about being a husband. As long as they were both able to walk away, there wouldn't be a problem. Besides, he wouldn't ever have to see her again.

He closed his eyes, then opened them suddenly. Of course he was going to have to see her again. She was moving into his house with her orphans. A premonition of danger filled him. He tried to fight the feeling, but it was too strong.

She'd promised to walk away and not look back, but it wasn't going to be that easy. As he stared into the darkness he wondered what kind of a price he would pay for this night.

Rebecca awoke to bright sunshine and the smell of coffee. She stretched against the soft sheets and opened her eyes.

This wasn't the children's home. This wasn't even the school auditorium where she'd spent the past few nights. She glanced around the unfamiliar loft, then gasped.

She was in Austin's bed.

She stared down at the wide mattress, at the decadent black satin comforter, then rubbed her fingers against the expensive sheets. Without thinking, she started laughing.

"I guess this means you're awake. How'd you sleep?"

The low masculine voice cut through her amusement. Rebecca glanced up at Austin, who was leaning against the kitchen counter. With the sunlight behind him, she couldn't read his expression, but his body proclaimed him wickedly male, in jeans and a worn sweatshirt pushed up to the elbows.

"I slept great," she said. "How about you?"

"Not bad."

She couldn't believe they were having this mundane conversation, especially after what had happened last night. He continued to stare at her. She didn't know whether to dive under the covers and hide, or toss the sheets and blankets aside and boldly offer herself up again.

He took the decision away from her by turning toward the counter. "Coffee will be ready in about two minutes if you want to wash up first."

"Okay." She reached for the robe he'd draped across the foot of the bed and slipped it on. When she stood up an aching soreness between her legs reminded her of their lovemaking. As if she needed reminding.

Once in the bathroom, she quickly checked her reflection in the mirror, searching for any changes. Her face looked the same, if a little pale. There was no visual proof of the difference in her body, but she felt the relief clear down to her bones. She wasn't a virgin anymore. Thank goodness. And Austin, she thought, giggling softly.

As she washed her face and brushed her teeth, she reveled in the sensual memories. He'd made everything perfect, bringing her exquisite pleasure, and ridding her of the reminder of her failure with Wayne. It was as if someone had lifted a great weight from her shoulders. She was free.

She wanted to do it again. She paused in the act of rinsing out her mouth. Would he want to? She'd read in an article in a woman's magazine that men liked to have sex early in the morning. Something about their hormones peaking. She knew it was shameful, but she would very much like to have him in bed with her again. Last night everything had been so new, she hadn't had a chance to pay attention to what was happening. Plus, it had been kind of dark and she hadn't been able to see much.

She reached for a towel and wiped her mouth, then grinned. She felt wicked and very much alive.

There was a window overlooking the back of his property. She looked out and saw the ground had dried. No doubt she would be able to drive her car right out. She turned toward her clothes hanging on the shower door. The dress and blouse were dry, as well. She thought about putting them on, but decided to wait. If she did manage to entice Austin back to bed, the robe would be less cumbersome than her dress.

Humming happily under her breath, she left the bathroom and headed for the kitchen. Austin stood where she'd left him, leaning against the counter. He'd set two cups on the table. She reached for the one lightened with cream and smiled.

"Good morning."

Instead of responding, he looked at her. Something dark and frightening flickered in his gray eyes, then he blinked and his expression was devoid of any emotion. Sometime while she'd slept he'd showered and shaved. His jaw was clean, his hair damp and brushed away from his face. She thought about him moving her clothes out of the way and then putting them back. Had he thought about her as he'd touched her things?

This morning his mouth was pulled into a straight line, but she remembered last night when he'd smiled at her in bed. They'd been naked then, touching. She'd been scared but willing, wanting him to be the one with her, in her. She took a sip of coffee and waited for him to speak.

The silence stretched between them. Her good mood began to fade. "You're angry again," she said, wishing he would stop staring at her as if he hated her.

"No. Concerned."

"Why? I promised not to have any regrets or second thoughts and I don't."

A muscle tightened in his jaw. He turned away. She gripped the mug to keep it from slipping out of her hand. He wasn't worried about her. Her second thoughts weren't the problem. *His* were.

"Oh, no." She set the mug on the table and stared at her feet. The floor was shiny with the morning sun reflecting off the polished wood. "You thought it was awful. You're sorry we did it."

"It wasn't awful," he said, his voice low and controlled.

"But you are sorry." She risked glancing at him. He stared out the big kitchen window. The stiff set of his back and shoulders spoke volumes. "Is it because I was a virgin?"

He nodded slowly.

"Why? It's no big deal. I'm the only one it affected and I wanted it gone. You did me a really big favor. I'm grateful."

He glanced at her and raised one dark eyebrow. "Grateful? I doubt that."

"Oh, Austin, it's the nineties. Don't get all macho on me. I have no claim on you. You made my first time terrific and I'll always be pleased about that. Everything went just the way I wanted it to. Can't you believe that? Is this some weird guy thing?"

"I guess it must be."

She wasn't sure, but she thought she saw a slight smile threatening at the corners of his mouth. "If you really want to believe it meant something or was some kind of gift, then consider it an early Christmas present."

"One I can't take back."

It might hurt to hear the truth, but she had to know. "Do you want to?"

He stepped close to her. She was glad she'd put her coffee cup down, because when he touched her face, she gathered enough courage to place her hands on his shoulders.

His kiss was soft and fleeting. When he would have pulled back, she raised herself on tiptoe and clung to him. Their breaths mingled; his heat warmed her. The pressure of his large hands caressing her back made her lean nearer and offer herself to him.

When he reached for the collar of her robe, she held her breath. In the bright morning light, she could see his face, the desire in his eyes. His black hair gleamed. She touched the damp strands, their coolness contrasting with his heat. His worn sweatshirt was soft against her fingers, his muscles hard. Long legs brushed hers.

As he lowered his head to her neck, her heartbeat increased. Her blood raced faster and hotter, her knees trembled. She told herself it was just her crush. It was just sex and the desire to experience it all again. It wasn't him. Austin Lucas wasn't the sort of man a woman willingly fell in love with. He wasn't the marrying kind. He was sin and seduction, sex and surrender—not commitment.

He nibbled along her jaw, then pushed the robe aside and licked her collarbone. When she moaned, he raised his head and looked at her.

She wondered if he could still read her mind. Yesterday he'd known exactly what she was thinking. She tried to hide her thoughts, then realized it was pointless. Besides, Austin already knew the truth about himself. He didn't want a woman to fall in love with him. Thank goodness her feelings were just an adolescent crush. Getting involved with him would be dangerous to her well-being. Better for her to remember her own limitations.

He reached up and cupped her face, then tenderly touched her mouth with his. He moved his lips back and forth, creating a lethargy that stole her strength, leaving her clinging to him. He whispered that she was beautiful. For a moment she allowed herself the fantasy that this was real. But the thought was too fantastic to imagine. He didn't want a woman like her in his life permanently. He didn't want anyone.

Did he ever get lonely?

The question surprised her. She must have instinctively stiffened when she thought it because he glanced at her and smiled. "What's got you looking so serious?" he asked.

"I was just thinking about you." At his frown she was quick to assure him. "Not in a good way." She paused. "I didn't mean that exactly. Of course I was thinking nice things, but not that nice. That is—"

He silenced her with a quick kiss. "I know what you're saying." He stepped back and drew her robe around her securely, then tightened the belt.

"What are you doing?" she asked.

"Covering up the temptation."

"Oh." She was disappointed. "Why?"

"Because it's safer for both of us. I'm going to order the furniture for the children tomorrow. When do you want it delivered?"

She allowed herself to be distracted by his question, mostly because she was on shaky ground. Had he stopped kissing her because of what she'd been thinking, or didn't he want her anymore? She could ask, but the truth was she didn't want to know.

She sat down at the table and sipped her coffee. There was a blank pad of paper and a pen. "May I?" she asked, pointing at them.

"Help yourself." He took the seat opposite.

"I'd like to look at the place this morning, then I can give you an idea of a delivery date."

"The house probably needs painting and cleaning."

She brushed her hair out of her face. "I've got plenty of volunteers." She made a few notes.

They discussed the logistics of getting everything done. When her list was two pages long, she looked up at him. "Any special rules?"

He shrugged. "I can't think of any except I want the kids kept away from the barn. There's lots of electronic equipment in there and some tools that could hurt them. I'll keep it locked when I'm not downstairs, but it would be better if they avoided the area."

"I can do that." She scribbled another note. With Austin's generous help, it was all coming together. "So between the— Why are you staring at me like that?"

He didn't answer. His gray eyes bore into hers. She'd seen him angry before, laughing, sarcastic and distant, but none of those emotions had prepared her for the darkness she saw flooding his irises. "Austin?"

He blinked as if coming out of a trance. "Did you plan last night?" he asked abruptly.

"Plan it? I don't understand."

"Figures. When I asked you if it was safe for us to make love, what was I talking about?"

She gripped her pen tightly in her hands. This was so embarrassing. "About, you know, sexually transmitted diseases. I've never been tested or anything, but you don't have to worry. There can't be a problem. I've never been with anyone else."

He flinched as if she'd slapped him. "That's not what I meant. When I asked if you were safe I was talking about birth control."

She felt her mouth open, but she couldn't speak. Birth control? Oh, no. She stared at him, at those fathomless gray eyes, at his unreadable expression, and thanked the Lord she didn't have a clue as to what he was thinking. She didn't want to know. Birth control. It had never crossed her mind.

Without thinking, she touched her stomach through the robe. It felt exactly the same. Panic flared, but she fought it down. She closed her mouth.

"There's no need to worry," she said. "It was just one time. There's no possible way I could get pregnant."

Chapter Five

Austin bent over the engine of his Mercedes, but he couldn't block out the sounds behind him. Straightening slowly, he reached for a rag and cleaned his hands. After tossing it down, he looked toward the slight valley through the grove of trees.

A large, empty house stood alone in a patch of sunshine. Grass stretched out fifty feet in each direction before blending into cultivated forest. Normally the house stood silently, a solid reminder of his achievements. He'd told the Realtor that he was buying the property because the barn and loft were perfect for his needs. What he'd never mentioned to anyone, what he'd barely admitted to himself, was that he'd bought it because of the house. The three-story building could easily hold all the kids from the children's home. It was a big old Victorian mansion, with more rooms than he'd bothered to count, two staircases and a master suite that could house a family of four.

He'd never spent a single night there. It was enough that he owned it. When he doubted himself, when he believed the lies his mother had told him as a child, when the foretelling of his future came back to haunt him, he walked to the top of the grassy knoll in front of the garage and stared at the empty, silent house. The big structure was his medal of honor, his proof that they'd all been wrong. He hadn't ended up a criminal in prison. He'd made it out. He might still be a bastard, but he was also his own man. He'd made his way.

Today, however, when he walked to the top of the knoll and looked down, the house was alive with activity. Volunteers had parked their cars near the front lawn. Children played in a side yard. He could hear their laughter and shrieks. Bits of conversations drifted to him. He caught a word, part of a sentence. It looked like half the town had turned out to help Rebecca get his house ready for the children.

Just two days ago she'd been naked in his bed, stirring softly in the bright morning light. Then she'd driven out of his life and he hadn't seen her since. He'd been half expecting her to show up and ask him to help. It was his house, after all. But she hadn't.

He watched as a little girl in bright pink pants and white T-shirt toddled toward the trees. Before he could start walking toward her, an older child, a boy of seven or eight, saw what she was doing and ran to grab her hand. He pulled her away from the trees and back into the center of the game they'd been playing.

Something tender and wistful caused Austin's throat to tighten. As soon as he recognized it, he banished the feeling. He was getting old and stupid, he told himself. Who was he trying to kid? He had no room in his life for children, or a woman, for that matter. He wanted his relationships on his terms. Casual sex, minimal conversation.

Nothing long-term. Nothing else was safe. Rebecca was smart enough to know that about him. That's why she'd left without looking back. As she'd so bluntly put it, he'd done her a favor. They were both realistic enough to look at that night for what it was. No ties, no questions about feelings or love.

Love. He shook his head. Love was an illusion. Something men said to get women into bed and something women used to trap men, then steal their money. He didn't want any of that in his life. He didn't even want a relationship. God help him, that was all he needed. Some clingy female cluttering up his space.

He was about to head back to his garage when a shiny new minivan pulled up in front of the Victorian house. Travis Haynes, the local sheriff, stepped out, then hurried around to assist his very beautiful, very pregnant wife down.

Austin told himself it was rude to stare, but he couldn't look away. He'd known Travis since they'd been eighth-graders in junior high. Elizabeth was the first woman his friend had ever found happiness with. They practically glowed when they were together. Travis had taken a lot of teasing from his brothers and from Austin when he'd fallen for Elizabeth. Austin wondered how much of their good-natured ribbing had been generated by envy.

As Austin watched, Travis hurried off, then returned quickly with a chair. He placed it in the shade and made sure Elizabeth was settled before going off to help the others. Another car pulled up behind the van. Kyle, Travis's youngest brother, got out and went to greet his sister-in-law. They talked briefly, then laughed. The sound of their amusement floated to him, taunting the silence around him and making him want to walk over and join them. He knew Kyle and Elizabeth would welcome him. There was certainly enough work for an extra volunteer.

He took a single step toward the house, then stopped and turned back to the garage. With a shake of his head, he banished all thoughts of the people working close by. He didn't need them. He didn't need anyone. He'd always been solitary. It was safer that way—easier to hide the truth from everyone. It wasn't as if he was lonely.

He made a few adjustments on the car engine. The Mercedes required a lot of work, but it was worth it. Like the house, he'd bought it because of what it represented. He didn't care what other people thought of his wealth—he flaunted his possessions for his ghosts. When the mocking voices from the past rose up to smother him, he silenced them with a list of accomplishments.

Sometimes he stared at his investment statements, unable to believe the balances in his accounts. He knew he'd been lucky. His ability to predict trends, to visualize a substance and then chemically engineer it, had earned him independence and a fortune. For whatever reason, God had reached down and touched his brain, allowing him to work his magic in his lab. Several large aerospace firms and the military had tried to buy out his patents, but he would only lease them, holding on to them for the future. He wasn't sure why. Certainly not for his children. He didn't have any.

Unless Rebecca was pregnant.

Austin straightened slowly. He'd done his best not to think about her. Hell, he'd even considered finding someone else to be his regular bed partner, but he couldn't seem to stir up any interest. For a brief moment he allowed himself to fantasize about the possibilities if Rebecca had been different. If she'd been experienced and willing to get involved with something unemotional and temporary.

"Yeah, right," he muttered, leaning against the side of his car. He had a bad feeling that if she was that type of woman, he wouldn't have wanted her in the first place.

He swore. He'd just admitted he wanted her at all. What was wrong with him? He couldn't be interested in a woman like her. She was the marrying kind. She'd been a virgin at twenty-nine. He wasn't sure he'd ever met a virgin over the age of eighteen before. Most of them were smart enough to stay clear of him. But not Rebecca. No, she'd come calling, practically throwing herself at him. Thinking her sexy thoughts and then staring at him with those big brown eyes. How was he supposed to resist that? It wasn't his fault.

He drew in a deep breath and let it out slowly. He was going to have to talk to her eventually. Find out if she was pregnant.

Pregnant. The thought made his blood run cold. Please, God, anything but that. He couldn't bring a child, his child, into the world. He knew what would happen—the same thing that had happened to him. No one deserved that kind of life.

When the horrors from his past threatened, he ignored them. In a few days he would go to the house and they would have a rational conversation. Like two adults. He was probably worrying about nothing. After all, they'd only done it once. What were the odds of her getting pregnant?

Before he could figure them out, a small sound distracted him. He turned toward the noise and saw a young boy standing on the driveway in front of the garage. He wore clean jeans with a blue T-shirt and scuffed athletic shoes. White-blond hair hung down to his eyes. The boy didn't say anything, just stood slightly outside the garage, looking in.

"Hi," Austin said.

The boy looked up. The tilt of his head caused his bangs to fall to the side, exposing big blue eyes. All morning Austin had heard the laughter and excited screams of the children as they played. The not unpleasant sounds had reminded him of his time in the Glenwood children's home.

However, the child in front of him didn't look as if he'd participated in any of the games. His expression was wary and sad, far too old for a seven- or eight-year-old boy.

When the child didn't return his greeting, Austin tried again. "What's your name?"

"David."

"I'm Austin." He held out his hand. The boy stared at him, then slowly moved into the garage. They shook solemnly. Austin gave him a quick smile, but the child didn't respond. His face was pale, as if he hadn't spent any time in the sun with the other children.

Something tugged at Austin's memory. David. Had Rebecca mentioned the boy when she'd explained why she needed the house? Was he the one who'd lost his parents and sister?

"Am I in trouble?" the boy asked, his voice low and quiet.

"For what?"

"Rebecca said we weren't suppose to come up here and bother you. I was just lookin'. I'll go back now."

Austin recalled the rest of the boy's story. He had relatives fighting over his parents' estate, but no one wanted him. Austin knew what it was like to be cast aside. As long as he lived he would never forget his own mother's angry words as she'd dumped him on another relative or friend.

Without trying, he remembered being in her old Mustang. She always made him ride in the back seat, as far away from her as possible. They'd pulled up in front of the house of one of his uncles. He'd tried to fade back into the dark upholstery so she would forget he was there with her, but it hadn't been enough. He could still hear the silence after she'd turned off the car's engine, then the strike of the match as she'd drawn it across the matchbook. He inhaled the acrid smell of sulphur and the scent of her cigarette.

She'd half turned toward him then, her hazel eyes staring at him, loathing oozing from her as visible as sweat.

"Uncle Fred said he'd keep you for a few weeks. I've got to get a job. You're just too damn expensive, Austin. Stop eating so much. And don't get your clothes dirty. You're a pain in the neck, kid. When I run out of relatives willing to take you in, I'm gonna dump you completely. So don't screw this up, you hear?"

Her hair had been the same color as his, black as midnight. Even then, at five or six, he'd thought her beautiful. And very cruel. He'd loved her and hated her with equal intensity. By the time he was eleven, she'd beaten and starved all the love out of him. When she'd finally made good on her promise to put him in a children's home, he'd almost been relieved.

He fought off the memory, mentally flinging it away from him, hating the weakness that allowed him to remember or give a damn. When he refocused on the garage, the boy was already turning away, prepared to go back alone to the new children's home.

"Do you like cars?" Austin asked.

David stopped in his tracks, then slowly looked back. "I used to. My family died in a car crash."

He spoke matter-of-factly. Austin was appalled. The boy must have heard adults saying the words over and over again for him to deliver them without emotion.

"Are you afraid of them now?" he asked.

David's mouth twisted as he thought about the question. "No. I don't think so. I wasn't there when it happened. I was spending the night with Randy. His mom let me stay with them until I came here."

Austin tried to imagine what the boy had been through. First he'd lost his entire family. Then, he had relatives who didn't want him, only his money. Finally he'd found some kind of peace at the children's home and the damn building had burned down. It was too much for anyone, let alone a seven-year-old.

Austin dropped to a crouch. He was close enough to touch the child, but he didn't. He remembered his own distaste when strangers had tried to cuddle him. That kind of affection had to be earned.

"Why'd you come up here, David?" he asked, careful to keep his voice low and friendly.

The boy shrugged. "Rebecca said you had a bunch of tools and stuff. I used to make things. You know, with my dad. I helped him make a bookcase once. He let me put on the varnish." David's thin chest puffed up with pride. For a second Austin thought he might smile, but his mouth remained straight.

"Maybe we can work on something together," Austin offered without thinking. He instantly wanted to call the words back. He didn't have the time or inclination to get involved with some kid. Besides, the problems with the estate would be settled and David would be moving on.

But he needn't have worried. David nodded, but didn't look enthused, as if too many people had made promises and then not followed through.

Austin rose to his feet. "We'd better get you back to the house before everyone realizes you're missing."

"They won't notice until dinner. Rebecca does a head count then. But I'll go back." David glanced up at him, as if searching his face for something. Before Austin could speak, he turned and started walking away.

"David."

The boy paused.

"I'll walk you back."

He looked surprised. "Really?"

"Sure. I don't want you getting lost."

David glanced through the trees toward the house, then back at him. "I can see everyone. I won't get lost."

Again Austin dropped to a crouch. This time he placed his hand on the boy's shoulder. He met his troubled gaze. "I was making a joke. I know you won't get lost. I'll feel better if I walk you back. Is that okay?"

David's white-blond eyebrows drew together. "I guess." He glanced at the hand on his shoulder. Austin thought he might pull away. He could feel the boy's bones through the thin material of his T-shirt. But David didn't step back, and Austin wondered if he'd misjudged the child. Maybe he wanted to be held and hugged. His parents had probably touched him. He might miss the contact. Unlike Austin, whose only regular physical closeness with his mother had been the back of her hand across his face.

Austin squeezed gently, then stood up. As they walked toward the other children, he tried to make conversation. "What do you think of the house?"

"It's big. I like the yard. There's no swings, though. At the other place there were swings."

"What else do you like to do?"

David shrugged but didn't answer. Before Austin could think of another question, he heard someone calling his name.

He looked up and saw Kyle jogging toward him. A deputy sheriff, Kyle was the youngest and tallest of the Haynes brothers—about six-two—with the Haynes-family dark, curly hair and good looks. He was a good kid who had a way with women. As Kyle came to a halt in front of him, Austin grinned.

"What's so funny?" Kyle asked. A lock of hair flopped onto his forehead. He brushed it out of the way with a familiar, impatient gesture.

"I was just thinking of you as a kid, but you're not anymore, are you?"

"Nah. I'll be thirty next year. Practically over the hill."

"Time to settle down and raise a family." Austin made the observation mockingly.

Kyle planted his hands on his hips and glared at his friend. "Yeah, sure. I'll find the right woman and get married right after I figure out the answer to world peace. Why are you just now showing up here? It's nearly two o'clock."

Austin glanced at David who was openly listening to their conversation. "This young man came to visit me. I'm bringing him back."

Kyle grinned and grabbed Austin's arm. "I don't think so," he said, hauling his friend toward the house. "You're going to help me paint."

Austin glanced at Kyle's jeans and shirt, for the first time noticing they were covered with flecks of white. "I don't have the time."

"Bull—" Kyle glanced at the boy. "Uh, make that I don't believe you. You're the one who donated this house in the first place, so it's your fault we all had to come and do work. The way I see it, you don't have a choice about helping."

"I don't, do I?" Austin allowed himself to be pulled toward the front steps. He glanced behind and saw David standing uncertainly on the lawn. He pulled free of Kyle's grip and turned to the boy. "Looks like they're going to force me to paint. You want to help?"

David stared up at him, his big eyes wide and blue. He wanted to believe him, Austin could tell. He wanted to participate and have fun, but he was afraid. Austin felt as if someone had reached inside his chest and crushed his heart. He knew exactly what David was thinking because he'd been there. The boy took a step closer.

"Looks like you've made a friend," Kyle said. "I didn't know you liked kids."

David froze. Hope fled his expression. "My aunts and uncles don't like kids, either." His voice sounded wary and far too old.

Austin told himself it would be easier just to walk away. David wasn't his problem. Rebecca or one of the other volunteers would take care of him. If they noticed one small boy standing on the sidelines. How would David grow up? Would he withdraw more into himself, or would he lash out, funneling his hurt into anger and rage, becoming a bully, hurting others before they hurt him?

Austin shrugged. "Kids are okay," he said, knowing if he made more of it he would be lying and David would know. "But if I have to paint, I wouldn't mind some help."

David swallowed hard. "Okay," he said, trying his best to sound casual, but unable to hide the eagerness in his voice. He ran up the stairs and waited by the open front door.

Austin glanced at Kyle. His friend grinned. "Isn't this interesting."

Austin gave him the ice glare. "Don't say a word," he growled.

Kyle's grin got bigger. "Who me? Never."

Two hours later, they'd almost finished painting a small bedroom. Austin glanced at the floor, then at the boy standing next to him. There was more paint on the newspaper covering the carpet and on David than on the walls, but the job was getting done. While Austin worked the roller, David carefully painted the baseboards and outlined the window. Austin would finish up around the glass later.

He listened to the sounds of conversation in the other rooms. They'd only run into a few people as they'd come into the house and been assigned a room to paint. No one had said anything about his joining in uninvited or the fact that David was going to help. He wondered what Rebecca would make of the whole thing, but so far he hadn't seen her.

"My room was blue," David said as he bent over the door. Austin had taken it off the hinges and laid it over two sawhorses. The boy worked slowly and carefully, making his brush strokes all go in the same direction. If he glopped paint up occasionally, Austin didn't think whoever was going to stay in this room would mind too much.

"You must miss it," Austin said.

"A lot. Sometimes when I first wake up in the morning, I forget. When I open my eyes, I can't remember where I am." David bit down on his lower lip.

Austin panicked at the thought of having to deal with tears. He didn't mind the kid helping him, or their talking about the boy's past, but he wasn't equipped to deal with any kind of pain.

"You got enough paint, there, sport?"

Momentarily distracted, David glanced down at the small tray Austin had given him. "I think I need a little more."

"Coming right up." He dropped the roller into the pan and bent over the paint can.

"Well, what have we got here? Two strong, handsome men painting a room. Be still my heart."

Austin didn't have to turn around to recognize that voice. He knew the owner intimately. Without having to close his eyes, he could see Rebecca stretched out naked, her pale body contrasting with his black satin comforter. Her dark hair fanning out over her shoulders, her eyes two parts welcoming and one part scared. He could taste her and feel her, and damn it all to hell, he was getting hard.

He picked up the paint can and held it in front of himself while he tried to think mundane, nonsexual thoughts. "Hello, Rebecca."

"Austin, what a surprise."

Her smile was as sweet as he remembered. Despite the fact that everyone at the house was cleaning or painting, she wore a dress. Some floral-print gauzy thing that fluttered around her knees and left her arms bare. The thin fabric brushed over her slender curves, hiding rather than accentuating, but he didn't need to see them to remember how they'd felt in his hands and mouth. That train of thought wasn't helping his condition, so he forced himself to study her face instead.

Her only concessions to the cleanup was that she'd pulled her hair back into a braid and wasn't wearing a scrap of makeup. Her gaze met his bravely, then ducked away. She seemed calm and in control, but he could see the blush on her cheeks.

"What brings you here?" he asked, pouring paint into David's tray.

"I heard you were helping us. I confess I thought Kyle was joking, but I see he wasn't." They were standing closer now. The small room got smaller. She had to tilt her head back to meet his gaze. "I'm so pleased you decided to come over. I'd wanted to ask, but I didn't want to intrude."

"Kyle shanghaied me into it."

"I see." She turned to David. "It was good of you to pitch in. Are you doing that door all by yourself?"

For the first time since he'd met him, David smiled. Then he nodded vigorously. "I did the baseboards, too."

Rebecca glanced around at his handiwork. "I'm very impressed. I told everyone this morning that you children didn't have to work if you didn't want to. You're the only one who's helped us." She bent down and fluffed his bangs, then kissed his cheek. "Thank you, sweetie."

David mumbled something under his breath and ducked his head.

Rebecca took the brush from his hand and put it on the tray. "There's lemonade and cookies on the lawn. Why don't you take a break and have a snack? When you're done, I'm sure Austin would like you to bring him a glass of lemonade."

David looked up at him. "That would be great, sport," Austin said.

"Okay. I won't be long." The boy ran out of the room.

Rebecca straightened and stared at her hands. She had paint on her thumb and forefinger. "I really appreciate your taking the time to work with him." She rubbed at the paint while she spoke.

"No problem. He found his way up to my garage. I was walking him back when Kyle insisted I help with the painting."

"Oh, no. I told everyone to stay away from you. I'll remind them again after dinner."

"I didn't mind."

She looked up at him then, her brown eyes wide with surprise. "Really?"

"Yeah, well, David's no bother."

"Oh, Austin."

He almost groaned aloud. That damned look was back in her eyes. The one that said she thought of him as a knight on a white charger. Women. He thought his behavior the other night would have chased away all her foolish illusions.

It was the wrong thing to think about, because it made him remember her in his bed and how his body had felt next to her. It also made him remember that she'd been a virgin and that they hadn't used birth control.

"Rebecca, we have to talk."

She rubbed at the paint one more time, then dropped her arms to her sides. "I know. But not now, okay? There are lots of people around and I don't want them overhearing this."

"Fine. We can do it later, but soon."

"I'm sure there's no problem."

He wished she was right. Life was rarely that simple. He set the paint can on the floor and picked up the roller. He turned his back to her and started on the wall. "I'll finish this room before I leave."

"Oh, you don't have to run off." She'd moved closer. Even with the windows open paint fumes filled the house. Despite their acrid aroma, he could still smell the faint scent of her body. Vanilla. Why did she have to smell like vanilla? "There's going to be a potluck dinner in a couple of hours. You're welcome to join us."

"No, thanks." He felt her moving closer. If she touched him he would be lost.

"But I— Oh, David, you're back already."

"I brung you lemonade, Austin."

He glanced down at the boy. "I appreciate this." He took the glass and downed it in four long swallows. "That was great," he said, handing it back.

David looked from him to the empty glass, then giggled. Austin smiled. He made the mistake of raising his gaze to Rebecca's. The starry-eyed stare was back. He clamped his lips together and tried not to swear in front of the kid.

"Are you staying for dinner, Austin?" David asked. "They're already setting up the tables. There's a big barbecue and corn on the cob and everything."

"I don't think I can..."

David clutched the glass tightly in his small hands. "You can sit by me."

Austin studied the youngster. Two hours ago the boy had stood outside his garage, all solemn and far too clean for a normal seven-year-old on a spring Saturday. Now he was smiling, not a lot but still smiling, and covered with paint. He looked...better. Happier. Austin knew he was a bastard through to his soul, but he couldn't deliberately hurt the kid.

"Sure, I'll sit by you," he said, knowing this was going to make Rebecca want to canonize him. When he got her alone, he'd make sure she understood he was absolutely the last person in the world to qualify for sainthood. If she could read his mind and know that all he wanted was her naked, in his bed, legs spread and her woman's place wet and hot, she would change her mind real quick. Only he wasn't going to tell her what he was thinking. The way his luck had been running, she would want to act out his fantasy.

David grinned, then handed Rebecca the glass and started painting the door again.

Rebecca leaned close to Austin. Too close. "Looks like you've made a friend."

They were the same words Kyle had spoken, but this time he didn't mind them as much. "Maybe. He's a good kid."

She stared into his eyes. He tried not to read her emotions. After a moment she smiled. "See you at dinner."

"Yeah, sure."

She turned to leave, pausing only to ruffle David's hair. The boy looked up, seeming to like the physical contact.

They worked for another hour and finished the room, then made their way to the cleanup station in the empty utility room. An older man was taking the dirty brushes and sending people to wash at one of the various bathrooms in the house.

"What have we got here?" the man asked. "Two fine workers by the looks of things. The bathroom by the front of the house should be empty by now, if you two gents don't mind sharing."

"We don't mind," David said, before Austin could answer.

As they turned away, the boy reached up and took his hand. Austin almost stumbled from surprise. He glanced down at David, seeing the child's hope and an expectation of rejection. His fingers were small and warm, sticky with paint. Austin squeezed them gently, then headed for the bathroom. As the boy chattered about the upcoming meal, Austin told himself the sudden tightness in his throat was from the paint fumes and nothing else.

Chapter Six

It was nearly eight in the evening when the last carload of volunteers pulled out of the makeshift parking lot and headed down the dirt driveway toward town. The setting sun caught the slightly rusted front fender of the old station wagon parked by the trees and reflected a single beam toward the wide front porch. Rebecca closed the front door of the mansion and dropped the key into her dress pocket, then moved to the stairs and took a seat next to Austin.

"That's the last of them," she said as she settled herself on the wooden step. He shifted to make room for her. She wanted to tell him not to bother, that she wouldn't mind if their arms brushed, but she figured he might not want to know about that. After all, two mornings ago he hadn't taken her up on her subtle offer to make love again. She didn't think it was because he hadn't read the intent in her eyes. Austin might have a few flaws, but stupidity wasn't one of them.

"You had a lot of people out here helping," he said.

His voice was low and controlled. She liked the sound of it, of him. When he spoke, she wanted to stretch like a cat napping in sunlight. Her body grew warm, her mind lethargic. It would be easy to start purring. She bit her lower lip to keep from smiling.

"Everyone has been very helpful," she agreed. She drew her knees up to her chest and wrapped her arms around them. The full skirt of her dress fell past her shoes. She stared out at the vast expanse of green lawn and the grove of trees beyond. The sun had slipped lower, until most of it was hidden behind the leafy branches. The slight breeze still carried on it the warmth of the day. Despite her bare arms, she felt no chill.

Without wanting to, she turned toward Austin. His profile fascinated her—the straight nose, the well-formed lips. Her gaze moved slightly to the right and she saw his gold-hoop earring. It was silly how that tiny piece of jewelry got to her. She supposed it was because this was Glenwood and men didn't wear earrings. Somehow it made Austin appear even more wicked. And tempting and—

"What did you say?" she asked, realizing he was speaking to her.

"I asked when you thought the painting and cleaning would be finished. The furniture is ready to be delivered anytime."

"Oh." She thought for a moment. "There are only two more rooms to paint, and they're pretty small. The kitchen has been scrubbed from top to bottom, so I'd guess by noon tomorrow. Is that all right?"

He looked at her. Pure gray eyes met and held her own. She wanted to see desire and affection lurking there. Of course she saw nothing of the sort. Austin kept his feelings carefully concealed. It was part of his charm, she admitted to herself. The mystery about him. Why was it women were instinctively drawn to men who were bad for them? It didn't make sense. Thank goodness her feelings for him was only a crush that would fade with time. Any woman who actually fell for Austin was destined for heartbreak.

"I'll call the man in the morning and have him bring everything somewhere between noon and two."

"That would be great. Thanks." She smiled slightly. "I know you don't want to hear this, but I really appreciate everything you've done for the children. First loaning me the house, then paying for the furniture. And you were terrific with David today. He had a great time with you. Since the accident he's been withdrawn and..." She stopped talking when he groaned low in his throat and rose to his feet. "What's wrong?"

"Stop looking at me like that," he commanded, pacing in front of the steps.

"Like what?"

"Like I'm some damn nice guy."

"But you are. Austin, you've proved it over and over. Face it, there's no way a man who opens his house to orphans can be all bad."

He swore under his breath. She pretended not to hear the word or notice the way he was rubbing his temple, as if he had a headache.

"Besides," she continued, "there are worse things than being a nice guy."

He stood in front of her, his legs spread slightly, his boot-clad feet firmly planted on the walkway. Flecks of paint had spattered his worn jeans and red polo shirt. "I am not, and I have never been, nice."

She shrugged, fighting a smile. "If you say so."

"I do."

The last rays of sunlight caught his long hair, making it shine. There was no hint of other colors in the dark strands, no red or brown, just pure black. Broad shoulders tapered to a narrow waist and hips. He was tall, strong and good-looking. A predator with a gentle streak that he didn't want to acknowledge. She didn't mind. Knowing it was there was enough.

When the intensity of his gaze started to make her nervous, she glanced around at the wide porch. It was big enough for a small dance to be held there. Everything about the house was oversize. It was a stunning home, but empty.

"Why did you buy this place?" she asked.

He looked up past her to the wide windows and the peaked roof. "Because I could."

That didn't make any sense. "Do you ever plan to live here?"

He shrugged. "I'm not sure. I like the loft. It's convenient and more my style."

"Then the house is just for show?"

He dropped his gaze to her face. "Exactly."

She wondered who he was showing it to. Judging from the lack of furniture and the dust on the floors, he hadn't spent any time in the mansion at all. So he hadn't bought it to impress women. Obviously he hadn't been inside the house for years.

"I'll do my best to keep the kids under control," she said. "They can be really hard on a place. You've been so generous. I don't want to repay that with broken windows and crayon drawings on the walls."

He moved to the stairs and took his seat next to her again. "Don't worry about it. I've already told you—I'm doing this because when I showed up at the home, the people there were good to me. I owe them. I wasn't the easiest kid in the world."

She turned her head toward him. "Gee, why doesn't that surprise me?"

He smiled slightly. "I guess it's pretty obvious I've never been a model citizen."

"You're not so bad." She released her knees and straightened up. "You didn't have to help out today, but I'm glad you did. I never thought David would enjoy spending time with a man. I'll make sure someone can work on a project with him in the future."

"He's a good kid."

Rebecca rested her elbows on her knees and dropped her chin to her palms. "The whole problem with his family makes me crazy. I can't believe his relatives don't want him. He's smart, funny, well behaved. What's not to like? I just don't understand people like that."

"How can you be in your business and still be so damned innocent?"

Austin's angry tone caused her to draw away from him. "What are you talking about?"

He gestured widely. "You work with these kids every day. You know about the abuse and neglect. Adults who use children for their perverted sexual pleasure. Parents who abandon their flesh and blood. Hunger, drugs, crime, they all prey on the young. You have to know about it, and see it. Why do you still believe in happy endings?"

"I'm not Pollyanna."

"You're damn close."

"I know bad things happen to children. But good things happen, too. Orphans find new families. Sick kids get better. Okay, so some don't find complete happiness, but I believe in doing everything I can to help. Why do you want to make that sound like such a crime?"

His mouth twisted at one corner. He shifted until his back pressed against the pillar at the top of the stairs and he was facing her. One long leg stretched out behind her back. The other bent at the knee with his foot resting on the second step. The toe of his cowboy boot was hidden by the hem of her skirt.

"You're trying to empty the ocean with a teaspoon."

"At least I'm trying. What are you doing to make it better?"

"Saint Rebecca."

Usually she was able to control her temper. The little things that annoyed most people rarely got to her. But Austin's cynical view of the world rubbed her the wrong way. "So what's your story? Why do you insist on seeing everything from the worst possible angle? I know you were in the children's home when you were a kid. Is it that you didn't get adopted? Do you think the system failed?"

He raised one eyebrow. "I couldn't have been adopted. My parents were both still alive."

"Then why were you there?"

She blurted out the question without thinking, then wanted to call it back. The sun had fallen behind the trees, leaving them in shadow. The cries of the night creatures began softly, building in sound and intensity with each passing minute. The smell of earth and grass, the coming cool of evening, reminded her that she was alone with Austin. Isolated with a man she didn't really know. They'd been intimate with each other. She knew a little about his body, his touch and his kisses, but almost nothing about his soul. He played the villain to hide a softer side. That she believed. But why he felt he had to conceal his gentleness she didn't know.

Something deep inside, some voice she'd learned to listen to, whispered that it was better she didn't understand him. She knew instinctively that learning the truth about Austin would be deadly. Not because the information would scare her away but because it would be too easy for her crush to blossom into something more dangerous. A woman would be a fool to care about a man like him. She knew that as surely as she knew the sun would rise tomorrow. Everything about him and his life-style screamed that he was destined to break hearts. Hers was already so fragile she wouldn't survive if it shattered again.

"You really want to know why I was at the home?" he asked, his voice deceptively lazy as if he didn't care about her answer. But her time with the children had taught her to look past the obvious. The sudden stiffness in his shoulders, the watchful expression in his eyes warned her that her answer carried some significance.

She didn't want to know. She would regret hearing his story. Yet the side of her that he mocked, the instinct to heal, was too powerful to be ignored. "Tell me, please."

"My mother wasn't much interested in raising a kid. She used to dump me with relatives while she went off and had a life. Eventually she ran out of family, so she left me on the steps of an orphanage up by Sacramento. When I turned out to be more than they could handle, they sent me here."

He spoke the words casually, as if they told a story about someone else. The urge to reach for him and hold him close almost overwhelmed her, but she forced herself to stay where she was.

"How old were you?" she asked.

"Ten or eleven. She came by every few months to take a couple of pictures of me." His mouth twisted. "She needed proof that I was alive to keep her meal ticket going."

"I don't understand."

He'd been looking out into the night, but now he turned his dark gaze on her. His eyes bore into her, as if he were searching down into her soul. She felt cold suddenly, although the temperature hadn't changed. She folded her arms over her chest and shivered.

"Blackmail." He let the single word hang alone for several seconds. "My father was—" he shook his head "—is a successful politician in Washington. Married, two kids, conservative constituency. He made the mistake of having an affair with my mother back when he was a nobody. She got pregnant and decided he was her meal ticket."

"She used you for blackmail, then left you in an orphanage?"

"No big deal."

No big deal? Who was he kidding? Rebecca stared at him, trying to absorb what he'd told her. How could any mother treat her child like that?

"I don't know what to say," she murmured. "It must have been awful for you."

"I got by."

She remembered Austin's care when he'd worked with David that afternoon. No wonder he'd handled the boy so well. He knew what it was like to lose everything. "You know what David's feeling," she said. "That's why he likes you so much."

"You're making it more than it was. I let the kid help me paint the room. Nothing more. I'm not like you, Rebecca. I don't believe the world's worth saving."

"That must make your life very lonely. How do you stand it?"

He glared at her. "I think I liked you better when you were spilling things and couldn't get out more than a sentence without blushing."

"I didn't know you liked me at all," she blurted without thinking.

"I don't generally sleep with women I dislike."

"But I seduced you. It wasn't your choice."

He leaned forward until they were close enough for her to feel the heat of his body. Excitement licked up her spine. "How the hell can you still be so innocent?" he asked. "Honey, you never had a prayer of seducing me. If I hadn't been interested, we wouldn't have done it."

She wrinkled her nose. "Big talk now that it's behind us. You keep your interpretation of what happened and I'll keep mine."

She studied the lines of his face. Stubble shadowed his jaw. The twilight pulled the color from his features, making his eyes look dark and mysterious. A waste of time. He didn't need any help to be more appealing. There was something too magnetic about him already. If only she could figure out what it was. She knew it was something about the way he was always alone. Maybe he challenged women on a primal level. Maybe females were instinctively drawn to a solitary male, wanting to bring him into the circle of intimacy.

"Now what are you plotting?" he asked. He moved a little closer. For a moment she thought he might kiss her. Anticipation made her body hum.

"I was wondering if you are ever lonely," she said without thinking, then could have cheerfully slapped herself.

Predictably Austin withdrew, pulling back until he was leaning against the pillar. He folded his arms over his chest. "Save it for the children. I don't need you trying to get inside to save me, Rebecca. Even if you had a prayer of getting the job done, I'm not interested in being saved. I like my world just the way it is."

"All right." She stretched her legs out in front of her, resting her heels on the lowest step, and folded her hands in her lap.

"Why don't I trust you?" he asked. "That was too easy."

"*I'm* not the difficult one. I'm straightforward, open, honest. You're the brooder. You can make fun of me all you want, but I'd like to point out that I'm a tiny bit closer to normal than you."

His gaze flickered over her face. A smile pulled at his firm mouth, but it wasn't humorous. "Let me guess. You're one of four kids?"

"Three."

"All girls."

She clutched her knees again, pulling them close to her body. "How'd you know that?"

His smile turned genuine. "Because you're such a girl yourself."

"What does that mean?"

"Look at you. You wear dresses all the time. Floral lacy things. You probably don't own a pair of jeans."

"It's hardly a crime."

"You were never a tomboy." He spoke with the confidence of a man who knows women. She wasn't sure if that was good or bad.

"You're right. I never wanted to play rough with the boys. I liked being a girl, and I like being a woman. I like doing female things. Cooking, being with the children."

"Don't defend yourself. I was making an observation, not a criticism."

His good humor had returned. Apparently he'd put her question out of his mind, but she hadn't. Did Austin get lonely? Did he really plan to spend the rest of his life living in his loft by himself? She couldn't understand that. All her life she'd wanted a husband and family. Back in high school and college, she'd studied hard because she'd wanted a career, but she'd always known that wouldn't be enough for her. She needed people around her. She needed a family. She liked the rhythm of life, births, holidays, the passing of the years. Sometimes her heart felt so full of love she thought it might burst open. She wanted a man in her bed, the same man, night after night. She wanted to feel her child growing inside her, then watch that child change from an infant to a toddler, from a teenager to an adult. She wanted to give her child the love-filled life she'd had when she'd been growing up.

She looked up at Austin. He was staring into the distance, his dark eyebrows drawing together in a faint frown. He was good-looking enough to make her weak with longing. There was just enough of a bad boy inside him to push her past reason. But he wasn't the one. She knew that. She needed someone like herself. Someone who believed in family values and shared her philosophy of life. She needed a man, not the temptation of the devil in disguise.

Funny that the devil had been the one to save her. Finally she felt like every other woman. Without the albatross of her virginity hanging around her neck, she was free to start looking for someone to share her life with.

Not someone like Wayne, she thought firmly. She'd loved him with all her heart, but it had been a young love. She would never know if it would have lasted through the changes maturation brought. She wanted to believe it would have, but she wasn't sure.

"We have to talk about it, Rebecca," Austin said at last, breaking the silence between them.

She knew exactly what he was referring to. "I'm not pregnant. I didn't try to trick you into anything. Why can't you let it go?"

"Because my luck isn't that good. When's your period due?"

She opened her mouth to answer, then closed it as color flooded her cheeks. She'd been doing so well with him, too. But with one simple question he left her embarrassed and gasping like a fish.

She ducked her head. "Ten days," she mumbled.

"The home pregnancy kits I looked at said you could check within three days of being late."

She stood up. "I can't believe we're talking about this. I'm *not* pregnant. We only did it once. What are the odds?"

"As long as there's a chance you are, we have to talk about it."

He rose to his feet, towering over her. She refused to be intimidated. "No, we don't. If I'm pregnant, which I'm not, then it's my problem. I don't want or need your help."

He grabbed her shoulders. "Damn it, Rebecca, I'm not going to be responsible for bringing a bastard into this world."

She shook herself free of his grasp. "It's not up to you. If I'm wrong, then I'm keeping this child and you can't make me choose otherwise."

He flinched as if she'd slapped him. Some emotion tightened his mouth briefly. "That's not what I meant," he said, his voice low and strained. "I can't..." He shook his head. "Thirteen days, then. Let me know either way."

He hurried down the stairs and toward the grove of trees that separated the house from the two-story barn. She moved to the edge of the porch. "Austin, wait."

He didn't stop, didn't even slow down. His long legs carried him farther and farther away, and then he was lost to the night.

Squeals of laughter carried across the bright green lawn. Rebecca smiled at the sounds, then sank back into the comfortable lawn chair that had been a gift from the hardware store in town. Tall, leafy trees provided shade from the afternoon sun, but the kids didn't seem to mind the June heat.

"I could get used to this," Elizabeth said from the chair next to hers. Rebecca's friend sipped on her icy glass of lemonade, then held the tumbler to her flushed face. "I've finally found a comfortable position. Do you think I could take this chair home with me and sleep in it?"

Rebecca laughed. "Go ahead. You need your rest." She glanced at her friend's rounded belly, stretching the front of her maternity blouse. The pale peach fabric set off Elizabeth's faint tan and brown hair. Even with her stomach sticking out and her ankles swollen, she looked beautiful. There was a contentment in her eyes Rebecca envied.

Elizabeth smiled at her. "I can't believe I have almost a month left. I feel like I'm going to go at any moment. I keep asking the doctor if she could have made a mistake and she just gives me that knowing grin of hers. It makes me crazy.''

"It'll be worth it," Rebecca promised. She raised herself into a sitting position, then swung her feet over the side of the chaise longue so that she was facing the other woman. "Soon you'll have a new baby. You must be excited."

"I am. But it's been so long since I had Mandy, I'd forgotten nine months felt more like nine years."

A loud burst of laughter caught Rebecca's attention. About ten of the children were playing a complicated game on the front lawn. They raced around, laughing and yelling to each other. Yesterday had been the last day of school, and to the children, summer stretched endlessly in front of them.

"They seem to have recovered from the shock of the fire," Rebecca said.

"Thanks to your hard work."

Rebecca shrugged. "Just doing my job. It's really the volunteers who deserve the credit. All the cleaning and painting. Plus Austin donating the house. We'd still be sweltering in the school auditorium if it wasn't for him."

Elizabeth grinned at her. "So how is it living so close to him? Are you getting over your crush or is it getting worse?"

"I haven't figured that out yet." Rebecca set her glass on the ground. "He's not exactly how I imagined him to be."

"Better or worse?"

She thought about her last conversation with Austin. She didn't know what to make of all that he'd told her. The horror of his past, the way he wouldn't admit to being a nice guy, his patience with David, his insistence on being a loner.

"Maybe both," she answered.

"That's definitive. By the way, I never got a chance to ask you before. What happened the night of the storm? Rumor has it you spent the night at his place. That couldn't possibly be true, could it?"

Rebecca saw the teasing look in her friend's eyes. Elizabeth was one of her closest friends. She trusted her completely. It would be a relief to tell someone what had happened. She opened her mouth to speak, but no words came. Rebecca tried again, then shocked herself and Elizabeth when she burst into tears.

"Rebecca?" Elizabeth scrambled into a sitting position as quickly as her distended belly would allow. "What's wrong?"

"Oh, n-nothing." Rebecca buried her face in her hands, trying to stop the flow of tears. She felt like a fool. "I d-don't know why I'm acting like this. I did spend the night with Austin and I'm really h-happy about it."

"I can tell." She felt the other woman's cool hands on her bare forearms. "Hush, honey. You're going to be fine. Take deep breaths."

Rebecca tried to inhale deeply. Her shoulders were shaking and her throat felt raw. "I'm overreacting, I think."

"I would guess so."

Rebecca looked up and glared at her friend. "You're not helping."

"I don't know what's wrong. How can I say the right thing if I'm completely in the dark?"

Rebecca sniffed. "I guess that makes sense." She straightened and wiped the back of her hand across her face. Elizabeth looked at her with growing concern. "I'm fine," she assured her. "Really."

"So what happened?"

"I—" She clamped her mouth shut. How was she going to say this delicately? "Austin was— He told me that—"

Elizabeth raised her eyebrows until they touched her bangs. "Yes?"

"We had sex."

"Oh, my." Elizabeth stared at her for several seconds, then started chuckling.

Rebecca glared at her. "You're not supposed to laugh. It isn't funny."

"Yes, it is. You've had a crush on him for years, then the first time the two of you are alone, you sleep together." She grinned broadly. "Little Rebecca, I would never have suspected that of you. How was it?"

Rebecca straightened her shoulders. "I can't believe you asked me that." She brushed away the last trace of her tears, then looked down and smoothed the front of her pale blue sundress.

"And?" Elizabeth asked.

Rebecca sighed. "It was wonderful. If you repeat that, I'll deny every word."

"My lips are sealed." Elizabeth leaned forward and squeezed her arm again. "Are you okay? The way you said it, I assume there wasn't any talk about having a relationship."

"Austin doesn't do relationships." She thought about all they'd discussed. She couldn't tell anyone about his concerns that she might be pregnant. She and Elizabeth were close, but even she didn't know about the whole virginity issue. "I'll admit that our night together didn't lessen the intensity of my crush, although I can hold a conversation with him now without making a complete fool of myself."

"That's progress." Elizabeth reached for her glass and took a sip, then tucked a loose strand of hair behind her ear. "What happens now?"

"I don't know. I still like him, but I've realized I don't know anything about him. He's always so apart from everything. He was generous in giving me use of this house and paying for the furniture. I think he's a nice guy, although he hates it when I tell him that."

Elizabeth tried to stand up. She leaned forward and pressed her hands on her thighs, but she couldn't get any leverage. Rebecca stood up and held out both hands. When her friend took them, she pulled her to her feet.

"Thanks." Elizabeth smoothed her short-sleeved, peach top over her belly and grimaced. "I look like a whale."

"You look beautiful."

"Thanks for lying. It makes me feel better." She rubbed the small of her back and stepped from between the chairs. "For what it's worth, I don't think any man likes to be called nice. It upsets their macho self-identity."

"I'll keep that in mind."

Elizabeth shaded her eyes against the afternoon sun. "Travis should be here any minute to pick me up. I'm going to grab my daughter and get out of your way. Call me if you want to talk."

"I will."

They hugged, then Elizabeth headed for the house. Rebecca lingered by the chaise longues, not wanting to leave her shady spot. She had tons of paperwork to fill out, but the thought of locking herself in her small office was too depressing. She felt restless and out of sorts. She didn't want to admit it, but she had the horrible feeling it was because she wanted to see Austin. He was just on the other side of the trees. It would be easy enough to stroll over there, but so far she hadn't come up with an excuse to go find him.

A low, rumbling sound broke through her musings. She turned toward the noise and saw a large truck turning the corner and moving onto the driveway. The heavy vehicle lurched forward slowly, rocking and swaying as it rolled over the uneven dirt road. The children outside stopped playing and came to gather around her.

"What do you think it is?" one of the boys asked.

"I don't know," she answered. "We haven't ordered anything that big."

The truck came to a stop about ten feet in front of the lawn. A burly man with gray hair jumped out of the driver's side, while a younger man stayed in the cab.

"I'm looking for Rebecca Chambers," the driver said, waving a piece of paper. "I got a delivery here."

"What is it?"

He peered at the sheet. "A playground set with extra swings."

"Let me guess. It was purchased by Austin Lucas."

"Yup. Where do you want it?"

Before she could answer, the children broke into cheers. One of her assistants, Mary, came out of the house to see what was going on. Rebecca explained about the equipment and asked her to show the men to the side yard. She watched the children lead the way.

Why was he doing this? He, who claimed to have no feelings about anyone, who had told her more than once he was a complete bastard, had bought playground equipment for the children. What was going on?

She took one last look at the kids, but they were too busy to notice her. Mary would keep an eye on them, she told herself, turning on her heel and heading through the trees.

Before she'd made it halfway through the grove she admitted she was using this as an excuse to see him. Before she'd made it out of the grove she'd admitted she didn't care if it was an excuse. She had to see him if only to have him yell at her. It didn't matter what happened when they were together. It had been less than a week since she'd seen him, and she missed him.

She shook her head as she marched past the garage and up the cement and brick pathway. If she was the swearing sort of person, she'd be saying something creative right now, but she wasn't. She balled her hands into fists and called herself a fool. At least that had a ring of truth.

At the door to the barn, she paused long enough to make sure her headband was in place and her dress smooth. Then she pulled open the outer door and stepped into the foyer. Before she could lose her courage, she grabbed hold of the door to the laboratory and yanked it open, then stepped inside.

She wasn't sure what she'd expected. Perhaps loud screeches from metal machines and smoke circling on the floor. She knew he invented something to do with heat-resistant substances but wasn't exactly sure what.

The long lab was surprisingly quiet. Computers hummed, as did the air-conditioning unit that kept the room a comfortable temperature. There were long tables against the walls, and shelves filled with equipment. The intimidating machines reminded her that Austin was both highly intelligent and incredibly rich. Obviously she was in over her head. What had she been thinking of, having a crush on him? He would never want someone like her in his life. He would want someone like him. A scientist maybe, or a doctor.

She looked around and wondered if she should just leave. It might be easier for both of them. Before she could duck outside, she heard a clunk, then footsteps. Austin came around one of the big computers. He wore jeans and a long-sleeved white shirt rolled up to his elbows. As he walked toward her, he pulled goggles off his head. When he spotted her, he stopped and stared.

"Rebecca. What are you doing here?"

She'd tried to prepare a rational speech. At the sight of him, it fled her brain. She felt as stupid and incapable of intelligent conversation as she had when she'd stood dripping in his garage.

She opened her mouth to thank him for the playground equipment, but those weren't the words that came out.

"If you want me to stop thinking about you, about that night, then why are you being so nice?" she asked without taking a breath. "Just stop it. Did you have to give the kids your house? Did you have to send over furniture? And now this. Playground equipment. How am I supposed to resist that? How am I supposed to put you behind me and date someone else? You're messing up my life, here, Austin. I don't want to get involved with you. You certainly don't want to get involved with me. I know you don't want me or anything, so please, don't do this anymore. I can't take it."

She stopped talking and waited for him to yell at her. She couldn't believe what she'd said. Her only saving grace was that it was the truth.

"Damn it, Rebecca, you think I don't know that?"

She stared at him stunned. "Wh-what did you say?"

"Do you think I like this thing between us? I don't. I hate it." He tossed the protective goggles on the desk and moved closer to her. "I'll stop being nice if you'll stop haunting me."

"I don't—"

She never got to finish her sentence and tell him she didn't understand. He stopped directly in front of her and placed his hands on her shoulders, then hauled her hard against him. Even if she'd wanted to protest, she couldn't have. He tilted his head slightly and brought his mouth down to hers.

Chapter Seven

Austin hoped Rebecca would bolt or slap him, anything to keep him from the madness that possessed him. She did neither. When he touched his lips to hers, she moaned softly and brought her hands up to his shoulders. Her slender body pressed against his.

She tasted as sweet as he remembered and she smelled of vanilla. When he brushed his mouth back and forth over hers, she parted for him, calling him into her. He told himself to back off, that she was more kinds of trouble than he could handle. He didn't know what it was about her that got to him. It could have been her innocence or that damn crush. He had a bad feeling that he was having one last fling with the world before shutting himself down completely. Who could say?

None of it made sense. Not her reaction to him, nor the way he couldn't stop thinking about her.

He slipped one hand under her hair behind her neck. She was warm and smooth to his touch. He threaded his fingers through her long, silken strands, wondering how they'd feel on his thighs, forming an erotic curtain as she took him in her mouth.

He groaned low in his throat at the thought, deepened the kiss and ground his hips against hers. She answered by pulling him closer still, gripping his shoulders and whimpering against his assault.

He knew it was a mistake, that he was playing with fire, but he didn't give a damn. He brought his other hand down from her throat to her breasts. He brushed across her slight curves, feeling the taut nipples through the layer of her clothes. She gasped at the contact. Her sundress had a long row of impossibly small buttons down the front. As he opened them one by one, he kissed the line of her jaw, then moved lower, planting more kisses down the side of her throat.

She held on to him as if she had no strength left. Her body trembled against his. When he'd unfastened the buttons down to her waist, he nudged her backward until she was against the desk. He shifted her so she sat on the raised surface. Only then did he look at her face.

Her flushed skin made her eyes look bigger. She met his gaze with an unfocused stare. Knowing he was ten kinds of fool and possibly the biggest slime ever to walk the earth, he took her headband off and tossed it behind her onto the desk. With one quick jerk, he pulled her dress down her arms. She wasn't wearing a bra.

He stepped back and looked at her. The long, flowing fabric was soft and romantic. Her hair fanned over her shoulders, partially concealing her naked breasts. She was the picture of seductive innocence and he wanted to take her right there, plunging deep inside over and over again until they were both shaken and exhausted.

She read his mind. Slowly her eyes focused on his face. Her gaze dropped lower, stopping at the obvious proof of his desire. Her welcoming smile ate away at his fading self-control.

"Yes," she whispered, tossing her hair back over her shoulders and baring herself to him.

"Damn you, woman," he growled, then swooped down on her.

He kissed her neck, her ears, her eyelids. He plunged his hands into her hair, holding her immobile. When he kissed her, he was violent, searching her mouth, biting her lips. He whispered exactly what he wanted to do to her, what he wanted her to do to him, in the most graphic of terms. As he licked her ears, he explained exactly how he would feel in her mouth, and then what she would feel when he did that to her. Even as his body got harder, aching with the need to take her, he waited for his actions and words to scare her off. He monitored her gasps of pleasure and surprise and waited for her to push him away in disgust.

She didn't. When he bent over to take one of her hardened nipples in his mouth, she breathed his name and pulled his head closer. When that wasn't enough, she parted her legs and pressed her damp center against him. His half-formed plan had backfired. She wasn't afraid of him—he was turning her on. Austin cupped her breasts in his hands and buried his face in her hair. He hadn't planned on making love with her on his desk, but why not? It wasn't as if she was still a virgin.

But she had been. They hadn't used birth control and he didn't have anything with him now. It was unlikely she did, either. She might already be pregnant with his child. What the hell was he thinking of?

He tore himself away from her and walked over to a workbench by the front door. He leaned against it, not wanting to look at her, not able to look away. She stared at him, obviously as stunned by the passion between them as he had been. She touched her fingers to her swollen mouth. "Austin?"

The air-conditioning clicked off, leaving only the hum of the computers. In the quiet of the large room, their breathing was audible. He tried to tune out the sound, along with the faint echo of his name. He did his best to ignore the pressure of his erection and the heat boiling his blood.

"How do you do that?" she asked, her voice quiet in the stillness. "You make every part of me tingle as if I've never really been alive before."

"Stop," he commanded. "Stop before you say something you'll regret."

She surprised him by smiling. "I have no regrets. Not about you, about what we did last week, or even about this." She waved her hand in front of her body, then glanced down. Her dress pooled at her waist, the short sleeves hung on her forearms. She was bare to his gaze, but didn't seem embarrassed. Casually she pulled up her dress and began to fasten the buttons. Her smile deepened. "Okay, I'll admit to one regret. That you stopped."

He pushed off the workbench and stalked toward her. "Don't play with me, Rebecca. You don't have the armor to survive in this league. If you don't watch your step, you're going to find yourself falling hard and getting hurt. I'm not interested in your gentle dreams of children and white picket fences. If you get in my way I'll take what you're offering, and when I'm done I'll walk away without looking back."

She finished fastening her buttons, then searched behind her for her headband. After securing it, she looked up at him. "Are you trying to convince me or yourself?"

He took two steps and closed the gap between them. Leaning forward, he gripped her shoulders. There was nothing passionate or gentle about his touch. He squeezed harder, not caring that he might mark her.

"Grow up," he growled. "Look around you. I'm not salvageable. Find someone else, someone like you. Someone who hasn't seen this world in all its ugliness. Someone who can still believe in happy endings."

Her brown eyes burned with conviction. "You believe. You just don't want to admit it." He knew he had to be hurting her, but she didn't flinch or try to pull away. "I'm not afraid of you, Austin Lucas. I know the truth."

"Bull. I told you I was placed in the Glenwood home when I was thirteen, but I didn't tell you when I left, did I?"

She shook her head.

"I stole a car when I was fifteen. The police caught me ten miles the other side of the Oregon boarder. I served my time in a juvenile facility until I was eighteen and they cut me loose."

"So? A lot of people make mistakes when they're kids. It doesn't mean anything."

He let her go and stepped back. Not because he was pleased with what she'd said, but because his level of frustration had increased his temper to a point where she was in danger.

"Listen to me," he said, his voice low and controlled. "Listen to what I'm telling you. I'm not a nice guy. There's no profit in being nice. I want to live my life by my rules. I've never been married because I don't see the point. I've had women in my life. Lots of women, but no serious relationship. Ever. Because I don't want one. I'm not interested in having one with anyone, including you. The sex was great, I'll admit that. But that's all it was—sex. Go home. Find yourself someone who wants to get married and have babies. Stop trying to fix me."

Rebecca stared at him without saying anything. Her big brown eyes searched his face as if he held the answers to her questions. He wanted to tell her he wasn't good for anything, but he doubted it would matter. Maybe he'd convinced her and maybe he hadn't. Either way, he wanted her gone from his lab, his property and his life. He wouldn't make her leave the house; he'd already given his word that the children could stay there. But he was going to make damn sure that they stopped running into each other. Every time he saw her he thought about their night together. Worse, he wanted to repeat it. Even knowing she was innocent and he was the wrong man to get involved with someone like her. Even knowing she had the power to rip him apart and leave him bleeding. Even knowing she might be the only one brave enough or stupid enough to keep trying to get inside. He wouldn't risk it. He'd learned that lesson too well.

She lowered her gaze, then nodded as if coming to a decision. "All right," she said, her voice steady. "I understand what you're saying. Just answer me one question. Why did you buy the playground set for the children?"

He was glad she wasn't looking at him just then. It made it easier to lie.

The truth would only hurt his case. Buying the playground equipment had been an impulse when he'd driven to Stockton a couple of days ago. He'd seen it from across the street and had made time to go into the store. The sturdy jungle gym had reminded him of the fun he'd had with Travis and his brothers all those years ago. He'd bought it because those memories were among his best, and because the equipment had made him remember how having friends in his life had made everything easier. But that was only part of the reason. He'd bought the equipment because little David had missed playing on the swings.

Without trying to he could see the pain in the young boy's eyes. The pain of loss and abandonment. He'd once felt like that, when his mother had dumped him on some unknown relative's doorstep. He'd stood on the porch and watched her drive away. At seven he'd been confused, half hoping she would come back and get him, half praying he would never have to see her again. He'd loved and hated his mother with equal intensity. Until he'd grown up enough only to hate.

He didn't want that for David. He wasn't willing to get involved with the kid, but swings were no big deal. No child should have to survive without knowing some kind gesture.

But the lie was cleaner. He shoved his hands into his jeans pockets. "I needed the tax deduction."

Rebecca raised her head. "You expect me to believe that? You could have simply written a check. It would have required a lot less effort."

"If you don't like my answer, maybe I should just take it back."

"Tough talk. I don't buy it."

He shrugged. "Believe what you want."

She slid off the table onto the floor and brushed at the front of her skirt. "I can't win with you. You're always trying to make our conversations about something else. I'd hoped we could at least be friends, but you obviously don't want that. And I know I'm not enough like your other women to entice you to, well . . ." Her voice trailed off as a faint blush stained her cheeks. She started toward the door.

"Wait." He grabbed her arm as she walked past him. Her skin was warm to the touch. Instantly his body reacted to her closeness. He dropped her arm and tried to ignore the pressure in his groin. "You just invited me into your bed."

"I . . ." She swallowed, then raised her chin slightly. "I wasn't going to ask you for any kind of commitment. I just thought that since you were between women, and we'd already done that and it was very nice, that we might, you know." She managed to get out her entire speech without looking away from him.

She was offering him exactly what he wanted. Hot sex, no ties. Yeah, right. He studied her face. The wide eyes, the full mouth, trembling slightly at the corners. Long curly hair tumbled over her shoulders. The warm weather and her time in the sun had turned her pale skin the faint color of honey. She stood before him, a virtual innocent. She'd saved herself for twenty-nine years and now she wanted to be his mistress.

"Why?" he asked.

She cleared her throat. "I could use the experience."

Terrific. She wanted a tutor. The hell of it was he wanted to say yes. "Explain one thing to me. If you were so in love with Wayne, why were you still a virgin when he died?"

"I made a mistake," she said softly. Clasping her hands together in front of her, she stared off into the distance. "I convinced him to wait. I thought coming to him a virgin on our wedding night would really be special. A magical moment. Something wonderfully traditional in a world overwhelmed by change." She looked up at him and smiled sadly. "It probably sounds stupid to you."

"Actually it doesn't."

"You don't have to humor me, Austin. I know the truth now. Wayne never pressured me, but I knew what he was thinking. I guess every guy would think the same thing. We did other things, but never that. I was proud of myself, thrilled about my precious gift."

Bitterness tainted her words, sharpening her tone. She swayed slightly and he thought about moving closer and offering comfort. He didn't. Even if she wanted him to hold her, he would only hurt her in the end. He shoved his hands deeper into his pockets and curled his fingers into his palms.

"Wayne was hit by a car while he was out jogging," she said. "He was paralyzed from the waist down. It was about three months before the wedding. I still wanted to get married, but he wouldn't. He told me he wouldn't saddle me with someone who was less than a man."

"He couldn't . . . ?"

She shook her head, then dropped her chin to her chest. "He died hating me for that. I told him it didn't matter to me, but I could see the truth in his eyes. Every day he saw me, I was a reminder of all he'd lost. But I was too much of a coward to let him go. I was there, with him, every day until he died. It took almost a year. They said complications, but I think he lost the will to live."

Austin exhaled a breath slowly. That night when he'd first realized what he'd done to Rebecca, he'd been shocked and unsettled. He'd never been with a virgin. He'd told himself it didn't make any difference. He hadn't believed it then and he didn't believe it now. Maybe it was cultural or part of a man's genetic makeup, but bedding her had been different from bedding all the other women he'd known.

"If it meant so much, why me?" he asked. "Why not wait until you were ready to marry someone else?"

She moved toward the door, then stopped and looked back at him. "Once Wayne was gone it didn't matter anymore. I wanted it gone. You were the perfect candidate. I knew you'd never want anything permanent. Besides, I found out nobody thought of my virginity as a gift."

He had, he realized, surprised that her words slipped past his defenses and lodged themselves deep inside. He felt a small sting, knowing she'd used him. Maybe it was fair that she had, even if he'd always done his best not to use women, seeking those who shared his rule and staying away from the innocents. Until Rebecca. He'd unknowingly crossed the line.

No, he told himself. That wasn't true. Even if he hadn't known how inexperienced she was, he'd been sure she wasn't like his usual bedmates. Her crush had intrigued him, her sweetness had lulled him into forgetting his own rules.

"You took a chance," he said. "I could have hurt you."

"Oh, Austin, give it up. You'd never deliberately hurt me."

"What have I done to earn that kind of faith? You don't strike me as a fool."

"You don't strike me as the bad guy. I guess we're even." She reached for the handle and pulled it. The door swung open. "You win. I'm leaving. You've made it clear you don't want to be my friend or my lover. I guess that leaves us neighbors and nothing else. Goodbye, Austin."

He let her go because it was easier than explaining why she should stay, and because, for once, it was the right thing to do. He'd hurt her. It was inevitable. She didn't understand why he wouldn't bed her, even though she'd made the offer on what she thought were his terms. He'd warned her that he was a complete bastard, but she hadn't believed him.

He headed back into the lab, hoping to bury himself in his work and forget about her. He laughed harshly. Not a prayer of that. For the next few days he would do nothing *but* think about her, until he knew whether or not she was pregnant.

What if she was? What if she carried a child? His child.

He didn't know. He didn't want to think about her growing big with his baby or bringing a life into this world. He would kill before he would subject anyone to the torture of how he'd been raised. If nothing else, those years with his mother had taught him that children need love, stability and normal parents.

But he was the wrong person to provide any of those things. Rebecca would be a good mother, he acknowledged. Leading with her heart was what she did best. The smartest thing for him would be to forget it and not get involved. Unfortunately he didn't have a choice.

She'd thrown herself at him and he'd turned her down. After almost a week that still hurt. Rebecca sat on the cushions in front of the bay window of her bedroom and stared out at the grove of trees that separated the large house from Austin's loft. From her second-story window she could see part of his roof and a bit of one wall. Not very exciting, she admitted sadly. Yet looking at that corner of his barn thrilled her. She could close her eyes and picture him sleeping in that big bed, imagine the black satin comforter covering part of his body, but leaving bare an arm or leg.

She drew in a deep breath and sighed. She was hopeless. Despite everything that had happened between them, she was still wasting her time on fantasies. Hadn't she figured out that he wasn't interested? She'd made it very clear that she was willing to have a "sex only" relationship with him. No emotional commitment, no ties. And he'd said no.

She buried her face in her hands, fighting the wave of embarrassment that washed through her. Why had she done it? In the heat of the moment, when she'd felt his hands on her body, she hadn't been able to think at all. The wonder of being that close to him had overwhelmed her, and she'd known that it would be worth any price to keep him in her life. Even the price of being his mistress.

She raised her head slightly and glanced down at the plain cotton nightgown she wore. It covered her from shoulders to calves, draping loosely over her slight curves. It wasn't the least bit seductive. She didn't own silk underwear or paint her nails or wear exotic perfume. She still got excited about Christmas, and sometimes, on Saturday morning, she watched cartoons with the kids. No wonder Austin had turned her down. She wasn't really mistress material.

He'd told her to find someone like herself or Wayne and settle down. She'd told herself exactly the same thing. Only she couldn't seem to summon up any interest in dating. A couple of men had called during the past week, but she'd turned them down. She wanted to be with Austin or no one at all. The thought should have horrified her. After all, it was time for her crush to start fading. It hadn't. She had a feeling it wasn't ever going to.

The more she'd gotten to know Austin, the more she liked him. The more she saw the side of himself he tried to keep concealed, the more she wanted to know his secrets and discover the real man behind the facade. She'd seen flashes of tenderness, and a gentle spirit. It would be a tough fight getting him to open up, but she had a feeling the rewards would last a lifetime.

She was a fool to dream. He wasn't for her. She should simply walk away and do her best to forget. But it was too late even for that.

Her gaze moved across the room to the open door to the bathroom. On the counter sat a small cup. The pink plus on the bottom made forgetting Austin all but impossible. She was pregnant.

For a few minutes she toyed with the idea of not telling him, then dismissed it. First of all, it wasn't her way to conceal the truth. She wouldn't be able to sleep if she was that dishonest. Second, on a purely practical level, he would find out the truth when she started to show. In a town as small as Glenwood, an unwed mother, even one who was almost thirty, was going to cause some talk.

Okay, she was going to tell Austin, but what was she going to say? She remembered what he'd said about his own father, how his mother had used him for blackmail. She shuddered. Austin was rich. Would he worry about that with her? Not that he would care if anyone knew he had a child, but did he think she would try to get money out of him?

Rebecca stood up slowly and stretched. She would have to tell him right off that she wasn't interested in his fortune. She'd always wanted children. This isn't exactly how she'd pictured everything happening, but the baby was a gift from God. She was a little shocked, but happy. It was all going to work out. Somehow. If he wanted to help out, she would accept the offer, but she wasn't going to trap him.

A baby. She touched her hand to her still-flat belly. It didn't feel real. A life was growing inside her, a child she and Austin had made in that moment of love.

She took a step toward her closet, then stopped. No, not love, she reminded herself. It had been about sex and nothing else. Austin didn't believe in love and she wasn't in love with him. She might be a fool, but she wasn't crazy. Falling in love with Austin was a guarantee of heartbreak. She liked him a lot, enjoyed his company, thought he was a great guy. That wasn't love.

When she had dressed, she went downstairs to help with the children's breakfast. After that she tackled the mounting paperwork in her office, but it was hard to concentrate. She kept trying to figure out what she was going to say to Austin and wondering how he would react.

Finally, when she couldn't stand not knowing, she called out to Mary that she was going for a walk, then left the house and headed through the trees to Austin's barn. On her way she passed the open garage. Voices stopped her, and she paused to investigate.

His Mercedes sat in the center of the garage, next to a large four-wheel-drive truck. There was a hall leading to another room. That's where the voices came from.

"Austin?" she called.

"We're in here."

We? Rebecca swallowed hard. Who was with him? A woman? She hesitated, wishing she'd taken the time to put on some makeup. All she'd done was wash her face and brush her hair, then pull on one of her favorite sundresses. She glanced down at the pale, floral-print fabric. Skinny straps held up the bodice. The dress showed off her slight tan and made her feel wonderfully feminine. She'd known she would need a boost of confidence when she faced Austin. Of course she'd just assumed they would be alone.

Stiffening her spine for courage, she walked across the garage and stepped into the workshop. It was a huge open room with big windows and a long workbench down the center. Toolboxes and saws and stacks of lumber had been pushed against the walls. At one end of the bench sat Austin and David. Between them was a small wooden box.

David grinned at her. "We're making a birdhouse. Austin's gonna let me paint it."

For once the shadows had been chased from the child's eyes. His color was good, his contentment genuine.

Austin cleared his throat. "I sort of reached a dead end in my research and thought I'd take a break. David was here, so we decided to build something together."

She stared at him for several seconds before she was able to put a name to the expression she saw lurking in his gray eyes. Embarrassment. She suppressed a smile. Austin was embarrassed at being caught working with the boy. They'd obviously been having a great time together. What was the big deal? Why couldn't Austin admit he liked the kid?

Men. She would never understand them.

"I think it's terrific," she said, moving closer and studying their project. "It's going to be very nice. Where are you going to hang it?"

"Outside my window," David said. He pointed to the metal loop at the top of the roof. "Austin said we can hang a hook under the eaves and I'll be able to see who comes to live in my house."

"Pretty neat." She ruffled the boy's blond hair. He looked up at her and smiled. The poignancy of his expression made her want to weep. If it'd been her choice, she would adopt David in a minute. As a single woman, she would have problems with his relatives. They'd mentioned they were willing to let him go to a family, but abandoning him to a single parent would look bad, even to their selfish minds. Besides, she already had a child of her own to worry about.

Instantly all her concerns about Austin and how he would react returned to swamp her. She glanced at him and saw he was watching her. Could he see her guilt? Had he guessed? She sent up a quick prayer to God to please transport her somewhere else, but He wasn't listening. She sighed. He probably *was* listening, but figured she had to go ahead and face the ramifications of what she'd done.

She squared her shoulders. Not for a minute did she regret making love with Austin. She didn't even regret being pregnant. It was telling Austin about it that was giving her pause.

She crouched down in front of David and smiled at him. "I have to talk to Austin, honey. Would you mind finishing the birdhouse another time?"

David leaned forward and gave her a hug. "I'll go to the house and ask Mary for a snack."

"You do that."

He turned toward Austin. "Can I come back tomorrow?"

Austin looked uncomfortable, then nodded. "Sure, sport."

David threw his arms around him and squeezed tight. Austin sat in his chair, frozen. He made no move to hug the boy back, although Rebecca thought she saw a flicker of affection in his eyes. David released him and scampered out of the room. She heard his running footsteps on the concrete in the garage, then there was quiet.

They were alone.

She stood up, edged back from the table and started to walk around the workshop, investigating the tools and supplies.

"What's up?" Austin asked. He remained seated at the workbench and bent over the birdhouse.

His not looking at her made it easier, she told herself, even as she wondered how he could be so casual. Of course he couldn't know why she was coming to see him. But it had been exactly thirteen days. Had he guessed? Maybe he didn't care.

She sighed. What was she supposed to say? She thought of several opening lines and discarded them all. Why was this so hard? All she had to say was *Austin, I'm pregnant.* No big deal.

She stood staring at a red toolbox and opened her mouth to speak. "It doesn't mean anything." That wasn't right. She tried again. "It doesn't have to mean anything to you if you don't want it to. It means a lot to me. Of course, why wouldn't it? I just don't want you to think it's about money. Yours. I don't want it or feel that a claim is necessary. It doesn't have to be disruptive. I guess you can ignore the whole thing."

"Rebecca? What the hell are you talking about?"

She turned to face him. He'd risen to his feet and loomed over her. Six feet four inches of confused male.

"I have a great job," she said. "Lots of support, friends, a decent income. I don't have my own place, but I'll be getting one as soon as the new home for the children is built. I think it would be a mistake for me to move out while they're in temporary quarters."

"I still don't know what this has to do with anything." His gray eyes locked on hers. He wasn't smiling. He wasn't doing anything but waiting and watching. It was unnerving, like trying to take a test with the teacher breathing down her neck. "Just say it."

"I'm pregnant."

Nothing about his expression changed. His mouth stayed in a straight line. His eyes continued to hold hers. Not by a twitch of a muscle did he give away what he was thinking. She waited, clasping her hands in front of her waist, nibbling on her bottom lip. The silence stretched between them until the room vibrated from the tension. Would he blame her? Did he understand that she hadn't done this on purpose? She'd never really seen Austin angry. Would he frighten her? She knew he wouldn't hurt her, but fear could be pretty upsetting.

She tried to think of something intelligent to say. Nothing came to mind. Just when she became convinced he was never going to say anything at all, he spoke. She'd spent the morning planning her response to any number of things he might say. She thought she'd planned for every contingency. She'd missed one.

"Rebecca," he said, his voice low but clearly audible, "will you marry me?"

Chapter Eight

Rebecca might have been beautiful and gentle, and terrific with kids, but she was an amateur when it came to hiding her feelings.

Austin watched her carefully, monitoring what she was thinking. Shock widened her eyes and drew the color from her skin. Her lips parted, but she didn't speak. Her fingers twisted together. She looked as stunned as when she'd turned around and seen him undressing that night in his loft. But she didn't recoil. That was something.

She was going to refuse, of course. He expected her to. Why would a woman like her want to marry a guy like him? After what he'd told her the last time they'd been together, he was surprised she'd come this close to him again. No doubt her sense of right and wrong had convinced her he should know about the baby.

Baby. He swore under his breath and stared at her stomach. He couldn't believe it. They were going to have a child together. Whether she wanted to or not, they were going to get married. No child of his was going to be born a bastard.

"You want to marry me?" she asked softly.

"Yes."

She held out her hands in front of her, palms up. "Why?"

"Because of the baby."

"This is the nineties, Austin. You don't have to marry a woman just because you got her pregnant. I would have thought you'd be the last person to care about convention."

"I don't care what other people think. This is between you and me. I want us to get married. I want my child to have a name."

There. He'd said it. He watched as understanding dawned in her eyes. He'd told her a little about his childhood and what had happened to him. Being the compassionate type, she would melt inside. It was a dirty trick, but he didn't care. He would do whatever was necessary to protect his child from the horrors of the world. Even if he had to lie, cheat and steal. He trusted no one. Not Rebecca, not even himself.

"I thought you'd be angry," she said shyly. "You're acting very calm about the whole thing. Did you guess?"

"No, but I'm not surprised. Life has a way of holding me responsible for my actions. I didn't think this time would be any different."

"That's not very romantic." She tossed her hair over her shoulders, leaving her face bare to his gaze.

"I know. I'm sorry. This isn't about moonlight and roses, but the proposal is genuine."

"If we get married, I'll be your wife."

"I know."

"But I don't love you."

For the first time since she'd made her announcement, he relaxed enough to smile. "I know. I don't want you to love me. I want to give the baby a name and a home. Nothing else. I know this isn't what you'd planned. Maybe you would have found another Wayne. Maybe you wouldn't have. You're still emotionally connected with him. When you're ready to let go of him and move on, we'll work something out. Being married doesn't have to change our lives all that much."

She drew her eyebrows together, as if she was mulling over his argument. "I don't..." She paused, then tried a different tack. "I do care about you, Austin, but marriage, gosh, that's so huge. It's really not necessary. I can take care of the child fine on my own. He or she can have your last name. I don't mind that."

He took a step toward her, closing the distance between them. When she tilted her head back so she could meet his gaze, he gently touched her cheek. Her soft skin burned him clear down to the black hole of his heart. "That's not good enough. I've got a lot of flaws, but running away from my responsibilities isn't one of them. You were the inexperienced one. I should have known better than to assume the birth control was taken care of. I didn't know you were a virgin, but I could tell you hadn't been around. Your pregnancy is my fault. I was too caught up with wanting to get you into bed to think the thing through. Now there's a baby to consider. I won't walk away from that."

"If I remember correctly, *I* was the one making all the offers. You resisted me, almost to the end." She smiled up at him, her expression teasing.

"Rebecca Chambers, I wanted you from the first time I saw you two years ago."

"Really?"

He nodded.

"Then why didn't you say anything? Ask me out?" Her smile broadened. "Although I probably would have expired right on the spot. The shock would have been too much."

"I would never have asked you out. You're not my type."

He was being honest with her. He wondered if it would scare her away. But Rebecca was strong, even if she didn't believe it about herself. He'd always suspected there was a core of steel inside her. She proved it now by not taking offense at something that was obvious to both of them.

"If I'm not your type now, I'd better learn how to be," she said. "After all, we are having a child together. Even if we don't get married, there are going to be a lot of joint decisions." She shrugged. "The list is endless. I don't even know where to start. What kind of parents are we going to be, Austin? I don't know the first thing about being a mother."

"You're with kids all the time. You'll be fine."

"I don't know." She wrinkled her nose. "I think it's going to be different when the child is ours. That is, if you plan to be part of your child's life."

Your child. He dropped his hand to his side as a coldness swept over him. She was worried about being a mother when she had years of experience being with children. How the hell was he supposed to be any kind of a father? He'd met his own father once about twelve years ago. The brief meeting had been hostile, with the older man threatening to have Austin arrested for trespassing if he ever dared bother him again.

Could he risk it? Could he allow himself to get involved with a baby, try to guide a young child, a teenager? What did he know about growing up? His life had been a collection of different homes and relatives, of knowing he didn't fit in and wasn't wanted. He had nothing to offer a child. He didn't know the first thing about being a father.

He turned away.

"Austin, wait." He felt her slender hand on his back. "Don't be afraid. I know you don't have a lot of experience with kids, but you'd be a great father. Look at how you are with David."

He shook off her touch and walked to the far side of the workshop. What did she know? Could she smell the fear, taste it, as he could? Was she able to see into the blackness and know the truth about him? Dear God, not that. No one could ever know. He barely acknowledged the truth himself.

They were so different, he and Rebecca. She came from a warm, loving home. Her parents were still married to each other. Her only act of defiance against all the rules had been sleeping with him. The irony caught him off guard. He was the only bad thing in her life, and she was his only act of decency. Of course he'd screwed that up royally by sleeping with her.

Why couldn't she have married Wayne and left him the hell alone? Wayne would have been a great father. He had probably been born to the job.

A little voice whispered that Wayne was gone and he was here. Rebecca wasn't carrying the other man's child. She wasn't Wayne's fiancée anymore. None of it helped. He was still jealous of a dead guy. Stupid, but true.

"I don't care if I know what I'm doing or not," he said, turning back to look at her. She stood where he'd left her. Waiting. How long would she wait, hoping for a miracle? Would he see that hope fade slowly, day after day, or would it die quickly? He couldn't lie to himself. If he convinced Rebecca to marry him she would believe in him, in them. She would want it all. He could offer her nothing but his name and his money. Eventually she would figure out it wasn't enough. But she would stay because of the child, and that was all that mattered.

"I'll do my best," he said. "I want us to get married and give our child a home."

"Why should I?" she asked. "I don't need to get married to have the baby. You don't need to get married to give this child your name. Why is getting married so important?" She folded her arms over her chest and tapped one foot.

He hadn't expected that kind of an argument. "I could take care of you," he said, not sure what she was looking for. "There's plenty of money. You wouldn't have to work if you didn't want to. What are you going to do when you're eight or nine months along? I can provide health care, arrange for a nanny, even a nurse. It's hard raising a child on your own. Believe me, my mother made sure I knew how hard. It would be easier if you had someone to help." *Most of all, I don't want my child to be a bastard.* But he couldn't bring himself to say that. Rebecca already knew about that part of his life.

"How practical," she said. "All the advantages are mine. What do you get out of it?"

I get to know my kid's okay. He didn't say that, either. "That's not important. Isn't it enough that I want to do this?"

"No." She walked toward him. When they were less than a foot apart, she placed her hands on his chest. "I'm not always a practical person. What if I want to marry for love?"

"I thought you loved Wayne."

Slowly she shook her head. "Wayne was the love of my youth. I'll never know what would have become of that. But he's gone. I've let him go. What if I want to hold out for love and passion? What if I want the fairy tale?"

His chest burned where she touched him. He could feel the heat circling through him. He could show her passion in a hot minute, but he suspected that wasn't all she was talking about. It wasn't just about sex. It was that something more. He'd seen it occasionally lurking in the eyes of a few of his lovers. Even though they'd known the rules of the game, sometimes they'd stared at him and he'd seen their hopeful expressions. He knew what they wanted, and he was confident he didn't have it to give.

"I don't know any fairy tales," he said. "I don't believe in love."

She didn't flinch or back away, and he was again reminded of her subtle strength. "Do you believe in anything? Do you at least like me, Austin?"

"Yeah. I like you."

"Tell me why."

Slowly he reached up and touched her hair. The long curly strands slipped against his finger. Raw silk, he thought. He could tell her that her hair was the most beautiful thing he'd ever seen and touched. But he didn't. He dropped his hands to her shoulders and his gaze to her breasts. He could tell her that she had driven him past reason in bed, that he couldn't stop thinking about her, of being with her, in her, touching her in wildly sensual ways she would never have imagined. But he didn't. His gaze moved back to her mouth and he could hear her voice, the sound of her laughter. He could tell her that he could listen to her talk for all eternity. Her beliefs, her innocence, her faith, all delighted and shamed him. He could tell her that she made him hope, even though hope was painful. But he didn't. He found a truth because she deserved one, but it was a safe truth.

"I like you because you think of the children first," he said.

She tilted her head slightly and pursed her lips together. "Okay. I guess I buy that. Kiss me."

"What?"

"Kiss me. I mean a real kiss. Kiss me like you want me."

Finally, something he could handle. As he bent his head closer to hers, he thought it was a strange request, then realized he didn't care. He'd spent the past several days remembering the last time he'd kissed her. It was definitely something he wanted to do again.

As always the first brush of her lips made him realize how warm and tender she was. She raised her hands to his face, holding him close to her. He tried to be gentle, moving softly against her mouth, but she wouldn't let him. She raised herself on tiptoe, and angled her head. Then her tongue pushed past his, invading his mouth, sending fire racing in all directions.

She sucked on his lower lip and murmured his name. Her hands slipped from his face to his shoulders, then down his back. Slender fingers reached for, then gripped, his rear. Involuntarily he tilted his pelvis forward, pressing his manhood against her belly. A minute ago, he hadn't thought of making love with her. Now his body was hard and ready.

Her tongue continued to play against his. He chased hers back so he could taste her sweetness. His hands roamed her torso, tracing the line of her spine, then circling around to cup her breasts.

He raised his head long enough to glance at the workbench. It was plenty long and wide, although it wouldn't be that comfortable. Of course, Rebecca could be on the top. Then he could cushion her from the wooden surface.

Before he could voice his opinion on the matter, her hand moved from his rear to his hip, across the front of his jeans to the length of his desire. She cupped him lightly. He sucked in a breath and arched against her, wishing there wasn't anything between his heated flesh and her palm. He wanted her like he'd never wanted another woman.

The thought was like being doused with cold water. His desire didn't fade, but his rational mind had a chance to take hold. He dropped one of his hands over hers. After squeezing gently, teasing himself with the potential release, he drew her fingers away. This wasn't supposed to be about him at all. This was supposed to be about the baby and convincing Rebecca to marry him.

He stared down at her, at the passion darkening her eyes. Her mouth was damp from his kisses, her face flushed. He could see the hard points of her nipples though the fabric of her dress.

"That was some kiss," she said, her voice throaty. "I like you, too, Austin. Does that surprise you?"

It did, but he just shrugged. He lowered his arms to his sides. She kept one of her hands on his waist. He hated that he liked the feel of her touching him.

"I like that you're good to me and the children. I like how you are with David. You want to think the worst of yourself. I'm not sure why."

It was because he knew the truth. But he couldn't explain that to her. He hoped she never had a reason to find out.

"I don't love you," she went on, "but I respect you."

It was enough, he told himself. Better, in fact. Anyone who cared about him too much would end up finding out he wasn't worth the trouble.

"And I will marry you."

He told himself that the emotion filling him was relief and that he pulled her into his arms to thank her and not to keep her from reading his expression.

"You won't regret it," he said, burying his face in her sweet-smelling hair. "I'm not Wayne or anything like him, but I'll do my best to be a decent father and husband." The words sounded foreign. What did they mean? Could he do it? He was going to have to try.

"I'm not looking for a replacement for Wayne." She pushed him back until she could see his face. "Believe me, I don't need another relationship like that. I want to marry you. For the baby, even for me a little, I think, and because of who you are."

He knew that if she really knew him, she would turn away in disgust. He could tell her, but she wouldn't believe it. "I'll do everything I can to keep you from regretting your decision."

She giggled. "That sounds ominous. This is going to be hard on both of us. How about if we both promise to try to make it work? Isn't that better?"

"Sure."

"So when's the, uh, wedding?" She blushed as she asked the question, ducking her head as if she expected him to get angry.

"How about in a couple of weeks? That'll give you time to hire someone to take your place at the home."

She stared at him as if he'd suggested she eat a live chicken. "Take my place? You expect me to quit my job?"

"No." He brushed a strand of hair off her face. "You'd mentioned you were going to be hiring someone to take over nights. Once you're married, we'll be living together. So you'll be sleeping here. With me."

"Oh, my." She bit her lower lip. "I hadn't thought of that."

"Did you assume we'd live apart?" For some reason the thought annoyed him, though he tried not to let on.

"No. Not really. I guess I didn't think about it at all. I just sort of figured we'd get married, but everything else would go on the same. I'm concerned about the children being alone at night."

"They won't be alone. Someone else will be with them."

"But after the fire, they need me."

"Why? Aren't they usually asleep? They probably won't even know you're gone."

He watched as compassion warred with the common sense of his argument. "But *I'll* know. I have to think about them."

He touched her chin, forcing her to meet his gaze. Sunlight filtered in from a window in the far wall, highlighting her features. He thought about the first time he'd seen her. It had been at some meeting about raising money for a new park. She'd made part of the presentation. In her flowing floral dresses, with her long hair and luminous skin, she'd reminded him of a stunning piece of art. Some perfect porcelain figurine, breathed to life by a tender wind.

Get real, he told himself. He had no time for fanciful thoughts. She was a woman, nothing else. But she sure was beautiful.

"You have to think about the baby," he said. "You can't keep running around using up all your time and energy. There's more than just you to consider."

"I hadn't thought of that," she admitted. "Okay. I'll hire someone. If there's a problem I'll be close enough to go right over. Two weeks, then."

He nodded.

"Can we invite Travis and Elizabeth?" she asked.

"We can invite anyone you'd like. If you have family or other friends."

Rebecca shook her head and stepped away from him. "I don't think so. Let's keep this private. Travis and Elizabeth are enough for me."

He remembered then that she was one of three girls. Had he destroyed her dreams of a big wedding complete with a team of bridesmaids and an orchestra to play the first waltz? What other dreams was he going to cost her?

"Maybe we could get married in the afternoon, then go out with them for an early dinner," she said.

"Fine."

But he wasn't thinking about the wedding. He was promising himself with an intensity he normally avoided that he would do anything, go to any lengths, to make Rebecca happy. Not because she might love him. God help him, that was the last thing he needed or wanted. But because she'd agreed to marry him. Because she was having his child. And because she was the only decent thing in his otherwise empty life.

Chapter Nine

The bride's dressing room in the back of the old Glenwood Christian church was big enough to accommodate a formal wedding party, including a bride in a gown with a cathedral train and a host of bridesmaids. Rebecca felt a little lost standing there alone. Her tea-length ivory gown didn't require petticoats or extra space. It hung straight from her shoulders and was fitted to just below the waist where it flared out, ending a few inches below her knees.

She turned around slowly, wondering if the ghosts of past brides would be friendly and wish her happiness, or if they would mock her solitary state. Maybe she'd made a mistake by not inviting some friends from town to be with her. It had been an impulsive decision made when Austin had told her to invite whoever she liked. As she listened to the silence and felt the presence of the ghosts, she finally admitted why.

She was afraid he wasn't going to be there.

In her heart of hearts she fully expected to walk up the center aisle of the church by herself and find the minister standing alone. It would be easier for her if only one or two people were witness to her humiliation.

Even as she tried to talk herself out of her negative thoughts, that insistent voice way back in her head whispered she was going to be abandoned at the altar. Austin would change his mind. He didn't really want to marry her. A man like him didn't want a woman like her. He could have anyone. Someone beautiful and talented, witty and comfortable in sophisticated surroundings. They would travel the world together, maybe on a yacht. Drink champagne and eat caviar. She'd never even seen caviar and, frankly, preferred it that way. Why would anyone want to eat salty fish eggs?

A sob caught in her throat, but she trapped it there. She wasn't going to give into the emotions raging inside her. She couldn't. If she started to cry, she might never stop. Then where would she be?

She glanced down at her watch. The slim, gold timepiece had been a graduation gift from her parents. She'd already written the telegram she was going to send them, informing them about the wedding. They would be shocked, but in time they would understand. She'd promised to bring her new husband home to meet them for Christmas. Of course if there wasn't going to be a wedding, then she wouldn't have to worry about her folks' reaction. See, she thought, there was good news in even the worst of circumstances.

She crossed the large, empty room and sat in front of the vanity. On the table in front of her was a floral headpiece, a bouquet and a small jeweler's box. She picked up the headpiece. Small, delicate ivory orchids formed a fragrant circle. She looked straight ahead and met her own apprehensive gaze in the mirror.

Her eyes were big, wide with nerves. Make that terror, she thought, trying to lighten her mood. Her smile was tentative at best, and quivering at the corners. She brushed her hair away from her face. She'd debated whether or not to wear it up, but in the end had decided that loose would be easiest. She'd been shaking since dawn and never would have been able to pin it properly.

She set the circle of flowers on her head and secured it in place. Long ivory ribbons fell down her back. She wore pearl earrings she'd had since she was sixteen. They'd been her grandmother's. Something old, she thought, touching them. The something new was her dress. She'd sewn a tiny blue ribbon into the lining of her right shoe. She glanced down at the satin-and-lace pumps. They matched the dress and had cost far too much, but they were beautiful. Even staring at them made her feel better about everything. She supposed she'd been foolish to indulge, but it was her wedding day. She owed it to herself to wear something special. For Austin. If he showed up.

Her heartbeat, which had finally slowed to normal, picked up again. Her hands grew cold and damp, and her stomach tied itself in knots.

"Please God, let him be there."

She'd whispered that prayer a thousand times through the long night and morning. Maybe it would help, but she doubted it. Since she'd accepted Austin's proposal, she'd been besieged by doubts. He would have been, as well. She was here today because she'd given her word and because it was best for the baby. And maybe, just maybe, because being married to Austin Lucas was her ultimate fantasy. It was crazy, but she couldn't ignore the thrill of excitement that rippled through her every time she thought about walking into his loft, knowing that she was his wife and that they would be spending the rest of their lives together. Not to mention the weakness that invaded her knees every time she reminded herself they would be sharing a bed. But he didn't have those fantasies. He was marrying her because of the baby. He could easily have changed his mind.

Before the doubts could overwhelm her again, the door to the bride's room opened. She looked up, expecting to see the minister's wife telling her it was time. Instead, Elizabeth stepped inside.

"Rebecca? Mrs. Johnson said you were in here. I got your note. What's going on?" Elizabeth blinked several times. The room was dimly lighted, compared to the bright sunshine of the June afternoon. She stared at her friend. As her eyes adjusted, she drew in a sharp breath. "Oh, my God. You're getting married!"

Rebecca rose to her feet and crossed the room. "Don't be angry," she said, touching Elizabeth's arm. "I really need your help. I'm not sure I can make it through on my own."

Elizabeth studied the flowers in her hair, then dropped her gaze to the lace dress. "Oh, my God. You're getting married."

Rebecca smiled. "You just said that."

"I can't believe it. When you called last week and asked Travis and I to be here, you mentioned a committee meeting. When you said to dress up because we were going out to dinner afterward, I never suspected this. I'm supposed to be your closest friend. I think I *should* be upset you never let on."

"Don't be." Rebecca led her over to a small love seat opposite the vanity. When they were sitting next to each other, she rested her hands on her knees and stared at the ground. "I was afraid to tell you. I didn't want anyone to know. But I couldn't go through this alone. For what it's worth, Austin wanted to let you both know right away. It was my idea to keep it a secret."

"You're marrying Austin Lucas?"

Rebecca raised her head and looked at her friend. "Am I crazy?"

"Maybe. This is all so sudden. Less than a month ago you were upset because you'd spent the night with him. Now you're—" Elizabeth gasped. "You're pregnant."

Rebecca nodded.

"Oh, my. This is one for the record books." Elizabeth patted her own rounded belly. "Enjoy the view of your feet while you still have it. Married and pregnant, all within a month. Are you sure this is what you want?"

"Yes. No. Oh, I don't know. Is it?" Rebecca twisted her hands together. "I'm terrified about all of this. I'm marrying a man I don't know that well, whom I don't love. But I like him. I respect him. We both want the baby. I think he'll be a good father. I think he needs me in his life, although he'd rather eat glass than admit it. Is it enough? Am I making a mistake?"

"Oh, honey. You should have told me. You shouldn't have to go through this alone."

Elizabeth put her arm around her shoulders and pulled her close. Rebecca absorbed her friend's warmth and support. "I was afraid to."

"Why? After what happened to me with my first husband, I'm the last person in the world to judge anyone. You know that."

Rebecca swallowed hard. "I almost didn't tell you at all. I was afraid he wouldn't show up. I thought it was better to face that by myself. But then, I couldn't get married without you being here."

Elizabeth drew back. "You were afraid Austin would leave you at the altar? Just standing there alone?"

Rebecca nodded miserably.

"Then you really don't understand your husband-to-be at all, do you? I know Austin is difficult at times, and mysterious. But he has a strong sense of honor. He's here. I saw him. He's a little pale under his tan, but he looks determined.''

Rebecca let out a deep breath. ''Thanks for telling me. I was panicked, wondering what I was going to do.''

Elizabeth leaned forward and took both her friend's hands. She squeezed them and smiled. ''You don't have to do this if you don't want to. Travis and I have half a dozen bedrooms that aren't being used. You're welcome to come live with us for as long as you want. We'd love to have you. Besides, you can see firsthand what you'll be getting into when you have your baby.'' She glanced down and patted her belly. ''Assuming I *ever* have mine. I feel like I've been pregnant for years.''

Rebecca studied her friend's kind face. Elizabeth had an impish smile. Love of life and laughter radiated from her almond-shaped eyes. She wore her brown hair pulled back in a French braid. Her skin glowed. Even the awkward shape of her body couldn't detract from her loveliness. She'd always been pretty, but loving Travis had made her beautiful. The love she'd been afraid to risk again had been returned to her tenfold. Her generous offer, given from the heart, made Rebecca's eyes dampen.

She stared at their clasped hands. Elizabeth's diamond ring winked back at her. Her friend was married, with one child, another on the way and many responsibilities. Yet she'd made the time and room for Rebecca.

''Thank you for inviting me to stay with you,'' she said. She sniffed and tried to smile. ''You're probably going to think I'm crazy, but I want to marry him. Part of it is because of the baby, but not all of it. I know I would have been fine on my own. But our child deserves to know both of us, don't you think?''

''I can't decide for you,'' Elizabeth said. ''You have to do what feels right for you and the baby. Is this what you want?''

"Yes. It is. *He* is. Not just because I'm pregnant. I like him. I think he's nice, no matter that he tries to tell me otherwise."

"Could you love him?"

"Yes." Rebecca spoke without thinking. At first she wanted to call the words back, but in the end she didn't. "It's scary, but I think I could. I've been wondering about my crush on him. Do you think my heart was trying to tell me something for the past two years but I wasn't ready to listen?"

"It's possible. Stranger things have happened." Elizabeth squeezed her hands, then released her. "But be careful, okay? Austin is a loner. He's never gotten involved like this before. I don't want to see you hurt."

"I don't think I get a choice in the matter." Rebecca stood up and forced herself to smile. "How do I look?"

"Stunning. Where did you find that dress?"

"I went to a shop in Stockton. I hope Austin likes it."

There was a tap on the door. Mrs. Johnson, the minister's wife, stuck her head into the room. "We're about to start the wedding, dearie. Are you ready?"

Rebecca nodded.

"Give me a minute to get to the organ. When you hear the music, you can go ahead and start up the aisle."

"Wait," Rebecca called before the older woman could leave. She grabbed Elizabeth's hand and pulled her to her feet. She was glad she'd invited her friend to be with her. "I have a matron of honor." She looked up at Elizabeth. "If you wouldn't mind. I'd prefer not to stand up there by myself."

"You won't be by yourself, you silly. Austin will be there." Elizabeth glanced down at her blue dress. It was simple, with short sleeves and a draped front that flowed over her extended belly. "I'm not dressed for a wedding, but

I wouldn't miss it for the world. Thank you for asking. I'm honored.''

Rebecca stepped close and they hugged. She held on, absorbing her friend's strength and quiet confidence. Then she stepped back and smiled at Mrs. Johnson. ''We're ready.''

''Good. I'll play something pretty for your friend. Then, when she's reached the front, I'll start the wedding march. Good luck.'' The door closed quietly.

Elizabeth laughed. ''I'm suddenly nervous. This is ridiculous.''

Rebecca walked over to the table and picked up her bouquet. The scent of ivory roses and tiger lilies mingled with her perfume. She studied the arrangement, then pulled out one of the lilies.

''Here. Matrons of honor should have flowers.''

Elizabeth took the blossom, then studied her. ''Do you have everything? Something old and all that?''

''I'm missing the borrowed something. Do you have a tissue?''

''I can do better than that.'' Elizabeth unsnapped a gold bracelet from around her wrist. ''Travis gave me this when I told him I was pregnant. It's a gift of love and promise. It'll bring you luck today.'' She slipped the bracelet on Rebecca's wrist and fastened it.

Outside the room, soft organ music began.

''I think that's my cue,'' Elizabeth said. ''Are you all right?''

''I'm fine. See you at the altar.''

Elizabeth gave her a quick kiss on the cheek. ''Austin is going to be there. I promise. You'll be fine.'' She started out the door, then turned back. ''Believe in the love, Rebecca. It can work miracles.''

When she was alone, Rebecca took one last look in the mirror. She stared at her reflection, hoping to find a hint as to whether or not she was making the right decision. She couldn't find any answers.

She studied her dress. The simple lines were so different from the beaded gown she'd ordered for her wedding with Wayne. Everything was different from the wedding she'd planned with Wayne. There was no church full of guests, no four-tiered cake, no family, no honeymoon in Hawaii. She'd played it safe and lost all her dreams. Now she was making new plans. They were different, but they could be just as satisfying if she let them.

Elizabeth had asked if she could love Austin. Could she? She thought she might if she could get through to him. Seeing him with David had helped her believe love might be possible. She'd seen proof he was a warm, caring man. He kept that part of himself hidden. In time she would find out why. For now it was enough to know it existed.

The music changed, becoming the familiar chords of the wedding march. Rebecca clutched her flowers more tightly in her suddenly damp hands. She grabbed the ring box from the vanity, then walked to the door, opened it and stepped out into the hallway.

The music was louder here. She made her way to the back entrance of the church. Wide double doors stood open. The sound poured over her, making her want to cry. She was getting married, alone, in an empty church, away from her friends and family. She wanted to call everything off. She wanted to sit down and sob her heart out. Instead, she took the first step into the sanctuary.

She stared past the rows of empty pews, past the stained-glass windows that filtered the afternoon sunlight, past Mrs. Johnson sitting behind the massive organ off to one side. Her gaze swept across the altar and settled on four people standing at the front of the center aisle.

She recognized Elizabeth, who smiled encouragingly, and the minister, then Travis, as best man. Swallowing her fear, she allowed her gaze to settle on the man she would marry.

He was there. Relief made her weak, but she forced herself to keep walking. Slowly, step after step, moving closer.

Austin faced the rear of the church, looking at her steadily. Nothing in his face or cool gray eyes gave away what he was thinking. She didn't care. It was enough that he was there and waiting.

Halfway up the aisle she faltered. She made the fatal mistake of allowing her gaze to dip below his face. He wore a charcoal-gray suit. Her steps slowed. At that moment she realized she'd only ever seen him in jeans. There was so much about her husband she didn't know. What kind of man was he? How would he treat her? What did he dream about, wish for? Where were his scars? Would he ever trust her, care for her? Would they grow old together?

She stopped in the center of the aisle. The music swept around her, but she couldn't move. This was insane. What had she been thinking of? From the corner of her eye she saw Elizabeth take a step toward her. Austin didn't move. Their eyes locked.

He spoke her name. Oh, his lips didn't move and there wasn't any sound, but she heard him. He didn't force her to come toward him. Instead, he held back, giving her the choice. She knew he wanted her to choose him. She could feel his thoughts as if they were her own. Then he smiled and her doubts faded. She took a step, then another. Effortlessly she reached the end of the aisle. Austin never once took his gaze from her face. When she was next to him, he held out his hand, palm up. She gave Elizabeth her bouquet and the tiny box containing his ring, and placed her fingers on his. As one they turned toward the minister.

"Dearly beloved, we are gathered here in the sight of God and this company..."

The minister spoke the familiar words, but she scarcely heard them. Rebecca could think of nothing but the man beside her. The heat and scent of his body swept around her, circling her in a cocoon of safety. She darted a quick glance at him, taking in his appearance.

Under his suit jacket he wore an ivory shirt, the exact color of her dress. His conservative blue-and-gray tie reminded her of a banker, but then she glanced up and saw the minister frowning at Austin's earring. She wanted to giggle. She liked his earring because it made her think of pirates, stolen women and forbidden love. She liked it because it was a part of him.

"Do you, Austin Lucas, take this woman to be your lawfully wedded wife?"

Austin repeated the vows slowly, carefully, as if each word was a promise. When it was her turn, her voice shook. Then she risked looking up at him.

"I do," she said.

He smiled. His smiles were rare jewels to be treasured. This one reached deep inside her, clear to her heart, and made her feel welcome. She smiled back. He squeezed her fingers and the last of her fears fled.

They were marrying because of a baby. Couples had been doing that since the dawn of time. Children were an affirmation of the future. A gift of joy. She looked at her soon-to-be husband and saw the questions in his eyes. He was wondering, too. They had much to learn about each other, but the discovery could be wonderful.

She sent up a prayer of thanks that she had made the right decision, that the feelings she had inside would blossom into love. She prayed that their child would be healthy and grow strong under their care.

Please, God, let me be enough to heal him, she thought. *And let him want to love me back.*

"The ring, please," the minister said.

Austin reached into his right jacket pocket and pulled out a ring. Rebecca stared at him with surprise. Of course he'd bought her a ring. She'd even bought him one. But she hadn't thought about it until this moment.

A thrill shot through her. What would it look like? What had he picked for her? She bit her lip as he brought the sparkling band to her hand, then slid it onto her finger. She froze, staring.

A circle of diamonds winked up at her. Pear-shaped stones nestled against each other, forming a pattern of brilliance. The ring was much heavier than the small quarter-carat solitaire Wayne had bought her all those years ago. Much more expensive. Austin could have bought a luxury car with the money he'd spent on this ring.

He was rich. She'd forgotten about that. It shouldn't make a difference, but it did. She sent up a prayer that Austin would know she hadn't married him for his money.

"It fits," he said, leaning forward and speaking softly in her ear.

"It's beautiful."

"I'm glad you like it."

She met his gaze and saw that he'd been nervous about her reaction. That tiny sign of insecurity made her relax again. She tilted her hand so the diamonds caught the light.

"I never imagined having anything this exquisite."

The pride that flashed in his eyes told her she'd said the right thing. It was going to be all right, she told herself.

"Is there a ring for the groom?" Mr. Johnson asked.

"No," Austin said.

Rebecca blinked. "Oh. I bought you one. Don't you want it?"

The minister stared at them as if they were insane. "You didn't discuss this ahead of time?"

She shook her head. "It doesn't matter, Austin. I don't want you to be uncomfortable." She tried to keep the disappointment out of her voice. It had never occurred to her that he wouldn't want to wear a ring. Of course many men didn't, and he worked a lot in the lab. She supposed it would get in his way.

"I didn't think you'd bother," Austin said. "I'd like to wear your ring."

"Really?"

He nodded.

She took the box Elizabeth held and removed the gold band. She'd spent the better part of an afternoon picking out this ring. It had been the same day she'd gone to buy her dress. The plain gold bands had been too plain, but anything with a stone hadn't seemed like Austin. She'd finally found what she wanted in a small store tucked on a side street. The heavy gold was engraved with a pattern that gave it a look of elegance. She'd been able to picture it on Austin's hand.

Now, as she repeated the words and slid it onto his finger, she was glad she'd bought it. She'd guessed at the size, but it fit perfectly. She glanced up at him and smiled.

"Thank you," he said. His eyes darkened with something she dared to identify as affection.

Her toes curled inside her satin pumps. They were going to make it. She knew that now. Her last prayer of the day was one of thanks.

Travis poured champagne into his glass. "I guess I don't have to tell you that this comes as a surprise."

"No," Austin agreed. "You don't."

He glanced around the private room he'd reserved in the back of the Country Inn restaurant. The minimum for parties was twelve, but he'd convinced the manager to make an exception. The order for several bottles of expensive imported champagne had helped. It was warm for June, but the dimly lighted room was cool. Lush ferns hung from the hooks in the bare-beam ceiling. The table had been set with fine china and crystal. Tasteful paintings graced the wall.

He hoped Rebecca was happy with the location. She'd been the one who'd wanted the dinner party. He'd offered to host something larger, with more of her friends, but she'd declined. Just as she'd declined his offer of a honeymoon. She'd said she couldn't be away from the children that long. To be honest, he was relieved. The last thing he needed was to spend time with her in a romantic location. It was going to be hard enough living together in the loft. At least there he'd been able to remodel the floor plan to make it more workable.

He looked up and realized Travis was staring at him patiently. "I'm sorry. What did you say?"

"I asked if you were going to tell me what was going on. I didn't even know you and Rebecca were dating."

As soon as the four of them had arrived, Rebecca and Elizabeth had ducked into the ladies' room. The two men were alone. Travis was the best friend Austin had ever had. Twenty-one years ago, Travis had stood up for Austin against his own brothers. A bond had been formed that day, one that had never been broken. There was a lot about Austin's life that Travis didn't know, but Austin had done his best not to lie.

"Rebecca didn't want to tell anyone until it was done. She asked me to keep quiet, so I did."

"But this is all so sudden. You'd always said you weren't interested in getting married." Travis leaned back in his chair. "Don't get me wrong. I'm happy for you. Rebecca and I have been close friends ever since she moved to town. I don't think you could have made a better choice. But why the rush and secrecy?"

Austin smiled slightly. "Come on, Trav, you're smarter than that. Why does any couple get married in a hurry?"

His friend frowned. "Elizabeth and I didn't want to wait because we were in love and because we couldn't live together during the engagement. Mandy is very impressionable. Something tells me that's not why you two did this." He frowned, thinking. Suddenly he straightened in the chair. "Holy— She's pregnant?"

Austin nodded. He hadn't been sure what his friend's reaction would be. Although he'd been bothered by Rebecca's request not to tell anyone about the wedding, in a way it had made things easier for him. He'd thought people might talk. That didn't bother him. He was used to that kind of attention. It came with his reputation. But Rebecca was different. She'd never done anything bad in her whole innocent life. No. She'd done one thing—she'd slept with him.

"Hot damn." Travis pounded him on the back. "Congratulations. That's terrific." He grinned and leaned close. "Scared?"

Austin smiled. "Terrified."

"Tell me about it. These women think it's so easy to be a father, but I'll tell you, it keeps me up nights." He shrugged. "I guess all we can do is our best. I know one thing for sure. I'm going to do a better job than my old man."

Austin wanted to say the same, but he didn't know what kind of father his old man had been. He'd been absent. Austin had only met him once in his life, and it had been ugly. He shook off the thought, not wanting to break the mood with unpleasantness from the past.

There was a noise by the door. Elizabeth entered with Rebecca following her. Both he and Travis rose and held out chairs for the women.

Rebecca paused before sitting down. Their eyes met. Makeup accentuated her brown irises, and high cheekbones. Her hair flowed around her shoulders and tumbled down her back in erotic disarray. A circle of small white flowers sat on her head. The ivory lace dress, the flowers, the tentative smile, all made her look like a sacrificial virgin.

Technically Rebecca wasn't a virgin anymore, but the air of innocence still clung to her. He wondered if it always would.

He stood behind her chair until she was seated. She rested her bouquet on the table between her and Travis. Austin sat on her right. Her left hand lay on the table, the diamonds in her ring gleaming in the candlelight.

He smiled slightly, remembering the stunned look on her face when she'd seen the ring. The wide-eyed stare had convinced him more than any words that she hadn't married him for his money. He would have sworn an oath that, until that moment, she'd forgotten he was wealthy.

He glanced from her hand to his own. The engraved gold band fit perfectly. He'd been surprised, as well, but pleased. Her gesture had erased some of the bitterness he felt about the day.

He glanced around the small table set for four and imagined what it could have been. He'd offered her a party for all her friends; he'd offered her a big wedding. She'd wanted no part of either. She hadn't told a soul about the baby or the wedding. He'd finally figured out why: she was ashamed of him.

Before he could say anything to her, Travis stood up and raised his glass. "I'd like to propose a toast. To the happy couple. May you be blessed with a lifetime of joy and love."

Elizabeth raised her glass. "Hear, hear."

Rebecca smiled. Austin waited, but she didn't drink. Then he noticed Elizabeth put her glass down untouched. Travis took a sip and smiled. "Smooth, Lucas. Only the best."

He glanced at Rebecca. She caught his eye and read his confusion. She leaned toward him. A strand of hair slipped off her shoulder and brushed against the back of his hand. A shiver raced up his arm.

"It's the alcohol," she whispered. "Neither of us can drink because we're pregnant. It's not good for the baby."

Understanding dawned. "Sorry, I should have thought of that."

"It's okay."

He motioned to a waiter standing by the door and ordered sparkling mineral water for the women. Soon the first course was served and everyone started chatting.

When the meal was finished and they were waiting for dessert, Austin glanced over and saw Rebecca staring at her hand. Travis and Elizabeth were talking to each other in low tones.

"What is it?" he asked, searching her face.

"I'm in shock, I think." She smiled.

He noted the shadows under her eyes. "Have you been sleeping?"

"Not very well," she admitted. "There's been a lot to do to get ready for the wedding and everything. I was up late packing."

He frowned. "I could have done that for you today."

She surprised him by blushing. "No, I wanted everything done so that when we got back to, uh, your place my things would already be there. Silly, huh?"

She bit her lower lip and looked anxious, as if she expected him to be annoyed. "No. I understand." But in truth he didn't. She'd been the one keeping the whole thing a secret. Why was she bent on getting moved into his place so quickly? He'd half expected her to tell him she wouldn't be moving in for a few days. He would have let her stay with the children for about a week, then he would have moved her over himself. It looked like that wasn't going to be a problem.

He told himself it didn't matter what she thought of him or the wedding. The important thing was that they were married and his child wasn't going to be a bastard. It was enough. Or it should have been. But he couldn't shake the feeling of inadequacy. Damn. He was thirty-four years old, respected in his field, successful, kind to animals, relatively thoughtful. Women in town whispered about him. He should have been a catch. So why had Rebecca kept the wedding a secret? Why didn't she want anyone to come and witness the ceremony? Why had she refused a big party? And why did he have to care so damn much? He should be happy. He didn't want her getting too emotionally involved with him. She obviously wasn't. Everything was going his way. In fact, he told himself, it couldn't be better.

Austin was quiet all through dessert and their goodbyes to Travis and Elizabeth. Rebecca wondered what she'd said to upset him. She didn't think it was because she wouldn't drink the champagne. He wouldn't want her risking the baby's health. So what was it?

He held open the passenger door of the Mercedes. She'd had Mary drop her off that morning, so her car, or rather the home's car, was back where it belonged. She'd made arrangements to have her things moved over to Austin's during the ceremony. Everything was all set. She glanced down at her ring. She should be as happy as could be. So why did she feel like crying?

"In a few months, as soon as the children have settled into their new place, we'll move to the big house," Austin said as he fastened his seat belt. "There'll be more room for you and the child."

"Are you moving with us, or are you going to stay in the loft?"

He'd already placed the key in the ignition, but now he turned to look at her. "I'd planned to move with you. Would you rather that I didn't?"

She blinked to hold back the sudden burning in her eyes. They'd been married less than three hours and already they were talking like strangers. "No, of course not."

"Then why did you ask?"

"Because of the way you phrased your statement. You said there would be more room for me and the child. As if you weren't going to be there."

He raised his hand, as if he was going to touch her. She leaned closer, but then he lowered his arm to his side and rested his fingers on the edge of his seat.

"I'm committed to this marriage," he said, not meeting her gaze. "I'm going to do the best I can to be a good husband and father. If you'll let me know what you expect of me, I'll do my best to oblige."

Hardly a romantic declaration, she thought grimly. But this was Austin, and he'd never pretended to be marrying her for love.

"I don't really have any expectations," she said. Although a little hand-holding and touching would be nice. But she couldn't say that to him. Couldn't he just know what she was feeling?

He rested his left hand on the top of the steering wheel. It was close to seven in the evening, and the sun was still up. Light glinted off the gold band on his finger. He was her husband. She was supposed to be able to say anything to him. Unfortunately it wasn't going to be that easy.

"I've opened accounts for you at all the major stores in the area," he said. "I know you lost a lot of your things in the fire. Feel free to buy whatever you want. We now have a joint checking account. I have someone who comes in and does the cleaning and I think we should keep her. I don't like that car you drive. In the next day or so, I want to buy you a new one. Maybe a minivan. Let me know your schedule and we'll pick a time that's convenient."

He continued with his list, explaining about life insurance, medical insurance and stock options. She felt more like a newly hired employee than a wife.

"Austin, stop. Why are you telling me all this?"

Finally he looked at her. She tried to read the expression in his unfathomable gray eyes, but his feelings were too deeply buried. "We're married. You're my responsibility."

"You make me sound like a puppy rather than a woman. Or a life partner. I know these aren't the best of circumstances, but if we try, I think it can work. I like you. You've said you like me, too. Please don't destroy everything we've built so far by talking about checking accounts and insurance. Tell me you're excited about the baby. Tell me you're terrified of picking out china patterns and don't want to change your flatware. Give me a hint that this wedding isn't the worst thing that's ever happened to you."

Before she could blink it back, a single tear rolled down her cheek. Austin sucked in his breath, then used his thumb to brush away the drop.

"Damn it, Rebecca, don't you dare cry. You're the one with the regrets, not me."

"Regrets? What are you talking about?"

"Don't pretend. I know what you've been thinking. You're embarrassed by this whole thing. Frankly I'm surprised you agreed to marry me at all."

He faced front and reached for the key. Before he could turn it, she grabbed his wrist. "Austin, wait. I'm not embarrassed to be marrying you. Why would you think that? I confess I'm a little apprehensive about making the marriage work, but that's about me. I'm not like those other women you've had. I'm not beautiful and smart and experienced. I don't know how to please a man or look good in an evening gown. I'm not who you would have chosen. I know that. But you agreed because of the baby. If anyone is embarrassed, it should be you."

He leaned back in his seat. "So why didn't you want people to know about the pregnancy and the wedding?"

She mumbled her reply.

He turned sharply and grabbed her shoulders. "What did you say?"

She flicked her hair back behind her shoulders. The evening sun hit him directly on the side of his face, highlighting the black in his hair and reflecting off his earring. He'd shaved recently; she could tell by his smooth jaw. The ivory shirt and tie, the conservative cut of his suit, were all out of character for the Austin Lucas she knew. He'd done it for her, so she would be more comfortable. And then he'd thought she was embarrassed to be marrying him.

Shame washed over her, shame and a growing awareness of how she'd misjudged this man. She'd had a crush on him, tempted him into bed so that she could be rid of her virginity. Never once did she give a thought to what her action meant to him. She'd used him sexually, the way men have used women for centuries. That wasn't right. She'd taken away his choices, married him and given him nothing in return.

"Oh, Austin, I'm so sorry," she whispered, and threw herself in his arms.

He held her close. She squeezed her eyes shut and tried not to cry. After a moment she got her emotions under control, but she didn't pull back. She liked the feel of his hard chest against her breasts and the way his large hands held her securely against him. He murmured soft words of concern, promising he would make her world right. But his was the world that needed fixing.

"I wasn't ashamed of you," she said softly, inhaling the masculine scent of his body. "I was ashamed of myself. I couldn't bear to think that people were saying I'd trapped you. I was afraid you'd get so upset at the talk that you'd change your mind. I thought you wouldn't show up."

There. She'd said it. Admitted her ugly truth and exposed the blackness of her deed.

He cupped her face and eased her back until he could see her. "Is that all?"

"All? It's horrible. Slimy. You must be disgusted." She closed her eyes and waited for his anger.

"You can look," he said, his voice low and teasing.

She opened her eyes. He smiled.

"You're not angry."

"You're right. It's okay to be scared, Rebecca. I'm scared, too."

"I never would have thought that."

"I'm just a man. No more, no less."

A good man, but she knew better than to say that aloud. He would flinch and probably withdraw.

"Okay," she said. "Let's not mess up this way again. No more wondering what the other person is thinking. Next time, ask me. And I'll do the same. Deal?"

She held out her hand. He glanced at it. "Deal." But instead of shaking, he leaned over and kissed her. It was a brief brush of lips, nothing more. But she experienced a reaction clear down to her belly.

He straightened in his seat. "Let's go home."

Home. She leaned back and relaxed. Everything was going to work out. She smiled lazily, thinking of the coming night. It had been almost a month since they'd made love. Not a day had gone by without her thinking about it, about him and how he'd made her feel. She wanted to experience his lovemaking again, only this time she wanted to be more a part of what they were doing, rather than just lying there. She closed her eyes and tried to remember exactly what Austin had done to her body so she could do those things to him.

But the recent activity and sleepless nights caught up with her. She must have dozed because the next thing she knew, they were parked in front of the barn and Austin was opening her door.

"Wake up, sleepyhead," he said, reaching over to unfasten her seat belt.

"Did I fall asleep? I'm sorry."

"It's all right. You're tired. Can you get out of the car?"

"Of course I can. I'm not an invalid."

She swung her legs around and stood up. But before she could take a step, Austin leaned over and swept her up in his arms.

"Put me down," she demanded.

"No. You need to be in bed. You're exhausted."

"Oh, I'm not that tired," she said, quickly giving up the fight and snuggling close to him. She wrapped her arms around his neck as he entered the barn and started up the stairs.

She sighed. It was so romantic. He was carrying her over the threshold and to their bed. Her body began to heat up at the thought of making love with him. She eyed his tie and wondered if she could pull it free or if she was going to have to figure out the knot. She wove her fingers through his hair, loving the feel of the silky strands. Her forehead rested on his shoulder. She turned her head toward his neck, ready to press her lips to his skin, when he came to a stop.

"Here we are." He slowly allowed her legs to touch the floor.

When she was standing, she kept one arm around him and smiled. "I can't believe I'm here," she said, reaching for his suit jacket. "It's all been a blur, but I think I'll remember this part." She tugged at the lapels, pulling the fabric over his shoulders.

He stepped back. "Rebecca, no."

"What?"

He placed his hands on her shoulders and turned her to face the room. She hadn't been in the loft since that first night, but she remembered every square inch of his home.

There had been a change. At the far end of the loft a room had been closed off. She saw the tall walls and the open door. Through it she could see the foot of a bed. Her gaze flew to the king-size bed sitting where it had before. Two beds?

"Austin? What's going on?"

"I knew you'd want the privacy. Some space of your own."

She clutched her hands together in front of her waist. "Separate bedrooms?"

"Yes. With your pregnancy and all. I thought it would be best."

Best for whom? She took a step back and bumped into the railing. Grabbing the wooden support, she stared at the walls that enclosed her solitary space. He wanted them to sleep apart. All her dreams for a sexual relationship, all her hopes for the future, vanished in the blink of an eye. No, they didn't vanish. They'd never existed in the first place.

"This is what you want?" she asked.

When he didn't answer, she looked at him. He was staring past her, gazing at something she couldn't see. He twisted his wedding band around and around, as if it was uncomfortable. It probably was.

She'd been fooling herself. He'd never wanted a real marriage at all.

She took a deep breath, determined to make one more try. "Austin, I'm your wife."

"I know," he said, and started for the stairs. "I've thought this through. It's for the best. For both of us."

Chapter Ten

Austin stood at the front window of the loft. From here he could see over the trees to the big house where the children were staying. He could see past that to the other side where a larger grove of trees separated his property from his nearest neighbor's. At night the stars glowed from the heavens and moonlight cast eerie shadows across the land. He knew. He'd spent each of the past seven nights staring out this window, listening to the silence and wondering how badly he'd messed everything up.

This morning was different. Voices filled the air. He drew his gaze from the horizon back down to the activity in front of the barn. Rebecca stood in front of the new Volvo station wagon he'd bought her two days before. Several volunteers were loading the vehicle under her careful supervision. At one point she turned toward the barn and glanced up. He knew she could see him standing in the window, but he didn't move back. Their eyes met. He wondered what she was thinking. She didn't smile or wave. She simply stared for a moment, then went back to what she was doing.

He hadn't seen her smile at him since the wedding. He had no one to blame but himself.

It would be easy enough to go downstairs and join in. Knowing Rebecca as he did, he was confident she wouldn't object. His helping might even go a long way to bridging the distance that had grown between them. If nothing else, she could use the help. The state had come through with the money to rebuild the children's home, but it would take a while to get the funding in place. In the meantime, the original lot had been cleared and a construction company had given them a break on the cost. Rebecca had met with the town council and together they had decided to earmark the annual Fourth of July carnival proceeds for the construction project. Austin had offered to pick up the tab until they received the state funding, but Rebecca had refused. He wondered if she would have agreed if he'd made the offer before the wedding. Before she'd seen that he'd arranged for them to sleep in separate rooms.

He continued to stare out the window. Rebecca was gesturing now, motioning to a box. A young man picked it up effortlessly and slipped it into the back of her station wagon. As she smiled her thanks, a shaft of sunlight caught her hair. The silky colors glowed brown, dark blond and red, rippling and changing with each movement of her head. Her skin had turned the color of honey. By the end of summer she would be brown, and there would be freckles on her nose. She would also be showing.

News of their marriage had swept through the small town of Glenwood. He'd deliberately avoided leaving his property for the past week. He'd known what everyone was saying. Rebecca had also stayed close, but he had a feeling it was more out of convenience rather than a fear of gossip. As innocent as she was, she wasn't expecting people to talk. He had to warn her before she left for the carnival.

Travis and Elizabeth had been discreet, only mentioning the wedding and not the pregnancy. Time enough for tongues to wag over that tidbit. He didn't care what people said about him; Rebecca was another matter. If she thought talk was rampant about their marriage, wait until people started counting backward from the baby's birth. He clenched his hands into fists and vowed to protect her. Then he released his fingers and called himself a fool.

Who was he kidding? The person he should protect Rebecca from was himself.

He'd hurt her by closing off a separate bedroom. He'd seen the flash of pain on her face when he'd first brought her here, and he'd heard it in her voice every day since. He'd hoped to do his best by her, but he might have known he would get it wrong. He'd never been around married people. He didn't know what being married meant. He only knew he had to keep Rebecca and the baby safe. If that meant making her unhappy, so be it.

Except he'd promised to be a good husband to her. He'd vowed to care for her for the rest of their lives. He hadn't even been able to accomplish that for a single day.

Maybe he should have paid more attention to the married couples he'd known when he was a kid. He frowned and raised his head to stare over the treetops. That wouldn't have helped, he reminded himself. He'd never had a close friend until Travis, and Travis's folks had been bitterly unhappy. Travis's father had made a habit of playing around, spending all his free time pursuing other women and ignoring his family. Not much of a role model there. Austin had no desire to be unfaithful to Rebecca. All he really wanted was to be with her in the most intimate of ways.

He turned slowly and glanced across the loft to the partitioned-off room. Maybe it had been a bad idea to build the second bedroom without asking her first. Given half a chance, he would jump at the opportunity to have her in his bed. But Rebecca was pregnant. A man was supposed to keep his animal nature to himself at times like these. It was hard enough being in the same house, hearing her footsteps, smelling the sweet scent of her body so close as she passed him in the kitchen. Having her in the same bed would be hell.

He massaged his temples. All this would have been easier if he hadn't seen the happiness in her eyes when he'd first carried her upstairs. She'd touched him and he'd thought he might explode right there. He'd wanted to take her to his bed, tell her that the separate room was for the baby. She would never have known it was a lie. But he couldn't. For once he was going to do the right thing and treat her as she deserved to be treated. It would be better for both of them.

So why did the right thing feel so wrong?

He turned back to the window, but everyone was gone. Then he heard the front door opening and the sound of footsteps on the stairs. Her tread was slow. Was it because she didn't want to face him? He was so damn confused about everything. He'd always known he didn't have a prayer of making a marriage work. That was why he'd always avoided commitment. He was bad at it. All he wanted was to make Rebecca happy. It had only been a week and they were both miserable. Would the kindest act be to let her go?

In his soul he knew the answer was yes, but his heart begged for mercy. Before he could make up his mind what to do, Rebecca reached the top of the stairs. She stepped onto the loft floor and crossed to where he stood by the window.

"The car is all loaded," she said, standing close enough to tempt, close enough to touch, but not touching. Did she torture him on purpose? He wanted to think she did. It would make it easier to dislike her. But he knew better. A kind and giving spirit governed her every action. If she thought her presence in his life caused him pain, she would leave him to the silence.

"Austin? What's wrong?"

He was surprised she knew to ask. Was she getting better at reading him, or was he getting worse at concealing his feelings?

He looked at her. She wore her hair loose. It fell down her back and moved in counterpoint to the graceful movements of her body. When most women would have worn shorts on such a warm summer's day, she was in a sundress with a full skirt. The peach material brought out the color in her eyes and cheeks. She wore something on her lashes and lips, but no other makeup. Her neck and wrists were bare, as were her hands, save for her wedding ring.

Without thinking he took her left hand in his. Slender fingers, strong yet feminine, curled around his. He studied the sparkle of the ring, liking the way it looked on her. As he'd wanted their first night together, he'd marked her as his. He'd claimed the woman, if not her body. He would make it be enough.

"What are you thinking about?" she asked.

He raised his gaze to hers. So many questions flashed through her eyes. He confused her. She tried to understand him and his moods. She tried so damn hard at everything. Had he even once made it easy?

"I was remembering our first night together."

"Why?"

He shrugged. "I was remembering how innocent you looked dripping on my floor and how I could read everything you were thinking."

She flushed and ducked her head. "You must have thought I was a real dweeb."

"I thought you were beautiful and very tempting."

"You regret that night, don't you?"

He released her hand and cupped her chin. Slowly he lifted her head until their eyes met. He owed her, so for once he would tell her the truth. "I regret the loss of your virginity and that I got you pregnant. I don't regret the baby."

"I don't understand."

"You should have saved yourself for someone you loved."

"You don't believe in love."

He smiled slightly. "You do."

"Okay. That sort of makes sense, but how can you be sorry you got me pregnant and not regret the baby?"

"I took away your choice, but the child is something special. I never thought I'd have that chance."

Her eyes misted over. He told himself it was an emotional reaction that had everything to do with hormones and nothing to do with him. He had a feeling he was lying, but he couldn't accept any other truth right now. He was already having enough trouble sleeping at night.

Her lips parted slightly. He could see her white teeth and the tip of her tongue. It would be so easy to bend forward and cover her mouth with his. Too easy. He drew back.

"You're leaving for the carnival?" he asked.

She nodded.

He folded his arms over his chest. "You need to be prepared for the talk."

"Oh. You mean people whispering that I trapped you into marriage? I probably deserve it."

He thought he'd taken care of her concerns about having "trapped" him, but obviously he hadn't. He wanted to assure her that was the last thing he was worried about. He couldn't. Then she would take heart and think there was a chance of making it work. She would only get hurt more. He had to keep her away from him for as long as possible. Better for her to leave because he was a heartless bastard than for her to stay and find out the truth. Her leaving then would destroy what was left of him.

"I doubt they'll have time to even think about that," he said, trying to keep his voice casual. "I have a certain reputation in town."

She smiled, some of the worry leaving her eyes. "I know."

"People are going to speculate about why I chose you."

"But I'm pregnant. Why else?"

"Travis and Elizabeth haven't told anyone. Unless you've been spreading the news, all anyone is going to have is news of the wedding. Nothing else. I just want you to be prepared for some unpleasant questions."

She glanced down at herself. After smoothing the front of her dress and brushing her hair off her shoulders, she looked up at him. Before he could step back, she closed the distance between them and touched his earring.

She was close enough that he could see the smoothness of her skin and feel her sweet breath on his face. Her smile made him want to pull her hard against him and hold her until the rest of the world faded like a bad memory.

"You mean they'll want to know why the town bad boy hooked up with innocent little Rebecca Chambers?"

"Exactly. Except it's Rebecca Lucas now."

"Is it?" she asked, her smile fading. "I suppose technically I *am* your wife." She dropped her hand and turned away. "All right, Austin. Thanks for the warning. I'll be on my guard against the gossip. I'd better leave. I'd hate the carnival to start without me."

"Rebecca, I'm sorry," he said, feeling her pain, but not knowing what to do about it. "I wish—"

"Don't," she said. When she reached the stairs, she looked at him. "I don't want to talk about it today. The sun is shining, the weather is warm. There's too much fun waiting to be had for us to talk about this now." She tilted her head slightly. "What are you going to do today?"

He stood stiffly, trying to act casual. He didn't want her to go, but he had no right to ask her to stay. "I have a couple of experiments I've been working on."

"Oh. All right. I'll probably be late." She hesitated, one foot on the stairs, the other on the hardwood floor. She opened her mouth and closed it, then muttered something that sounded surprisingly like "damn." Only Rebecca never swore.

"Do you want to come with me?" she asked quickly. "You don't have to, of course. I just thought it *is* the Fourth of July and I hate to think of you here by yourself. It's not just that. I'd like us to be together and—" She clamped her mouth shut. "Forget it. It was a dumb idea."

He shouldn't go. The more time he spent with her, the harder it was to turn away from her at night. The more they were together, the more he hurt her and the closer he came to his own self-destruction. Besides, he hated carnivals.

She started down the stairs. He tried to look away, but he could see the slump of her shoulders.

"Rebecca," he called before he could stop himself.

She paused. Before he could think of a nice way to say no, she held out her hand. She didn't speak; she didn't have to. The pull of her offer was as powerful as the tide. He moved toward her, a single wave being drawn away from the safety of the shore and back into the welcoming depths of the ocean.

It was just one day, he reminded himself. She *was* his wife. It was his duty to be with her. His acceptance had nothing to do with the warm feeling of contentment that began inside of him, growing large enough to start filling the black hole of his soul.

Rebecca waited while Austin dropped off the last of the supplies she'd brought. He wouldn't even let her carry the paper bag filled with napkins.

"I'm pregnant, not dying," she said, planting her hands on her hips and trying to glare at him. It didn't work. All he had to do was raise one eyebrow in that way of his and she melted like a snow cone in the early July heat.

"Stop arguing," he said pleasantly. "The quicker you leave me alone to finish this, the quicker I'll be done and we can go get some of the cotton candy you've been eyeing."

He picked up a heavy box containing canned goods for the cooking booth. His muscles flexed underneath his cream polo shirt. She watched the shifting in his arms and back, and felt herself grow weak at the knees. No matter how he'd rejected her, despite the long talks she'd had with herself as she'd lain alone in her solitary, cold bed, he got to her. He always had. She had a feeling he always would.

When the last box was on the counter of the booth, Austin turned to her. "Anything else?"

She shook her head. "We're done." She glanced at the workers inside, already starting on the chili. "I'll be back in a couple of hours to spell someone."

Mary glanced up, her gray hair curling around her face. "Don't worry about me. I plan to spend my day right here. I'm sure some of the youngsters would like a break. But first you go have some fun. You've been working too hard. Austin, I expect you to show your bride a good time."

Rebecca held her breath, worried he wouldn't appreciate the older woman's good-natured interference. He surprised her by smiling and tipping an imaginary hat. "Yes, ma'am. I'll do just that." He glanced at Rebecca. "All right, bride, where do you want to go first?"

"There," she said, pointing to the cotton-candy kiosk set up by the tallest of the roller coasters.

As they crossed over to the stand, he frowned slightly. "Are you sure it's safe for you to eat?"

"I'm fine," she said, taking her place in line. "I haven't had a moment's morning sickness. I feel great."

She had a few symptoms of pregnancy, but she didn't want to go into detail now. Her breasts seemed a little bigger to her, and they were tender. She got tired in the middle of the afternoon. Part of her wanted to share her small discoveries with him; part of her didn't want to find out he didn't care. It was easier to hold it all inside and wait until she knew for sure.

Around them crowds of people surged in different directions. Teenagers lined up for the wild rides. Adults tried their skills at several games. Pies, cakes, jams and preserves, along with photographs, quilts and farm animals were being judged in the two main pavilions. Tonight a local country band would provide entertainment. A dance floor was being set up around seven, with fireworks to follow at dusk.

How long would Austin want to stay? Would he dance with her in the moonlight or would he find an excuse to avoid her?

Before she could decide, the ten-year-old in front of her paid for his cotton candy and it was her turn. She pointed to one of the sugary treats. Before she could slip her purse off her shoulder to pay, Austin passed the man a bill.

"Thank you," she said, faintly surprised.

"My pleasure. Is that your lunch?"

"Yes, but I had an extra serving of vegetables last night, and I promise to behave at dinner." She pinched off a wisp of the pink floss and stuck it in her mouth. "So there."

He shook his head. "You're awful."

"I know. Isn't it great?"

Without thinking she swirled a thin length of the candy around her index finger and offered it to him. Their eyes met. Her good humor faded as she steeled herself to be rejected yet again.

His gray eyes darkened with an emotion she couldn't identify. For a moment she thought it might be pain, but that wasn't right. Why would her simple gesture hurt him? She studied the handsome lines of his face, the hollow cheeks, the firm jaw and straight mouth, and wondered why it had to be him. Why couldn't she have fallen for someone less complicated?

The sounds of the carnival—the screams from the people on the rides, the call of the barkers, the excited conversations disappeared. The world seemed to stop and tilt slightly until she wasn't sure she could maintain her balance. The wisp of cotton candy trembled in the warm afternoon breeze.

Then Austin leaned forward and took the treat in his mouth. His warm lips closed around her finger, his tongue swept her skin clean. Tingling rippled through her, from her hand clear down to that secret place that ached for him.

His eyes held her captive. Slowly, as if he feared she would run away, he raised his hand to her face. He cupped her chin, touching her reverently. She wanted to weep at his gentleness. He brushed her hair back, smoothing it over and over again. Her gaze dropped to his mouth and she silently begged him to kiss her.

Their bodies didn't move, yet they strained toward each other. Her heart ached. Sexually her body was ready to be taken by him, but even stronger than that was the flood of tenderness. She wanted to hold and be held, to protect and be protected, to find refuge and to provide a haven. She wanted him to let her in enough for her to fall in love with him.

Impulsively she decided to tell him.

"Austin, I—"

"Well, well. I'd heard the rumors, but I hadn't thought they could be true."

Austin dropped his arm to his side as if he'd been scalded. He turned toward the voice. Rebecca looked, as well, then wished she hadn't. It was the redhead. The one in the fancy car who had driven to Austin's house twice a week for months:

"Jasmine," he said. "What are you doing here?"

The woman smiled, revealing even, white teeth and not one wrinkle in her classically beautiful face. Rebecca stared at her perfectly made-up eyes, at the coral-colored lipstick, then lower at the knit shirt clinging to large, well-shaped breasts. Her confidence nose-dived into her shoes and whimpered.

"I'm doing my bit for the children's home." Jasmine turned her attention to Rebecca. "This must be your lovely wife. Such a pleasure to meet you."

"Thanks," Rebecca mumbled, trying not to notice that the other woman's eyes were an enchanting color of green. Not boring brown, but green. Cat's eyes. Everything about Jasmine screamed sophistication, from her designer sandals to her tailored shorts. Rebecca tried not to remember she'd recently bought her sundress on sale for less than twenty dollars. Or the fact that her underwear was cotton. She told herself it didn't matter that her breasts were smaller than pumpkin seeds and that she was still holding a half-eaten stick of cotton candy.

She realized the other woman was staring pointedly at her left hand. "May I?" she asked.

Rebecca raised her fingers to chest level.

Jasmine studied the ring. "It's beautiful. Austin, you always had exquisite taste. I wish you both every happiness."

The words all sounded right, but Rebecca could see Jasmine staring at Austin as if she'd been without food for a week and he was her favorite dish.

"Thank you," Austin said. He glanced at Rebecca. "Shall we go?"

Her battered ego took solace from the fact that he didn't seem inclined to linger in the presence of his former lover.

Maybe he was trying to avoid being tempted by what he could no longer have, she thought glumly.

She said goodbye and they left. Rebecca was proud of herself for not turning around to see if the other woman was watching them, and soon they were swallowed up by the crowd.

"It's over between us," Austin said, his low voice carrying to her, despite the cacophony around them.

She stumbled. As quickly as that? He'd never even given their marriage a chance. Her stomach lurched and she dropped the rest of the cotton candy into a nearby trash can. "If you say so."

Austin stopped walking and turned to her. "You sound as if you don't believe me. I assure you I took my wedding vows seriously. I have no intention of straying."

She exhaled a sigh of relief. "You're telling me it's over between you and Jasmine."

"Of course. What did you think?"

It was too silly to explain to him. Why had she been so quick to jump to conclusions? Because Austin wasn't acting like her husband. Had she been so different? she wondered suddenly. Had she acted like his wife?

"I appreciate your telling me that," she said. Maybe he was waiting for her to set the tone in their marriage. Before giving herself a chance to change her mind, she slipped an arm though his. "What do you want to do first?"

The sun beat down. It was already in the eighties. Despite that, she felt a chill as Austin stiffened. Would he pull back? She didn't want him to. Just as she was about to lose hope, he relaxed.

"How about checking out the pavilions? It'll be cooler inside."

She nodded. They walked across the carnival grounds, ducking around running children and talking about the fund-raiser.

One little boy barreled right into Austin's jean-clad legs. Austin grabbed his shoulder with his free hand. "Go a little slower, okay?"

The boy nodded, grinned, then took off, running just as hard as he had before. Austin shook his head. "Kids."

"Oh, I would guess you were just as much of a terror when you were a kid."

"Probably," he agreed. "I never spent a lot of time at places like this, but I would have found a way to get into trouble."

"Your mom didn't bring you to local fairs?" she asked.

He shook his head. He started to pull away from her. Without thinking, she grabbed his hand. "Austin, don't. We can talk about something else if you'd rather."

They'd reached the entrance to the first pavilion. There was a short line. When they paused to wait their turn, she thought he might tug away.

"Please," she whispered, knowing she was leaving herself open to heartbreak.

He shuddered and she wondered what he was thinking. Then he slipped his fingers between hers and squeezed gently. "My mother couldn't be bothered taking me anywhere, except away from her," he said, not meeting her gaze. "It's not that it bothers me to talk about it so much as there's nothing to say about her. She spent her time looking for a rich man to support her. When it was going well, she left me alone. When it wasn't she used me to blackmail my father."

Rebecca could feel his pain. She wanted to say something comforting, but suspected he wouldn't accept it. Instead, she held on to his hand. "That would be hard for any kid to take. Do you ever see her?"

The line moved forward and they entered the building. It had a partition down the center, and both walls were covered with photographs. It was cooler inside, and people spoke with hushed voices.

"No," he said quietly. "After college I went to work for a research-and-development company and made my first big breakthrough with heat resistant material. I won an award, including a cash payment. There was a write-up in the paper and it got picked up by a wire service. About two weeks later my mother showed up at my door wanting her cut of the money."

The fingers gripping hers tightened. She could see the tension in his shoulders and back. His jaw thrust forward. His hurt and shame were as tangible as the building around them.

"It's the last time I ever saw her."

"I'm glad you threw her out," Rebecca said fiercely, knowing she would be happy to tell his mother what a horrible, evil person she was to have mistreated her child. How could anyone dare to wound a young boy, then have the nerve to approach the man and expect something for her abuse?

"I didn't send her away," he said, pulling his fingers free of Rebecca's. He tucked his hands into his pockets and rocked back on his heels. "I gave her the money."

He turned toward the closest photograph and stared as if the sunset on a farm was the most interesting picture he'd ever seen.

The empathetic side of her was almost overwhelmed by the waves of pain radiating out from him. He'd let his mother use him. Why? She closed her eyes. Because the small boy inside still needed a mother's love.

Oh, Austin, she broke you into so many pieces. Could he be mended? Was she strong enough to help? Was she strong enough to walk away? She didn't have either answer.

"It's getting late," he said, still studying the photograph. "We'd better get you back to the booth."

She nodded, unable to speak.

They didn't talk as they made their way through the crowds. The sun was hotter now. Rebecca felt perspiration on her back. She was grateful to duck under the awning around her booth. Mary was serving up chili. One of the teenage helpers smiled gratefully when offered a break.

"Don't work too hard," Austin said, his voice impersonal. They hadn't talked since his confession. Rebecca wanted to get through to him, but she didn't know the right words. She wasn't even sure there were any.

"Rebecca, look what I got!" David came running up, carrying a small red bear. "I won it at the ring toss. All by myself."

"Good for you." She bent over his prize. "It's wonderful. I've never won anything. You must be very talented." She brushed his hair out of his face. "Are you thirsty? There's soda in that cooler." She nodded toward the white box in the back. David left the bear in her care and ran off.

"How's he doing?" Austin asked.

"He's fine. I've spoken with the family lawyer, but he doesn't have any good news. David's relatives are talking about putting him up for adoption. Even with the promise of his inheritance, none of them want him." She shook her head. "I don't understand people sometimes. How can they be so awful?"

Austin surprised her by bending over the rope cordoning off the booth and kissing her fiercely on the mouth. "Don't ever stop expecting the best of people. Promise?"

She touched her hand to her lips. "Sure."

David reappeared with a soda. "Austin! I didn't know you were here, too. Did you see my bear?"

"It's great." He crouched down and smiled at the boy. "You want to go on a ride with me?"

The boy yelped with excitement. "Yeah! Wow! That's great. Rebecca, we're going on rides."

"I heard." She didn't dare look at Austin. Her eyes were misty, and she knew he would tell her to quit making him into a hero. He would remind her that he was just a bastard, not a nice guy at all.

"We'll be back in a couple of hours."

"Perfect," she said, watching them walk away.

"Rebecca, you're pretty enough to be a decoration, but we need another pair of hands here to serve the chili," Mary called.

Rebecca laughed, then reached for one of the big aprons lying across a table in the back of the booth. "I'm coming." Still watching David and Austin out of the corner of her eye, she made her way up to the front and started taking orders.

Two hours later, she was ready for a break. Mary, one of the few people who knew about her pregnancy, insisted she get off her feet.

"I'm too hot to protest," Rebecca said as she was ushered to a folding chair in the shade of an elm tree behind the booth. She'd barely taken her first sip from her glass of water when Austin and David came around the corner.

They were both laughing. David's action-figure T-shirt was definitely dirtier than she remembered. There was a new stain on the front that looked suspiciously like chocolate ice cream. Austin's eyes had lost their troubled expression. When the boy saw her and called out, Austin glanced in her direction. For once, his smile was easy and welcoming.

"Did you have fun?" she asked as David crawled into her lap.

"Yup. We went on a roller coaster and the Ferris wheel twice."

Austin dropped to the ground beside her chair and leaned against the trunk of the tree. "I'm glad I didn't eat more of your cotton candy. My stomach isn't that young anymore.''

Rebecca leaned close to David and ruffled his hair. "How old is your stomach?''

The boy laughed at the question. His blue eyes crinkled with delight. "It's as old as me. Seven." He held up the appropriate number of fingers.

She smiled back and glanced at her husband. But Austin wasn't laughing. He was looking at her with the oddest expression. As if he saw something he wanted more than life itself, but couldn't have. For a second she thought he was aroused, but then she saw the bleakness in his eyes and the straight line of his mouth.

She wanted to ask what was wrong. He wouldn't tell her, though. He would deny there was a problem. What was it? Envy? She bit down on her lower lip. For what?

"My bear liked the rides, too," David said, holding up the small stuffed animal.

"Did he?" she asked, paying only half attention to the conversation.

David nodded. "He had fun today. Like me."

"Like you?" Rebecca cupped the boy's face in her hands. "I can tell you had fun. You have dirty cheeks and ice cream on your shirt." She dropped a kiss on his nose. David giggled.

She glanced at Austin. Unabashed longing swept across his face. For her? No. It wasn't like that.

Understanding dawned. To test her theory, she casually rested one hand on David's back and used the other to brush his hair out of his face. Austin looked away as if it had become too much to bear.

It was the touching that got to him, she thought sadly. Not the sexual contact between a man and a woman, but the loving contact between friends, between an adult and a child, between a mother and her son. She remembered all she knew of his early life and suspected no one had ever taken the time to hold him. He was hungry for physical human contact. Excitement gripped her. Had she just found the way to reach her husband?

"Rebecca!"

A familiar voice called her name. She looked up and saw Travis hurrying toward her. Elizabeth followed more slowly.

Rebecca set David on the ground and stood up. Travis was pale, his breathing rapid. "What's wrong?" she asked.

Elizabeth smiled. "My handsome prince is falling apart." She winced, then drew in a deep breath. "Finally, after being two weeks late, I think it's time."

"Oh, God, what can I do to help?" Rebecca asked.

Elizabeth took her husband's arm. "Would the two of you mind coming with us to the hospital? I think Travis is going to need someone to hold his hand."

Chapter Eleven

The waiting room at the hospital was painted a cheerful shade of yellow. Sofas and chairs lined the area. A TV blared from one corner. On a table sat a collection of parenting magazines.

Rebecca smiled as she watched Austin and Kyle pace the floor. Austin was as unreadable as ever, although she thought she saw tension in the set of his shoulders and the line of his mouth. Kyle didn't bother to hide his feelings. He was almost as pale as Travis had been when he'd gone in with Elizabeth.

When Rebecca had first moved to Glenwood, Travis had given her the rush. She'd been ready for a relationship, but within ten minutes of their first date they'd both admitted to a distinct lack of chemistry between them. Instead of lovers, they'd become close friends. She'd seen firsthand the trail of broken hearts left by the Haynes boys and their good buddy Austin. Funny to think such a short time later that both Travis and Austin were married men. At least in Travis's case, it had been a bond formed by love.

"Do you think she's going to be all right?" Kyle asked as he paced in front of her. He still wore his khaki deputy's uniform. His hair was rumpled from his constantly running his fingers through the curls.

"Elizabeth said she had Mandy in about eight hours with no trouble. A second child is supposed to be easier than the first. She'll be fine." She patted his arm.

He gave her an absent smile, then continued his path across the room and back. When Austin stalked by her, she stepped in front of him.

"How are you holding up?" she asked.

He shrugged. "Better than him," he said, jerking his thumb at Kyle. "I hope Jordan and Craig get here soon and calm him down. His brothers always did a better job of that than I could."

"So you're not worried at all?"

His gray eyes held hers. "About Elizabeth? No."

The unspoken comment was that he was worried about her. She bit back a smile, not ready to let him know that his concern pleased her. She glanced around the empty waiting room. It was time to test her theory about Austin's behavior earlier at the carnival. Did he secretly long for the comfort of a woman's touch? What if she'd misjudged the entire incident with David, and Austin turned away from her? She reminded herself that they were already sleeping in separate rooms. It couldn't get much worse.

"I'd like something to drink," she said, placing her fingertips on his forearm. "I saw a soda machine in the hallway. Will you please come with me?"

"Sure." He glanced at Kyle, still pacing. "Want something to drink?"

"Scotch?" the deputy asked hopefully.

"Sorry."

Kyle shook his head. "I'll just stay here in case there's any news."

Rebecca led the way to the double glass doors that opened onto the hallway. Even in the maternity ward, hospital smells overwhelmed everything. The combination of antiseptic and the lunch that had been served several hours before made her wrinkle her nose.

When they reached the soda machine, Austin fished several coins out of his pocket. He handed them to her. "Can you drink anything here?" he asked.

"Sure." She studied the displayed labels. "I have to avoid caffeine, but that's all." She dropped in the coins, then bent over and collected the cold can. When she handed Austin the remaining change, he chose a drink for himself, then they started back toward the waiting room.

A mother, her baby in her arms, was being wheeled down the hallway. Rebecca stepped to one side to let her pass. When Austin moved next to her, she took advantage of their closeness to take a small step back, bringing her shoulder in contact with his chest.

Instantly heat flared between them. She told herself to ignore her sexual urges. She was conducting an important emotional experiment.

After the woman had been wheeled past, Rebecca waited before moving. Austin didn't slide away. That was good. When she couldn't think of an excuse not to start walking, she kept her pace slow, making sure their arms brushed. At the entrance to the waiting room, Austin held the door open for her. She had to struggle to keep from grinning. He wasn't avoiding her, even though she'd spent the past fifteen minutes practically glued to his side. She dared to be hopeful.

Kyle looked up as they entered.

"Any news?" she asked.

He shook his head. "Do you really think Elizabeth is going to be okay? What if something happens to her? Jeez, Travis can't lose her now. He's the only one of us to find somebody worth keeping."

"Kyle, you're overreacting," Rebecca said. "Women have babies all the time. Elizabeth is young and healthy, and she's already had one child. There's no reason to be afraid."

The door opened and a strange man stumbled in. His pale features were drawn. He looked as if he hadn't slept or shaved in three days.

When he saw the other people in the room, he smiled weakly. "My wife and I just had a boy. Almost eight pounds." He sank onto one of the chairs and shuddered. "Oh, God, I don't know how we got through it. The pain kept coming. I don't know how she stood it. I told her to scream, but she wouldn't. I tried to help. I tried to remind her about her breathing." He dropped his head into his hands. "It was horrible. I just wanted to run. It's not like in the movies, ya know? How can I ever face her again?"

Rebecca watched the rest of the color drain from Kyle's face. Even Austin looked a little shaken. She walked over to the man. "How's your wife now?"

"Fine." He looked up at her. His eyes were bloodshot. "Her folks are with her, and everyone is happy. Like it never happened. Not me. I'll carry this to my grave." He lurched to his feet. "I'd better go check on her." He glanced around at the three of them and smiled vaguely. "Good luck." The door swung shut behind him.

Kyle dropped onto the nearest chair. "Elizabeth is going to die."

"No, she's not," Rebecca said briskly. "Men. You're less than useless. Try to keep a positive outlook, Kyle. If something was wrong, we'd have been told."

"If there was time," he said morosely.

She crossed to Austin and smiled up at him. "I give up."

Austin didn't look much better than Kyle. "Aren't you worried?"

"A little," she said. "But childbirth is a normal part of a woman's life. Elizabeth will be fine."

Before he could answer, she wrapped her arms around his waist and leaned against him. She forced herself to relax as she waited to be pushed away. Austin stood immobile for so long she thought he might not even be aware of what she was doing. Then he brought his arms up and encircled her body, holding her close. She breathed a sigh of contentment. Looks like her idea had been dead-on. He needed the touching he'd been deprived of so many years before. He needed to know he was loved, not just desired.

"I didn't mean about Elizabeth," he said, resting his chin on her head. "Are you scared for yourself? When it's your time?"

"I try not to think about it," she admitted. "Sometimes it's frightening to think about going through labor. I don't deal all that well with pain. Then I think about having a baby, and I know it will be worth it in the end. Birth is a natural part of the cycle of nature. I want children, and this is how I'm going to get them."

"I wouldn't want anything to happen to you."

Her heart fluttered. That statement was the closest Austin had ever come to admitting he cared.

"I feel responsible for the pregnancy," he continued. "Bad enough that your life has been turned around without anything else making it worse."

Okay, so that wasn't exactly the romantic declaration she'd been hoping for, but it was enough.

The door behind them opened. They both turned and saw Travis come in. He was still dressed in green scrubs. The color had returned to his face, and he was grinning like a fool.

Rebecca smiled at him. "Well?"

His gaze swept the room. "Where are my other brothers? Or couldn't they get away?"

"Right behind you," came the gruff response. "Nice of you to wait until we got here."

Jordan and Craig entered the waiting room. Craig, a cop in Sacramento, was still in uniform. Jordan, the black sheep and only fire fighter in four generations of policemen, was wearing jeans and a T-shirt.

Travis turned and held out his arms. The two tall men moved into his embrace. Kyle crossed the room to be included. The four Haynes brothers clung to each other, communicating silently what they could not put into words. Rebecca felt a lump forming in her throat. When she had her child, her sisters would come up to be with her, as would her parents. The warmth and support of her family would allow her to get through whatever she had to.

She turned to Austin, ready to share the moment. He stood stiffly, his hands balled into fists at his sides. The stark pain was back in his eyes. His expression of longing tore at her. In that instant, when she saw down into the empty, hungry part of his soul, she realized he'd spent his entire life on the outside looking in. Although he'd made friends with Travis and his brothers, not once had he been pulled inside the circle of closeness.

Slowly, cautiously, so as not to startle him, she placed her hand on his back. He relaxed slightly, but didn't acknowledge her presence. Still, it was enough that she could be with him and that she knew the truth about him. Tonight she would take the next step in her campaign.

Travis looked up and saw Austin standing beside her. He broke free of his brothers and walked over. He held out his right hand. When Austin took it, Travis shook once, then jerked him into his embrace. Rebecca had to swallow back her tears.

"You never told us, Travis," she said, sniffing. "What did you have?"

He released Austin and grinned at Rebecca. Bending down, he kissed her on both cheeks. "A girl."

"What?" Craig stared at his brother. "Did you say a girl?"

Kyle raised his eyebrows and placed his hands on his hips. "That's not possible. There hasn't been a girl born into this family in four generations."

"There is now," Travis said, grinning like a proud papa. "She's as beautiful as her mother."

Craig shook his head. "A girl. I have three boys. Dad had four boys. He's one of six boys. So how did you get a girl?"

Travis puffed out his chest. "Just lucky, I guess."

"I think it's because you were in love," Rebecca said.

Craig stared at her as if she'd grown another head. Kyle laughed out loud. Only Jordan didn't smile. "I think she's right," he said.

While all the Haynes brothers looked very similar with their dark, curly hair and handsome features, Jordan was the loner. As Rebecca met his gaze, she realized he'd always been the one most like Austin. Although Travis was her husband's closest friend, Jordan shared his inclination to stand outside the circle and look in. He was the quiet one, the rebel the other brothers never ceased teasing about becoming a fire fighter, instead of a cop.

The other brothers gathered around Travis and started slapping him on the back. She looked up at Austin. "Maybe we should go look at the baby."

He nodded and placed his hand on the small of her back. Before they could leave, Jordan stopped them. "I never got to congratulate you," he said, looking at Austin. "You got lucky. Don't let her get away."

"I won't," Austin answered.

Rebecca wanted to believe his comment meant something, but she was sure he was just being polite. Then Jordan turned to her. "I hope you're happy," he said, his tone sincere. Then he touched her face with his fingers and bent to kiss her. The brush of his lips was quick and warm, and overwhelmingly sad. In that split second of connection, she felt his emptiness. Startled, she tried to read his expression. Like Austin, Jordan Haynes had learned to hide what he was thinking.

"Maybe you should find someone of your own," she said, drawing her eyebrows together.

"Unlikely," he replied, and walked back to his brothers.

She stared after him. What *was* Jordan's story? He was the best-looking of the brothers and all of them were easy on the eye. If the stories were true, he'd always been the quiet one. What had happened to make him withdraw?

As they approached the nursery, she shook off thoughts of Jordan. As much as she liked all the Haynes brothers, right now her husband required her full attention.

They stopped in front of the glass wall separating the nursery from the hallway. "They're so small," she said. A black-haired infant directly in front of them waved a fist in the air and made sucking motions.

"Oh, my." Her breath caught in her throat.

Back in the waiting room, with Kyle and Austin so nervous, she'd been able to handle the thought of having a baby. She wasn't showing, she didn't feel sick, and she'd only missed one period. Although she knew in her head she was pregnant, she didn't really feel any different. Even the conversation about going through labor hadn't affected her.

But now, staring at these tiny infants, she felt the heavy responsibility settle on her shoulders. This wasn't an intellectual discussion about some event far off in the future. This was real. She was actually going to have a baby.

A nurse walked into the nursery. "Which one would you like to see?" she asked.

"Baby Haynes," Rebecca said. "She was just born."

"Let me see if she's cleaned up." The nurse disappeared into a back room. Seconds later she returned, a tiny child nestled in her arms. She moved to the glass partition and brushed the pink-and-ivory blanket away from the baby's face.

The little girl, so small and red-faced, opened her big eyes and blinked fuzzily. Her mouth was the shape of a tiny rosebud. Even with her blotchy skin and wisps of light brown hair, she was beautiful.

"Oh, Austin, isn't she wonderful?"

When he didn't answer, Rebecca glanced at him. He was staring at the infant as if she was the most precious thing he'd ever seen. Rebecca felt her eyes start to burn. She blinked to hold back the tears. Then Austin reached for her hand. His fingers slipped between hers and he squeezed.

Together they watched the newborn snuggle deeper into the blankets and fall asleep. Rebecca didn't bother to brush away the tears, not even when Austin put his arm around her and pulled her close. When his free hand touched her still-flat belly, she smiled with contentment. They were going to have a child. Pray God they found their way together and were able to give their baby the warm, loving home every child deserved.

Austin picked up the television remote control and started hunting through the channels. From his place on the sofa he could see Rebecca cooking in the kitchen. After they'd left the hospital, they'd talked about going back to the carnival, but Rebecca had admitted to being tired. He certainly didn't need to spend any more time in the crowds, avoiding gossip and old lovers. So they'd come home.

The news show couldn't hold his interest. He glanced up and watched his wife move from the stove to the counter and back. His wife. He'd never planned to say those words. He'd never thought he would get involved, get married or have a child. It had happened so quickly. He hadn't lied that morning when he'd told Rebecca that while he might regret getting her pregnant, he didn't regret the child.

But it scared the hell out of him. He grimaced, remembering the man who had come into the waiting area and talked about the torture his wife had gone through to have their child. He could still see the horror in his eyes and hear the fear in his voice.

Austin hit the remote again and switched from the news to a baseball game. As much as he wanted a child, he would give his life to keep anything from happening to Rebecca. He couldn't bear knowing he'd hurt her by their living arrangements; he would never survive if he knew the pregnancy would do her harm.

They were going to have a child. He leaned back on the sofa and tried to absorb the words. They'd had little meaning until he'd seen Travis's daughter. She'd been so tiny. How did anyone take care of something that small? How was he supposed to know what a baby needed or wanted?

"It'll be about ten more minutes until dinner," Rebecca called.

"Fine. Do you want me to set the table?"

She looked up and smiled. "Already done."

She'd taken her shoes off when they'd come upstairs. Her hair was pulled back in a loose braid, with a few wisps floating around her face. Her dark eyes flared with life and contentment. From the first moment he'd seen her, he'd thought she was beautiful inside and out. Time had convinced him his initial assessment was correct. Rebecca was one of those rare souls who truly believed there was good in the world. She didn't use sarcasm in her speech. She thought the best of everyone until proved otherwise, sometimes even after seeing proof that person had no good side.

God knows why, but she thought he was worth saving. It didn't matter what he told her about his past or how much he unintentionally hurt her. She continued to believe he had a heart of gold. Today he'd seen that damn light back in her eyes when he'd taken David on a few rides. Why did she have to make a big deal about it? The kid had been alone. Anyone would have done the same thing. Besides, he'd had time to kill until Rebecca was done with her volunteering.

But she didn't see it that way at all. She'd looked up at him, her eyes glowing with pride, her heart on her sleeve. He'd felt like slime. The sharp pain in his chest had been one part joy, two parts fear. Because it was too easy. It was just a matter of time until this whole thing blew up in his face. The second he started to need her and depend on her, he would lose her.

The problem was, he admitted to himself, it was already too late. Even though they slept apart, he couldn't imagine the place without her. The whisper of her perfume kept him awake long after she'd fallen asleep. The sound of her laughter echoed in his lab, taunting him throughout the day. Needing her would make him vulnerable. Not needing her would snuff out the light in her eyes.

With a certainty that crawled over him like the cool, smooth belly of a snake, he knew he had to let her go. Let her go, or hold on for all he was worth. And he couldn't do that. Ever. Holding on, caring, meant exposing himself. Once his dark secret came to light, he would crumple and blow away on the wind. Then she would know the truth. That inside there was nothing worth loving. The black hole of his soul sucked in all the light and let none escape.

But his arms ached to hold her close. Not just to make love, but to be near her, touching her, being touched by her. All afternoon she'd been next to him, brushing against his body, resting her hand on his arm. Little touches. They'd been a balm to his wounds. He'd horded the memories, storing them to feed on in the long winter to come.

He would let her go because it was the ultimate act of kindness. To bind her to him was unconscionable. A woman like her shouldn't be tied to a bastard like himself.

She hummed under her breath. The sweet sound called to him. He glanced at her face, at her slender body, at her still-flat stomach, and knew he had to let her go before it was too late. Once their child was born, he would never be able to survive losing her.

His gaze returned to her face. Their eyes met. Rebecca studied him as if she knew exactly what he'd been thinking and didn't like it one bit. Before he could turn away, she slid the pan off the flame, turned off the stove and walked over to him.

"I don't think so," she said.

"What are you talking about?"

"Whatever you're planning. You've already made enough rules without asking for my input. I suppose it's my own fault for letting you. I should have spoken up right away. After all, we're partners in this marriage. Don't you agree, Austin?"

There was a light in her eyes he'd never seen before. The strength he'd always admired seemed to steel her spine as she got closer.

"Yeah, right," he mumbled, not sure what she was talking about. He reached for the remote and punched off the TV.

"They've been your rules, put in place for your convenience. That's about to change." She knelt on the soft next to him, then slid one knee over his thighs so that she was straddling him. Raising her hands high, she unfastened her braid. When her hair was loose, she brought her forehead down to touch his. The dark, curly strands provided a curtain of privacy.

"It's time for new rules. *My* rules." She shifted her weight from knee to knee, then sank onto his lap. Her panties rested against his crotch, her hands touched his shoulders. "Rule number one. More touching." She pressed her breasts against his chest. "Lots more touching."

He told himself to pull away. He knew this was a mistake. One of them was bound to get hurt. But he couldn't move. Her slim arms were like bands of steel. Or maybe he just wanted them to be. Maybe he was tired of pushing her away and hiding from the things she made him feel.

She bent closer and brushed his lips with hers. Instantly fire flared between them. Heat rolled through his body, settling in his groin. By the time she'd leaned forward and nibbled on his ear, he was already hard.

"Oh, Austin, I'm your wife," she whispered, dragging her mouth back to his. "Don't keep shutting me out."

The second kiss wasn't quite as fleeting. She pressed against him, moving slightly. The soft pressure taunted him. Of their own accord, his hands slid up her calves to her thighs. He slipped under her full skirt and touched her warm, bare skin. She shivered against him.

"Don't resist me," she said softly, then swept her tongue across his lips.

He moaned low in his throat. His mouth opened. Slowly, so slowly he thought he might go mad, she pushed her tongue inside. Tentatively tasting, savoring each moment as if it was precious.

He brought his hands up her legs, feeling her muscles tense and release as he held her hips, then slipped back to cup her rear.

She wrapped her arms around his neck and breathed his name, then angled her head and plunged into his mouth again. Her kiss changed from searching to demanding. When he responded, she bit down lightly.

"Stop being a jerk," she said, pulling back and glaring at him. "I mean it. We didn't get married under the best of circumstances. I'll admit that. But so what? We can still make it work between us. But we both have to try." Her brown eyes searched his. "I can't do it by myself. You have to let me in. Just a little. I know you don't want to expose your feelings. That's okay. But you have to give me something to work with."

His hands stilled on her body. "I don't know if I can."

"Try. Today at the hospital when we saw Elizabeth and Travis's baby, I knew we weren't pretending anymore. This is very real. We have to be ready to provide a home for our child."

Or end it now, he thought grimly, knowing he didn't have a hope in hell of letting her walk out that door tonight. It wasn't just because he was hard and ready and the dampness of her panties told him she was just as willing. It was because if he pushed her away he would hurt her, and right now he wasn't strong enough to face that. And, a small voice reminded him, if he sent her away, there would be no one to hold him and care for him....

"I know you have secrets," she said. He stared at her, wondering when she'd learned to read his mind. She went on as if she hadn't noticed. "You don't have to share them with me. What's more important is that we make this marriage work. That we respect each other. That we work on building a bond between us."

He touched her face, then ran his fingers through her long hair. The bond she spoke about was already in place. He could feel the silken ties wrapping around his heart and squeezing. She didn't know what she was asking. It was too late. It had been too late for years. Didn't she know that everything he loved or tried to love had been destroyed?

He'd desperately loved his mother and she'd returned those feelings with abandonment and betrayal. He'd wanted to know his father, but the old man had threatened to put him in prison if he ever approached him again. Even when he was just fifteen and he'd loved this town and his friends more than anything in his life, he'd managed to screw it all up by stealing a car. Just because he knew it wasn't going to last. Rather than wait for the pain, he'd created it himself so he could meet it on his own terms.

He didn't want to mess up with Rebecca, but it was inevitable. Somehow, sometime, he would say the unforgivable, lash out in fear and destroy the bond she sought to weave between them.

"Austin," she said, cupping his face in her hands, "it's not supposed to hurt that much. I'm sorry."

"It doesn't matter."

"Of course it does. You matter to me. Very much." She traced his nose, his mouth, then the line of his jaw. Last of all, she touched his earring and smiled. The tenderness in her gaze made him flinch. "I don't need you to love me back," she said softly. "Just let me in enough to love you."

Desire to believe battled with panic and fear. Panic and fear won. He gripped her waist and lifted her away from him. When he was free, he sprang to his feet and retreated to the far side of the room.

"Don't," he said hoarsely. "Don't love me." His muscles were tight, his arms rigid at his sides. His chest tightened and it was hard to breathe. "I'll save you the effort of even trying. It won't work, you know. I'm not worth the trouble. Never have been. Now get the hell out of here."

Chapter Twelve

Rebecca rose to her feet slowly, fearful that if she moved too quickly he would bolt. He stood alone on the far side of the room, fighting his feelings. Their eyes met. His anguish was so deep, so gut wrenching, she thought she might break in two just watching him. She raised her hand, as if she could touch him from across the distance of the room.

"No," he growled, and turned away.

He stared out the window at the twilight as if it held the answers to his suffering. He stood in the same place he did each time she left the loft. He always watched her go. Sometimes, when she reached the grove of trees that separated the barn and garage from the main house, she turned back and saw him staring down at her. The sadness in his expression was what had made her come back night after night, even knowing he had shut her out of his bed and his heart.

"I'm not worth the trouble," he said.

He'd spoken the words with the certainty of someone who had heard them a thousand times before. No doubt he had his mother to thank for that. A woman who would dump her child on relatives, then abandon him in a children's home, would easily express her displeasure by telling her son he wasn't worth the trouble.

Often during the busy workday at the home, harried adults would discuss whether or not a child was worth saving. Should they bother to solicit for adoption, knowing most couples wouldn't want to take on that kind of responsibility? She constantly warned her staff that the children overheard more than everyone thought, that they remembered and passed on the bitter judgments. How many times had Austin heard himself discussed? She knew enough about his past to guess the phrases they would have used. Troublemaker. Bully. Antisocial. Unredeemable.

Words tossed around by professionals who sometimes forgot words could be the harshest blows of all. Like the children now in her care, he had been cast aside, unwanted.

He'd proved them all wrong. His accomplishments and generous spirit had long since convinced her of that. He'd fought his way out, forged a new path and stood as a testament to the power of determination. Despite the odds against him, despite his lack of emotional support, despite the deepest, most tragic scar of all. The belief that he wasn't worth the trouble.

She studied the breadth of his shoulders, the strong musculature of his back. Jeans hugged narrow hips and outlined powerful thighs. He wasn't a child anymore. He'd long ago left that part of him behind. He was a man, with a man's sensibilities. She'd been a fool to think she could heal him with a couple of pats on the arm. She might never be able to heal him.

But he was her husband; she had to try.

She'd asked him to open up enough to let her love him. As with the children she provided for, she couldn't make him an empty promise. Not if she wanted him to learn to trust her. She would only get one chance, if that. She couldn't make a mistake.

She shook her head at her earlier belief that she'd found her way in by figuring out he hungered for physical contact. So what? Of course he did. Most victims of abuse did. It wasn't the key; it was a symptom. She would have to risk everything to get through to him.

She studied the set of his head, so proud. Her gaze dropped to her left hand and the diamond ring that proclaimed her as his wife. From the very first moment she'd stood dripping on Austin's garage floor several weeks ago, he'd come through for her. Offering her refuge from the storm, giving his house to the children, warning her away from him, even when she'd wanted nothing more than to have him make love to her.

Later, when he'd given the playground equipment to the children and then married her because she was pregnant, he'd been supportive, giving, generous and kind. He was her husband. She hoped she would be able to give back as much to him.

She took a step closer to him. He stiffened, but didn't move. Another step, then another, until she stood directly behind him. Not touching, not doing anything to send him running, she breathed in the scent of him and searched for the right words.

"I still remember the first time we met," she said softly. "I don't remember anything about what committee meeting it was, but I can see the room." She closed her eyes. "You were wearing a white shirt, rolled up to your elbows, jeans and boots. I was new in town. I walked in and you were the first person I saw. I couldn't move. I couldn't even breathe. When the lady at the desk asked me my name, I couldn't answer her. I felt like I was thirteen and meeting a rock star."

She opened her eyes and stared at the weave of his polo shirt. In front of him through the window, she could see the darkening sky. There was a light on in the living area and an overhead lamp on in the kitchen, but their illumination didn't reach as far as the window. Shadows crept in around them, cocooning them in the protective cloak of night.

"You wore an earring," she continued, smiling at the memory. "I'd never known a man who wore an earring before. You were forbidding and dangerous, and I couldn't stop thinking about you. That night I don't think I slept at all, remembering the meeting. Hearing your voice in my head gave me the shivers."

She drew in a deep breath. His silence unnerved her. She wanted to poke him in the side and make sure he was awake. She smiled slightly. Of course he was awake. But couldn't he say something and make this a little easier?

"You made me feel alive inside," she went on, "as if I'd been missing out on the best part of life and suddenly it was available to me." She paused to collect her thoughts. Now came the hard part. "The first time I met Wayne, I knew he was the man I was going to marry. There was no flash of lightning, no sense of danger, just a rightness, as if I'd met the other half of myself." Interesting how both men had provided her with a sense of completion. She'd never thought of that before.

Despite her declaration, Austin didn't move. She said, "I was with a friend of mine at a pep rally. We were both freshmen. My friend was this skinny little guy, one of those nerdy science types who was always getting beaten up. That day was no exception. Two tough guys grabbed him. I was screaming for someone to help, and then there he was. Wayne waded into the trouble, punched out both the bullies and rescued my friend."

Austin turned and looked at her. In the darkness, she couldn't read the expression in his eyes. "A real hero," he said, his voice cold.

Then she remembered how he'd told her about his first meeting with Travis. How he'd been the bully, picking on everyone. The fights covered the pain, she thought with a flash of insight. She should have seen that before. It made perfect sense.

They were standing so close his breath fanned her face. If she stood on tiptoe she could kiss him. It would be a mistake to do that now, she told herself. He wasn't ready. If the truth be told neither was she.

"He was a hero to me," she said softly. "When he'd done away with the other two guys, we introduced ourselves. He offered to walk me to my next class, and that was it. From that moment on, we were together."

"A touching story. Thanks for telling me."

She ignored his sarcasm. "I have a point here. Marrying Wayne was logical. There was never another choice. We dated, we fell in love, we got engaged. There weren't any tests along the way. The only fight we ever had was about me wanting to save myself for marriage and wanting to put off the wedding until I had my master's degree. Being a normal male in his twenties, Wayne was frustrated by my stubbornness." She shrugged, suddenly embarrassed to be discussing something so intimate.

Despite the darkness she stared into his eyes, hoping to see a glimmer of what he was thinking. His gray irises gave nothing away. Was he bored, angry, hurt—what? She couldn't tell.

"Yes, well, after the accident everything changed."

"You've told me this part, Rebecca. You wanted to get married. He didn't. He died hating you. So what?"

She told herself he was being cruel on purpose. It didn't help. Rather than let him see he'd gotten to her, she lowered her gaze. Her eyes widened. His hands hung at his side, balled into tight fists. She could see the strain around his knuckles. He wasn't quite as disinterested as he wanted her to believe. The small sign gave her hope.

"The 'so what' is that I didn't try hard enough. What I realized later was that I should have forced the issue of marriage. I believe Wayne wanted me to prove that I loved him by making the arrangements, anyway, and risking his rejection. I never did."

She placed her palm on his chest, in the center, close to his heart. He didn't move away. The steady thudding gave her courage. "I'll always care about Wayne—he was my first love. I'll carry those feelings with me always. I'll also always know that I failed him in the end. Not because I stayed a virgin. That was my choice. If I'd known what would happen, of course I would have wanted us to make love. But I couldn't know that ahead of time. Given the same set of circumstances, I still would have wanted to save myself for the marriage bed."

"You belong in a different time, Rebecca Chambers," Austin said gruffly. "You're out of step with the rest of the world."

"I don't think so. And it's Rebecca Lucas, Austin. I'm your wife." He didn't answer so she went on, "All my choices have been easy ones. I've never had to look inside myself and search out the difficult solutions. Until you. I never believed I was very strong. The fire taught me differently. I survived that. I took care of the children. I'm not dismissing the help I was given, but I was the one responsible and I did it."

He swore under his breath, then reached up and placed his hand on the side of her neck. "You've always been pure steel. I've known that from the start."

"That sounds like the beginning of a goodbye." When he started to speak, she touched a finger to his mouth. "No. Not yet. I'm not done. I went into this relationship with my eyes open. I knew exactly who and what you were that first day I came here, dripping on your floor."

He jerked his hand away, as if her gentleness burned him. "You never knew. You still don't know. You see what you want to see, not the truth."

"How do we know you're not the one with the cloudy vision?"

Before he could speak the sky behind him burst into a thousand sparks of color. Seconds later, a muffled *boom* shook the building. He turned, pulling her with him, so they both faced out the window.

Fireworks from the main park in town were clearly visible above the trees. Reds, greens, blues and whites exploded, washing away the brilliance of the stars. Their beauty hurt her eyes.

"This is what you see," he said, pointing to the display. "This is what you imagine me to be. You're wrong." There was a moment of calm before the show continued. He gestured to the black, smoky night. "This is reality, Rebecca. There's no magic, nothing noble here. Just the absence of light."

"Oh, please." She moved in front of him and grabbed his shirtfront. "I came into this fully aware of what I was doing. I chose to stay here and invite you into my bed. I wanted to be here, with you. I still want to be with you. You didn't force me or coerce me. When I found out I was pregnant, I chose to marry you. I *want* to be your wife." She wished she were big enough to shake him, but that wasn't possible. She settled for wrinkling his shirt. "I'm making a permanent commitment to you. I'm willing to work through all the hard stuff, the boring parts, the past, the future and everything in between. I know you think you're not worth the trouble. You're wrong. You are. Let me inside, Austin. Trust me so I can learn to love you. Let me give you what you've always wanted."

He started to back away. The fireworks cast colored shadows on his face, making him seem otherworldly, as if he really were the devil. She hung on tighter.

"No!" she cried. "I won't lose you. Not now. Trust me, please. Just a little. You're a good and decent man. Kind, generous, sensitive. Even loving, if you'd give yourself a chance."

His eyes bore into hers. Silence crackled around them, broken only by the booms of the fireworks. He took her hands in his and pulled them from his shirt.

"You lead with your chin," he said. "It's a good way to get it busted."

"You'd never hit a woman," she said confidently.

"It's a metaphor."

"To hell with metaphors."

He raised his eyebrows. "What did you say?"

"Oh, Austin, I'm not interested in metaphors and analogies anymore. Let's just deal with us. Can you trust me even a little?"

He didn't even pause before answering. "No."

She felt as if he'd slapped her, but she plunged on. She'd made her commitment; there was no turning back. "I'll make you trust me. I'll prove myself a thousand times if necessary. I'm not going to leave you or hurt you or betray you. I'm going to be here for the next fifty years. Maybe longer if I keep my looks."

He smiled faintly. "You will."

"Believe me."

The smile faded. "I can't."

"Then believe this."

She rested one hand on his shoulder and reached the other to the back of his neck, pulling him down toward her. She raised herself up to kiss him. When he would have resisted, she breathed his name.

He relaxed enough to let her kiss him, but he didn't respond. His mouth stayed closed, his lips didn't move and his arms hung at his sides.

She exhaled her frustration. "Just once give in, would you? Why do you have to be so stubborn?" She tried to think of a way to get through to him. Something deep inside her whispered that if she could get back into his bed, she would have a better chance of making things work. Of course there was a chance the voice doing the whispering belonged to the parts of her he'd awakened with his masterful touch. Which meant her desire was more selfish than she liked.

She glared up at him, loving the way the evening stubble shadowed the lines of his jaw, causing him to look even more forbidding. "Why do you have to make everything so difficult?" she asked in frustration. "I'm already pregnant. What's the worst that could happen now?"

The worst was that he would start to believe, Austin thought, fighting against the will of his body and his soul. Only his mind stood firmly on the other side, watching as if from a distance. The cold logic that made him successful in his chosen field reminded him that his relationship with Rebecca was doomed to failure. By keeping his distance as much as possible, he would minimize the risk.

But she wouldn't want to hear that. Not from him, not now. "You'll be the death of me, Rebecca," he said.

"No." Her smile was sweet and pure. "I'll be your salvation."

"I'm long past saving. If you had any sense, you would have already figured that out."

She opened her mouth to protest. He didn't let her. Before she could make a sound, he raised his hands to her hair and slid his fingers through the silky strands. Gently he tilted her head toward him. A brilliant rocket burst in the sky, showering them with red light, turning her eyes the color of velvet and her skin the sweetest cream.

He lowered his head until his mouth was almost touching hers. Their breaths mingled. "Why do you haunt me?"

"Because I'm your destiny, Austin Lucas. You can't escape me."

She was right, he thought sadly. She was his destiny, but he wasn't hers. She belonged to a gentle man, someone who would cherish her innocence and giving spirit. Not Wayne, not even himself. Somewhere a stranger waited to claim his ladylove. But not tonight, he told himself fiercely. Tonight she was his.

He tugged on her hair, pulling her head back farther, exposing her neck. Bending over her, he kissed the skin beneath her ear, then moved lower to the hollow of her throat. He tasted her, licking and nibbling, enjoying her soft moans of pleasure. She trembled in his embrace and he was lost.

The madness overtook him, wiping out all thoughts of walking away. She clutched at his shoulders and chest, the diamonds in her ring catching the faint light from the kitchen and living room. The flash of brilliance reminded him that she was his wife. He had to claim her or die.

Releasing her hair, he slipped one arm under her legs and the other under her back. He swept her up in his arms simply because he could. She clung to him, burying her face in his shoulder. With quick kisses she traced the line of his collar, then tasted the place where his stubble gave way to smooth skin. She whispered his name, taming him for the moment, and exhaled her satisfaction.

As he crossed the living room, he glanced into her face. Her eyes were clear and trusting. She didn't fear him or their joining. Had he been a different kind of man, he might have read the flickering light as affection, perhaps even love, but he didn't want to know that. It would only make things more difficult later. He would take her to his bed, mark her, claim her, because she wanted him. That desire had taken away his ability to choose. He would pay any price, suffer any pain to have this night and as many nights as she would grant him before leaving. He would hold back the shattered bits of his heart, knowing they were an unworthy offering, and resist the need to pray for a miracle. As he'd said, he was long past saving.

He saw the open door to her bedroom, but he didn't take her there. Instead, he stopped in front of the king-size bed covered with the black satin comforter. How many nights had he lain awake remembering how she'd looked naked in his bed? He wanted her there again, only this time, instead of burning in the presence of a memory, he would feel her body against his.

Slowly he lowered her to her feet. She stared up at him, patiently waiting for him to lead the way. Her trust mocked his weakness. She was strong, fearless. It never occurred to her that the price for this moment would be high. She'd confessed to him the secrets of her life, of her soul, in an attempt to make him understand. He understood completely; it just didn't change anything. She lived by rules he didn't understand. He envied her simplistic belief.

Then she smiled at him. "You are too handsome by far," she said, touching his cheek. "I think that was my downfall. That and your earring."

He took her hand and kissed her palm. Her eyes widened as he licked the tips of her fingers. Her breathing quickened instantly.

She was such an innocent. She'd only been with a man once in her life. He hadn't known then, hadn't taken the time to seduce her. Regret swept through him, convincing him that this time had to be different. He returned her smile. At last they were treading in territory he knew something about.

He kissed the back of the hand he held, then urged her to sit on the side of the bed. When she was seated, he knelt before her. Once again he slipped his hands through her hair, but gently this time. Teasing, instead of punishing.

"Rebecca," he whispered.

She blinked sleepily. "I love how you say my name."

"Rebecca," he whispered again, lower this time, sensually. "Beautiful Rebecca. Relax. Trust me."

"I do."

The echo of her wedding vow caught him low in the belly. He fought not to flinch. He wanted it all to be real, but it was just an illusion. The woman before him would disappear as the fireworks had done, leaving behind the smoke of his existence and nothing else.

He wove his fingers through her hair, moving lower, dividing it into two sections. He drew her hair over her shoulders, baring her back. His fingers found the zipper of her dress and lowered it. Most of the time she didn't wear a bra, but today he could feel the thin strap in back. He unfastened it, as well, but made no move to take off her clothing.

He leaned close and kissed her cheek. Soft kisses. Lightly he moved over her face, her eyes, her nose, finally her mouth. Brief brushes, lip to lip, never lingering, teasing her into wanting more. She reached for his shoulders. He drew back with her hands in his. Turning them palms up, he rubbed his thumbs around and around, circling her skin, heating it. Then he brought her palms to his mouth. He sucked the most center spots, making her straighten with surprise, then gave his attention to each of her fingers, drawing them into his mouth, tasting the salty length, nibbling on the sensitized tips, before withdrawing and allowing the warm night air to continue his work.

The floor was hard beneath his knees, but he didn't notice any discomfort except that between his legs. His hardness grew with each moment he spent with her. In time he would take his release and it would be all the better for waiting. In time. This was for her.

He released her hands, then drew her to her feet. As she rose, her dress stayed in place. Still on his knees, he hugged her close, burying his face on her flat belly. He breathed in the scent of her, savoring the lingering fragrances of the carnival, the sunshine, the heat, and myriad other smells that would forever mark this day in his memory.

He lowered his hands to her knees, then drew them up under her dress and along her thighs. When he reached her hips, he raised his head and looked up at her.

"Pull up your dress," he said quietly.

His hands held her in place. A shudder rippled her body, then she reached for her skirt. Inch by inch the flowing fabric slid up her legs, exposing her shapely thighs. When the fabric was bunched around her waist, he leaned forward and pressed his lips to her belly, just above the elastic of her panties.

The room was silent around them, except for the faint sounds from outdoors and the rapid cadence of her breathing. With his index fingers, he tugged her panties down a few inches. He turned his head so his stubbled cheeks brushed her sensitive skin. Her breath caught. Back and forth he moved, teasing her in an erotic dance of sensation. Her legs began to tremble. He searched for her belly button and traced the small circle with his tongue. Her muscles rippled in reaction.

Slowly, so slowly he could hear her mentally screaming at him to hurry, he lowered her panties to her ankles. Supporting her at her hips, he held her steady as she stepped out of them.

He turned his attention to the dark curls at the apex of her thighs. Here the heat was more intense, her scent more captivating. Gently, carefully, he brought his mouth to her. She stiffened in shock, then her legs started trembling harder, as if she was having trouble standing. His own need pulsed painfully against the fly of his jeans. He brought his hands down from her hips to her woman's place and used his fingers to part the curls.

When her most sensitive spot was exposed, he touched it with the tip of his tongue. He didn't move, he just held the contact. She tasted of the forbidden, of sweet sin and promise. She gasped his name. He brought his mouth to her and suckled her. She grabbed for his shoulders, letting the dress fall over him, cushioning him in darkness. Her knees buckled and he caught her as she fell.

Her dress slipped off one shoulder, exposing her bra and part of one breast. As he stood up and drew her to her feet, her dress slipped down to her waist. Without his urging, she pushed the garment over her hips and to the floor. Her bra followed.

This time she didn't cover herself. She sat on the side of the bed, then slid onto the comforter. Her gaze was glazed with passion, but underneath, he felt the trust. It should have scared the hell out of him. It should have, but it didn't.

He tugged his shirt out of his pants, pulled it over his head and tossed it aside. Then he moved onto the bed and knelt between her legs. The night hid the subtleties of her body from him. He reached to the nightstand and flicked on the light.

"What are you doing?" she asked, blinking in the sudden glare.

"I want to see everything."

"Why?"

He smiled. "Looking at you turns me on."

"Really?" She sounded surprised. "But you've seen it before. After those other women, how can I be very exciting?"

He would have laughed except he knew the question was genuine. "Look at me," he said.

"I am."

He shook his head. "Not in the face."

She apparently hadn't forgotten how to blush, he thought, trying not to grin. She lowered her gaze to his midsection, then dropped it to the place where his hardness strained against his jeans.

"I think you're plenty exciting," he said.

She smiled slowly, that sensual smile that spoke of a female's power over a male. When she reached to touch him, he grabbed her wrists and pinned them above her head. She didn't struggle. Her surrender was absolute.

"Do you want me to let you go?" he asked, eyeing her full mouth and needing to kiss it.

"Never," she said.

She wrapped her legs around his hips and drew him closer. Her wet core brushed against the rough fabric of his jeans. Pleasure made her arch her head back. When she opened her mouth to draw in a breath, he covered her lips with his and plundered her softness.

This time there was nothing gentle about his possession. His tongue swept inside her mouth, claiming her, daring her to fight back. The strength he'd always believed in caused her to accept the dare and duel with him. Tongues circled against each other, sending electric impulses through his body. He grew hotter, harder, more ready, as the pressure in his groin built.

He drew his head down her neck and bit her tender skin. She gasped. Suddenly he had to touch her, all of her. He released her wrists and covered her breasts. Already taut nipples scraped his palm. Although she didn't know about it, he had a secret stash of books on pregnancy in his lab. While she was at the house, he would read chapters, preparing for his child's birth. He remembered now that most pregnant women had extra-sensitive breasts, so he was careful when he stroked her curves. And he licked gently when he drew the hard points into his mouth.

She clutched at his shoulders, digging her fingers into his skin. Her hips continued to rock against his. She was bringing herself pleasure. He wondered if she knew. He grinned against her breasts. Somehow he doubted it. She was too easily embarrassed to take control in bed. In time she would be the tiger. His organ flexed at the thought.

He straightened and looked at her. The bedside lamp exposed the flush on her face and chest. Teeth marks faded on her shoulders and neck. Her nipples stood at attention, begging for his touch. He glanced down to where her curls pressed against his jeans. When he moved back, he could see the wet spot she'd left on him.

Her hands clutched at the comforter. He took them in his and brought them to her center. "Open for me," he said, placing her fingers on either side of her most secret place.

She swallowed hard and complied.

He rested his hands on her knees and pushed them back toward her chest and out slightly. He could see her most womanly place, feel the heat. She was ready for him, and he was more than ready for her, but it wasn't time. He wanted to hear her cries of pleasure first. He wanted to drive all thoughts from her mind and leave her empty of anything save ecstasy.

He lowered himself on the bed and nipped the back of her thigh. She jumped, then giggled. With his index finger, he traced a line from her tiny point of pleasure to the place that would send him to paradise. She shivered and whispered his name.

He planned to taunt her with her release, to build slowly and make her shake with need. She would cry out, scream and shatter, all for him.

But when he touched her with his tongue he couldn't think about anything but her. Thoughts of technique, of skill, disappeared. He'd been with other women, but that disappeared, as well. His chest and throat tightened as he tasted her sweetness. There was a connection between them, between their bodies. He would bring her pleasure, exquisite pleasure, but honestly. Because he wanted to, rather than because he had something to prove.

So he listened to her breathing, felt the urging pressure of her fingers on his face, shoulders and in his hair. When he could have paused, playing the game, he kept his rhythm steady. And when she asked him to stop, he did, raising his head until their eyes met.

"Be in me," she said. "Make love to me."

His hands shook as he unfastened his jeans. It was insane, he told himself. This was no big deal. He'd done it countless times before. Still he trembled as he undid the last button. His knees threatened to give out when he bent down to pull off his pants. It wasn't the need making him weak; it was the woman. Rebecca. Perhaps in his heart he'd always known what would happen. Perhaps that was why he'd avoided her bed until now.

When he returned to kneel before her, she reached for him to guide him inside. Her touch was tentative but loving, and almost his undoing. Her heat swallowed him, her muscles caressed him. The light of love in her eyes blinded him.

He looked away because he was a creature of the shadows. He plunged in deeply, wondering if she was his greatest sin or, as she had promised, his only hope of redemption. He had meant to shatter her, but he was the one who was shattering.

Her hips moved in time with his, her hands pulled him closer. He couldn't hold back, even though he knew she wasn't ready for their final ascent. He slipped his hand down her leg and dipped his thumb into her moistness. When he found her most sensitive spot, he circled in time with her thrusts, touching lightly, quickly, urging her over the edge.

His performance was juvenile at best, his technique laughable. Another time he would analyze what was wrong with him. This moment it was enough to match her rapid breathing, to gaze at her face, watching her eyes flutter closed as she arched her head back. He held on to his control until her muscles contracted around him, milking his hardness, sending him into oblivion. He plunged deeper and deeper still, holding her hips and hoarsely calling out her name.

When they had found their way under the covers, she snuggled against him.

"I'm not going back into that room," she said, then yawned. "I don't care what you say. We're going to make love every single night and you can't do anything to keep it from happening."

He had a bad feeling she was right. "What about the other room? Do you want me to take the walls down?" he asked.

"No." She rested her head on his shoulder and sighed. "The baby can stay there." Her fingers trailed across his chest, then she tucked them under her chin and closed her eyes. "I'm never going to leave you," she said quietly. "No matter what. You'll see. I'll make you see...."

Her voice trailed off as she fell asleep. Austin lay on his back and stared up at the ceiling. He could hear the regular sound of her breathing. Something had happened to him tonight, something that scared the hell out of him.

Through a combination of events he didn't understand, she'd gotten through to him. She'd found a way past the barriers and reached into the blackness to leave a small light. Its flame burned inside him. He could feel it. In time the blackness would swallow it whole, leaving him once again without hope. It would be worse, though, for the promise she'd given him. Because as surely as he knew that flame would die, he knew she would leave. She thought she'd learned his deepest secret, but she was wrong. There was something else, something far worse than she imagined. And when she knew the truth, she would leave as the others had left. Once again, he would be alone.

Chapter Thirteen

"Okay, the glue should have dried on the wing," Austin said, stretching across the workbench and picking up the white piece of plastic. "Looks like we're ready to paint. Where'd we put the brushes, sport?"

David slid off his chair and collected a brown paper bag from the corner. "They're still in here. We never unpacked 'em." When he handed Austin the sack, he glanced longingly at the wing of the plane. "What color are you gonna paint it?"

"I'm not the one doing the painting. You are."

David stared up at him, his big blue eyes wide with excitement. A grin split his face. "Golly. That's cool." The smile faded. "What if I mess up?"

Austin recognized the sudden distress and silently cursed the circumstances that had made the boy fearful. David wasn't stupid. He knew what his relatives fought over. No doubt he'd figured out that even the promise of his parents' substantial estate wasn't enough to make any of his relatives willing to take him. In the month since the carnival, he'd gone from a bright, inquisitive child to a fearful one. He questioned every move he made, did his best to behave perfectly, as if finding the right behavior would make someone want him.

Austin knew what that kind of pain was like. He wanted to tell David it would get better in time, but it wouldn't. All that would happen was that he would cease to care. He would lie awake in the night and refuse to admit he was bleeding on the inside.

Austin spread out a sheet of newspaper and set the wing in the middle. After opening the pattern so the boy could see what colors were supposed to go where, he uncapped the first small container and handed him a brush.

David worked slowly and carefully, trying to copy the pattern exactly. Austin wanted to tell him it was no big deal if he went outside the lines. He was a kid; he should have fun. But he didn't speak. Partly because he knew David wouldn't understand and partly because he didn't want the kid to care any more than he already did.

Since the carnival, David had been a regular visitor to his workshop. At first Austin had resented the interruptions. He needed to concentrate on his work. In time he'd grown to expect the soft squeak of the door opening, then the hushed footsteps as David stepped inside. He let the boy continue to visit because Rebecca had mentioned that he was still not joining in with the other children. He stood on the outside, watching them play, but never entering the circle. Austin knew all about that, too.

David dipped his brush in the paint and drew a straight line along the edge of the wing.

"Great job," Austin said. "This is going to be the best plane anyone has ever seen."

David smiled up at him. "Will it be done by next Tuesday?"

"It can be. Why? What happens next Tuesday?"

"It's my birthday. I'm going to be eight."

"So you want the plane ready for your party?" All the children had parties on their birthday. He knew. Rebecca was always roping him into taking care of the balloons. He and the helium-tank dealer were spending far too much time together.

David nodded. "My uncle Bob said he might come for my birthday. I want to show him what I can do."

His hopeful expression tore at Austin's heart. He wanted to pull the boy close and protect him against the bastards of this world. He shook his head. Austin was one of them. Would he also protect the child from himself? He had no answer. He only knew it tore him up inside to see David so eager and know he was bound to be disappointed.

"Sure, we'll have the plane ready by then," Austin promised.

David bent over the wing. "Are you coming to my party?"

"I don't know, sport. I have to give a presentation in Kansas on Monday. I don't think I'll be back in time."

"But you *have* to be there, Austin. You're the one I want there the most. More than Uncle Bob."

Even as the child's words warmed him, he fought against the urge to run. He didn't mind spending time with David, but he didn't want to get too involved. "I'll try," was all he promised.

David nodded, but his shoulders slumped and he stopped being quite as careful with the paint. Austin stared at him and swore silently. He was messing up again, this time with an innocent child. The problem was he was as wrong for the kid as he was for Rebecca. This was turning into a disaster.

They continued to work in silence. Finally Austin couldn't stand it anymore. "Why don't we finish this up tomorrow?" he said.

Instantly David put down the brush and started cleaning up. Austin stared at him, not sure what to say or do to make things better. Should he even bother to try?

Footsteps in the garage drew his attention. He looked up, recognizing the sound of his wife.

"Are you two hiding out in here again?" she asked as she came in from the garage. "What is it about hammering and sawing that's so interesting?"

David looked up and returned her smile, but he didn't answer. Austin knew she was smart enough to figure out something was wrong. He steeled himself for her questions. But she didn't ask any. Instead, she crouched down beside the boy and draped her arm around his shoulders.

"What have you been doing?" she asked.

"Working on the plane."

"Show me, please. Is this the wing?"

David nodded.

"Did you paint it yourself? It's a very good job."

Slowly her questions drew him out until he was once again chatting animatedly. While David explained what they'd done and their plans for the plane, Rebecca kept her arm around him and used her free hand to brush the hair from his eyes and touch his face. Constant contact and reassurance. Austin recognized her technique; she used it on him.

In the past month, she'd kept her word. She hadn't gone back to the bedroom he'd built for her. Every night she'd shared his bed. Every night they'd made love. As much as he'd tried, he'd never been able to reclaim his distance. He could only be with her, in her, and feel the moment.

He leaned back in his chair and studied the woman he had married. She wore her thick hair pulled back in a ponytail. The August heat made everyone irritable, but Rebecca looked calm and cool in a loose white dress. The waist was set low, around her hips, and the skirt flowed out around her knees. It wasn't see-through or low cut. Except for the fact that it was sleeveless, there was nothing sexy about the dress.

Yet looking at her now got to him. It made him want her. She didn't even have to touch him. If he closed his eyes he was able to see her as she'd been last night, on top of him, riding him like a pagan queen. As he'd suspected, she had a wild streak of passion far beyond what she'd known about herself. She was flagrant and daring in bed, yet every morning she looked at him with the calm, loving eyes of a Madonna.

Here, in the confines of his workroom, with her safely occupied by David, he could admit the truth. He adored being with her, next to her, inside her making love. More than that, he lived for the sound of her voice, the way she walked, her innocence, her belief in him, the light in her face when she smiled at him. He admired everything about her. But he refused to love her. That final step of faith was beyond him. It always would be. He couldn't trust her. Even more, he couldn't trust himself. Something would happen and she would leave. Not loving her was the only thing that would keep him alive in the aftermath.

Rebecca stood up, drawing his attention back to her. "It's almost lunchtime, David. Why don't you head on back?"

The boy slid out of the chair and obediently headed for the door.

"You want to finish this tomorrow?" Austin called after him.

David shrugged.

"I thought you wanted it done in time for your party?"

David stopped by the doorway and looked back. Disappointment filled his blue eyes. "It doesn't matter now," he said, then left.

Austin grimaced.

"What was that all about?" Rebecca asked, taking the boy's seat and picking up the wing.

"He told me he wanted to have the plane done by next week so he could have it at the party. I guess he changed his mind."

"Why?"

He had a suspicion, but if he was right, it meant that he'd started to matter to the child. That was dangerous for both of them.

It wasn't about him, he assured himself. David wouldn't notice if he was at the party or not. "I'm not sure," he said, then realized he'd just lied to her for the first time.

She set the wing down, then leaned forward and placed her hand on his arm. "I really appreciate your taking the time to work with him. It means a lot to him."

"No big deal." He'd kept his voice gruff on purpose. At the unfriendly tone, he saw Rebecca frown. He knew he confused her. She kept trying to get close to him and he kept backing away. He wanted to tell her it was a mistake to keep trying, but he couldn't. For some stupid reason he needed her to try, even though it was useless. In the back of his mind, he kept waiting for a miracle. There wasn't going to be one. He was long past believing in anything good happening. But he couldn't shake a sense of expectation.

His gaze dropped to her stomach. There was the barest hint of rounding in her belly. He could feel it when they were together at night. He ached at the thought of having a child. It filled him with wonder. At the same time he prayed she would leave him before their baby was born. He couldn't survive losing them both.

"You're not listening to me," she said impatiently.

"I'm sorry. What were you saying?"

She shook her head. "No. Tell me what you were thinking. You had the oddest look on your face."

He couldn't lie to her again. "I was thinking that you make me very happy."

Her smile was slow and sweet, filled with promise. "Do I? I try. It's important to me. Well, of course it is. I mean, I'm your wife. Every wife wants her husband to be happy. Well, not every wife. Some wives might hate their husbands, especially if they're getting a divorce. I'm not saying I want to get—"

"Rebecca?"

She clamped her mouth shut. Faint color stained her cheeks. Her eyes held his, then slipped away. "Yes?"

"You're babbling."

"I know. I was embarrassed by your compliment. Thank you. I'm glad I make you happy." She bit her lower lip. "You make me happy, too."

"Do I?" The thought surprised him. "How?"

"There's that thing you did last night." Her grin was teasing.

He was surprised to find himself feeling a twinge of hurt at her words. He didn't want their relationship to be just about sex. Which was insane, he told himself. He was the one so damn set on keeping her out of his life.

"You make me happy by being with me," she went on. "By helping me and supporting me, by holding me. And mostly by talking to me like I'm an intelligent person."

"You are."

"A lot of guys hate that."

He leaned forward and brushed her lips with his. "A lot of guys are wimps."

She giggled and tilted her head so their foreheads touched. "I'm worried about David," she said.

He straightened. Great. So she'd figured out he'd hurt the child. He tried to think of a defense, then realized he didn't have one. He deserved whatever she was about to say.

"He's been talking about one of his uncles coming to his birthday party," she said.

"He mentioned it."

"The uncle isn't going to show up. He hasn't called or anything, but I've been working with this family for three months now. They don't want anything to do with David. I don't understand them. They make me crazy." She stared at her lap and twisted her ring. "You . . ."

He braced himself. He told himself he could handle any criticism she might make. He'd always known he wasn't perfect.

"You . . ." She took a deep breath. "This is so hard."

"Just spit it out."

"I don't spit," she said, giving him a quick smile. Her mouth twisted. "I thought maybe we could adopt him."

He stared at her, sure he couldn't have heard her correctly. "You want the two of us to adopt David?"

She nodded. "I know it's asking a lot. We're still trying to put the marriage together. I'm pregnant. This is the worst possible time. But he needs us, Austin. We would be good for him. And I've seen you working with him. I know you care about him."

"No." He stood up and glared at her. "You want me to be some kid's father?" He laughed harshly. "Hell, lady, you should have been here about twenty minutes ago. I nearly sent the kid into tears because I told him I couldn't make his birthday party."

"But you're going to be in Kansas next week. It's a business trip. That's hardly your fault."

"I could get back if I wanted to. The point is I don't give a damn about some kid's party. I don't care about him or any of those other children. I don't want to adopt him. That's final. Do you understand?" He stopped when he realized he was yelling. He closed his eyes briefly and struggled for control. "Rebecca, I'm sorry."

"No," she said, standing. "You're not. You're still fighting all this, aren't you?"

He didn't answer.

She sighed. "I know it's only been a month, but I thought I was making a difference."

He thought she was, too, but it was too dangerous to admit that.

"I love you, Austin."

He stared at her, the words hanging between them. He couldn't speak.

"I've loved you for a long time," she continued. "I thought it was about my crush, or sex, but it's not. I love you. Flaws and all. Even knowing you might never be able to love me back. I suppose I'm a little crazy. I can't help believing in you."

"Don't," he whispered, backing away from her. "Don't love me. Don't believe. I won't let you."

"Austin, wait."

But it was too late. He stalked out of the room and toward the barn. Instead of entering the building, he walked around it, heading into the trees. He had to be alone. He couldn't let her find him. What if she was able to convince him to believe? No, it couldn't happen. He wouldn't let it.

Adopt David. She was crazy. He would end up destroying the child, just as he'd destroyed everything he loved. What about his own child? What about Rebecca? He didn't want her to love him.

He trekked through the woods, his thoughts going around and around. Nothing was real. Nothing made sense.

The sound of laughter caught his attention. He turned toward the sound. He'd come through the trees to the section that separated the barn and garage from the main house. He could see children playing on the grass. The playground set he'd purchased gleamed in the bright August sun. There were ten or so children, from very young to preteen. They were having fun running around and calling out in the pattern of some intricate game.

He stood outside the circle watching as he always had, as David did. Even as a young boy he'd never fit in. Going from place to place, being dumped where he was never wanted, wondering if his mother would come back for him, praying she wouldn't, praying she would. How confused he'd been. A lonely child. No one had taken the time to know him. Until that day in junior high when Travis had seen past the bully to the scared boy inside. Until Rebecca had believed enough to love him.

He leaned against one of the trees and fought the emotions welling up inside him. He knew what she wanted. A single step of faith. It was so damn hard. But if he didn't take it, he would lose her. He wanted to reach out. He wanted to trust.

Then he remembered even if he did reach out, she would leave, anyway. He would find the one way to drive her from him. As he had with everything he'd ever cared about.

He would never be Wayne—a good, decent man. He would always be the dark loner. In time she would figure that out, as would David. It was better to stay outside the circle. Safer for all of them.

Rebecca tied off the last balloon and attached the ribbon tail. "I miss Austin," she said, staring at the bouquet of balloons she'd spent most of the morning finishing. Streamers flowed down from the high ceiling in the house's giant family room. Most of the furniture had been moved out to clear space for games, although two tables had been pushed against the far wall. One was for the cake and ice cream, the other for presents.

"It is difficult when your husband goes away, leaving you to take care of decorations all by yourself," Elizabeth said, then laughed.

"Okay, I'll admit I miss him for more than his balloon-blowing-up technique, but right now that's most on my mind."

"When does he come back?"

"This afternoon. His plane gets in early enough for him to make it to the party, but I'm not sure he will."

Elizabeth stood up and stretched. Except for her full breasts straining against her T-shirt, she didn't look as if she'd had a baby just a month before.

"I thought Austin liked David," she said.

"He does. It's just difficult to explain." Rebecca grabbed three balloons and walked them to the corner of the table. She bent over and began tying them to the leg. The bright decorations floated in the air. "He's concerned about getting too involved with David, then having him leave when this whole mess with his family is settled."

"Rebecca." Elizabeth joined her. "You'd mentioned something about wanting to adopt David. Did you talk to Austin about that?"

Rebecca secured the knot and straightened. "He doesn't want to."

"I'm sorry."

"It's for the best." She tried to smile, but had a feeling it came out shaky. "At least that's what I keep telling myself. Oh, Elizabeth, I'm so afraid. What if I've made a terrible mistake? I keep trying with Austin. I'm just not sure I'm getting through to him."

"You are." Her friend patted her arm. Her eyes darkened with concern and encouragement. "I know it's hard now, but you have to keep plugging away. Remember what Travis went through with me? He was ready to get married and I didn't even want to see him again. He had to give me time and room to come to my senses. You have to do the same. It's worth it in the end, I promise."

Rebecca glanced down at her wedding band. "But we're already married. I feel as if we've done this whole thing backwards. First we make love, then I get pregnant, then we get married and now we're getting to know each other. I think even a strong relationship would have trouble with that sequence of events, let alone one that's brand-new."

Elizabeth leaned forward and hugged her. She smelled of baby powder. The sweet scent made Rebecca want to cry.

"Give yourself a break. So it's not going perfectly, but it is better, isn't it?"

Rebecca shrugged. "Sometimes I think so. Sometimes I feel like I'm banging my head against the wall."

"You're stronger than any old wall. For what it's worth, I think Austin is desperate to love someone. He just doesn't know how. Show him the way. Keep believing. If not just for yourself, then for your child." Elizabeth glanced at her stomach and grimaced. "I can't stand the fact that you aren't even bloated."

"I am." Rebecca smoothed the front of her dress tight across her midsection. "See?"

Elizabeth snorted in disgust. "I think I'm going to hate you through this pregnancy. You'll probably gain all of fifteen pounds, never get puffy and look perfect two days after giving birth. I'm still fighting to *lose* fifteen pounds and I've been dieting for almost five weeks."

Rebecca grinned. "They must all be in your chest because you look great."

Elizabeth glanced down at the front of her blouse. "Travis is kind of excited about that part. I haven't told him most of it will go away when I stop breast-feeding. I hate to disappoint him." She glanced at her watch. "Speaking of Travis, I've got to run. Little Julia is going to be hungry in about a half hour, and that's one activity Travis can't do for me." She leaned over and kissed Rebecca's cheek. "Hang in there. Keep believing. And if you ever need a break, there's always a room waiting for you at our place."

"Thanks."

Rebecca watched her friend leave, then turned back to the decorations. She was determined to make the party special for David. It was his first one without his family. She'd put the word out in town, and she knew enough about the community of Glenwood to know the people would come through for the little boy. If only Austin would do the same. It would mean so much to David.

She collected another three balloons for the far side of the table. It wasn't all for the child, she admitted. She needed Austin to show up for David because it would give *her* hope for their future. But deep in her bones, she prepared herself to be disappointed. She was beginning to wonder if her husband was ever going to change.

By two-thirty, the party was in full swing. Several people from town had come by to drop off presents for David. The table was stacked high with packages. Some of the children in the home had made him gifts, others had used their candy money to buy something small. Sounds of conversation and laughter filled the room. Despite the hot August afternoon, a lot of the children were outside playing, although the adults stayed in where it was cooler.

Rebecca glanced out the rear bay window and saw David in the center of the activity. For once, he wasn't standing on the outside watching. She breathed a sigh of relief. At least that was going right. Now if only Austin would show up. For the hundredth time in twenty minutes, she checked the door to the family room. Nothing. Then she heard a commotion toward the front of the house. She hurried out, telling herself she was foolish to hope.

As she rounded the corner into the hallway, she saw Kyle setting a large cake on a table by the front door.

"Beware handsome men carrying gifts," he said when he saw her.

"Thanks for getting the cake," she said, trying to keep the disappointment from her voice.

Even so, Kyle must have heard something. He walked over to her and put his arm around her. Brown eyes, as dark as midnight, met her own. He squeezed her hard against him. "You're disappointed because I'm not wearing shorts." He motioned to his jeans. "I know it's difficult for you. You probably spent most of last night dreaming about seeing my legs this afternoon. But in your condition—" he patted her stomach "—I thought the excitement would be too much. I didn't want to be responsible for you fainting away at my feet."

She swatted his arm and stepped out of his embrace. "You have some nerve."

He winked. "Ain't it terrific? Makes you realize you married the wrong man, huh?"

She planted her hands on her hips. "If you ever thought any woman really cared about you, you'd run in the opposite direction."

Kyle's grin faded, leaving him looking devastatingly handsome and just a little lost. "Maybe not."

Rebecca refused to be sucked into a conversation with him. "You always say that when you're between women. Then when you get involved with someone, you can't wait to dump her before she dumps you. What is it about you Haynes men, anyway?"

For a second she thought he might answer her seriously. But that went against Kyle's sense of fun. He bent down and grabbed her around the waist, then raised her in the air and twirled around. "Because us Haynes boys are too good-looking. No one can stand it. That's why you had to marry that sorry dog Austin, instead of me."

"Put me down, you savage."

He lowered her to the floor. "Can you handle the cake? I've got a present for David."

"Sure." She picked up the cake and carried it to the family room. When she set it on the table, she saw David had come inside.

"How are you doing?" she asked him, then straightened his party hat. "Having fun?"

He nodded, but didn't smile. She knew he was missing his family, but he was being a good sport. She gave him a quick hug. "Kyle is here. He's bringing you a present."

"Is Austin home yet?"

"No, honey. He hadn't arrived when I checked an hour ago. He might have had to take a later flight," she said, then told herself it was stupid to lie for Austin. He wouldn't care that she was trying to make him look better to the boy, and it wasn't like her not to tell the truth. Austin would have left a message if he'd taken a later flight. He always told her where he was going to be. No, he was probably already home. He could come to the party if he wanted to.

"Where's the birthday boy?" Kyle asked as he came into the family room. He was holding an impossibly large present. "Someone left this for him in my car." He glanced around. "Rebecca, do you see David?"

David smiled. "I'm right here," he said, crossing to stand directly in front of Kyle.

"Where?" Kyle looked on both sides of him, over his head, then turned and looked behind him. "David? Where is that little guy?"

David giggled. "Kyle, I'm right in front of you."

Kyle looked down. "Oh, there you are. You know you shouldn't hide on your birthday. People might think you didn't want presents." He lowered himself to his knees and placed the huge box on the floor. "Happy birthday, David. This is from me and Jordan."

"Wow!" David plopped down next to him and tore at the wrapping paper. "Thanks. What is it?" He pulled off the large sheet covering the top and stared at the picture of an elaborate train set. "Oh, Kyle! This is so great. Rebecca, look. It's a train!"

She bent down and studied the picture. "It's wonderful." She glanced at Kyle. "It's going to take a lot of work to put it together."

Kyle grinned. "I'm off for the rest of the day. I have tools and stuff in my car. I thought we could work on it tonight after everyone is gone."

"You sound as excited as David."

He shrugged. "Hey, birthdays are for everyone. Glad you like it, David."

The boy gave him a wide grin. "Thanks." The front door opened and closed. He looked up expectantly. One of the men from the town council came into the room. David looked down at the box and bit his lip. Rebecca's heart went out to him. He was waiting for Austin. She said a quick prayer that he wouldn't have to wait very long.

Chapter Fourteen

By the time all the presents had been opened and the cake served, David had given up trying to pretend. Rebecca watched him standing on the edge of a game, observing but not joining in. Several of the children invited him, but he stood stubbornly alone, waiting for the one person who wouldn't come.

He'd asked her once about his uncle. When she'd said she hadn't heard from him, he didn't seem too surprised. Austin was another matter. Over the past couple of months, Austin had become important to the boy. Rebecca fought her anger, knowing it would accomplish nothing. Her husband was acting true to form. She shouldn't be surprised, but she was. She'd hoped he would change.

A loud truck engine broke through her musings. She turned toward the sound. The children stopped their game to watch the large vehicle make its way across the dirt road. Her stomach clenched tightly. She had a bad feeling she knew what this was about.

Two men got out of the cab. "We're looking for a little boy named David," one of them said.

David stepped forward. "I'm David."

The taller of the two jean-clad men grinned. "Happy birthday, son. Someone sent you ponies to ride."

A cheer went up from the children and they all rushed toward the truck. David stood rooted in place. Rebecca walked over to his and put her hand on his shoulder.

"Here." The man thrust out a card. "Let me get 'em unloaded and you can have the first ride."

David turned the card over and over in his small hands. She squeezed him and fought her tears. When he opened the card and read the message, she already knew who had sent the gift.

"They're from Austin," he said, confirming her guess. "He says he's sorry he had to miss the party."

The men led eight ponies from the back of the truck and lined them up. "You ready?" the taller man said, approaching David. "We've got a special pony for you."

Rebecca felt his body stiffen. "I don't want to ride any dumb pony," he said, and threw down the card. He turned and ran toward the house. She took a step toward him, then stopped. He needed some time alone. She would give him a few minutes, then see how he was doing.

"Is there a problem, ma'am?" the man asked.

She shook her head. "He's thrilled about the ponies. It's just he thought someone important to him was going to come to the party and he didn't. Go ahead and start with the other children."

She watched the first kids being placed on the back of the docile animals. Oh, Austin, she thought. You really blew it this time.

She looked back at the house, then at the woods separating this property from the barn. Quickly making up her mind, she called out to Mary that she would be gone for a few minutes, then she headed through the trees toward the loft.

As she passed the garage, she glanced inside. Austin's Mercedes and truck were parked next to the new wagon. He *was* home. She cursed him under her breath, then felt embarrassed by her own use of swear words. That man was a bad influence on all of them, she thought, making her way to the barn and opening the front door.

"Austin Lucas, what do you think you're doing?" she called as she marched up the stairs.

"Rebecca?"

When she reached the second floor, she could see him standing by the bed unpacking. He turned to face her. "What's wrong?"

She laughed harshly and planted her hands on her hips. "You're asking me what's wrong? Typical. You create a problem, then you don't want to deal with it."

He put the jeans he was holding on the bed, then shoved his hands into his pockets. "What are you talking about?"

"David."

He frowned. "Look, I'm tired. There was a thunderstorm last night. I didn't get any sleep. I had to get up early to catch my flight and I just got in. I thought about what happened before and I sent him a present. It should be arriving at any time."

"It's already here."

"So what's the problem? Are you telling me David doesn't want to ride a pony on his birthday?"

"Yes. That's exactly what I'm telling you." She shook her head. "Why can't you see what's right in front of you? It's not the gift. He's got plenty of presents. This is his first birthday without his family. He's lonely and scared about the future. You're the one person who's gotten through to him. He doesn't care about any ponies. He wants to see you. He wants to hear you wish him happy birthday and give him a hug. He wants to know you care."

Austin turned back to the bed and dumped the remaining contents out of his suitcase. "What makes you think I care?" he asked, zipping up the sides.

"You make me want to scream," she said, holding her arms out in front of her. "Why are you so stubborn? What is so terrible about admitting to having any gentle feelings? It won't hurt, I promise. He's just a small boy. He needs you."

"I'm tired," he said coldly, and walked to the closet concealed in the wall.

She stepped closer to the bed. "Damn you, Austin, don't you dare turn away from me. Who did it? Who beat it out of you? Who made you think you had to be hard to survive? Why isn't it okay to care? Why isn't it okay to love someone?"

He slammed the door shut and glared at her. "Love is a myth, just a line men use to trap women into sex and women use to trap men into marriage. It doesn't mean a damn thing. It never has."

There was a darkness in his gray eyes, a determination she hadn't seen before. It was as if he'd found a way to shut the door in her face, and he was never going to open it again.

He didn't believe anymore—if he ever had. Not in David's feelings for him, or hers. Her promise of love had meant nothing to him.

"Then that's it," she said. "You're not going to come see him."

"No."

They stood staring at each other, poised like characters in a play. She prayed for a sign that she hadn't made the worst mistake of her life. God chose not to oblige.

An iciness settled over her, freezing her blood and opening a crevice in her soul. It didn't matter what she'd said or how she'd tried to convince him of her feelings and her commitment. He didn't care. He didn't believe. He was and always had been a stranger. She'd created a facade and put it over the real man. It had all been make-believe.

Without saying another word she walked away, down the stairs and out into the bright August afternoon. The heat of the sun should have warmed her, but she didn't feel anything except cold.

What had she done? What was she going to do? A part of her said to keep trying, but her heart whispered it had always been too late.

It was dusk when Austin made his way over to the house. He hadn't seen Rebecca since she'd stormed out of the barn. He couldn't blame her. He'd been a real jerk. The funny part was he'd done it on purpose.

When he came out of the grove of trees, he looked around. The children had long since gone inside. He looked down at the shoebox-size package in his hand. This was his real present. If David still wanted it.

He stared at the big house knowing he didn't have the courage to walk up there and knock on the door. He couldn't face Rebecca right now. Not knowing what she thought of him.

He started to turn back when a flash of color caught his eye. He stepped to the left and saw David sitting alone under a tree in the backyard. His red shorts and red-and-white shirt looked much the worse for wear. Stains covered the fabric, grass, punch and something that looked like chocolate cake.

So the kid had had a great birthday, he told himself. David probably hadn't even noticed he hadn't shown up.

Yeah, right, he thought, wondering when he'd stooped low enough to start lying to himself.

He walked around the house to the backyard. David was staring at the ground. The slump of his shoulders hit Austin in the gut. He'd stayed away out of fear. Because he wasn't man enough to face a little boy. He deserved to be shot.

"Happy birthday," he said quietly.

David snapped his head up. His blue eyes widened, then he scrambled to his feet and raced across the lawn. "Austin!" he yelled, holding out his arms.

Austin dropped the package, bent down to gather the boy close to him, then pulled him up to his chest. "Hey, sport, how's it going?"

David wrapped his thin legs around Austin's waist and buried his head in his shoulder. "You came. You really came."

"It's your birthday, isn't it? I wouldn't want to miss that for anything."

The boy clung tighter, hanging on as if he never wanted to let go. Austin absorbed the slight weight, wondering why he'd worried it would be a burden. Then David raised his head and looked at him. "I was scared you'd be too busy." His lower lip trembled. "My uncle Bob couldn't come. I didn't miss him like I missed you." He sniffed. "And my parents. I tried really hard not to miss them. But kept 'membering." He choked on a sob. "I want my mommy and daddy."

Tears poured down his face. Austin wrapped his arms around the boy and held him closer. With one hand, he stroked his back, then his head. "It's okay to cry, David," he said, his own voice a little froggy. "I understand."

Hell, who better? He knew exactly what it was like to be left alone on birthdays and other holidays. His mother had done it to him countless times. Once he'd gathered his courage together and the next time he'd seen her after his birthday, he'd asked her if she'd remembered he'd turned nine. She'd looked back at him and snapped, "No. And I didn't get you a damn present, either, so shut up about it."

That was twenty-six years ago and the words still had the power to hurt him.

The child's sobs tore at his heart, reminding him of all the times he hadn't let himself cry. Crying was weak. It let his mother know she'd won. Silence had been his only victory.

Still holding David, he crouched down and picked up the present, then made his way over to the tree where the boy had been sitting. Austin lowered himself to the ground and arranged David on his lap. The sobs had lessened, but not let up completely. Austin continued to hold him, murmuring occasional words of comfort, wishing he knew what else to do.

Rebecca wanted to adopt this boy and bring him into their family. He was probably better off in the home. At least there he was around adults who knew what they were doing. They weren't as broken and flawed inside. They wouldn't thoughtlessly wound him.

Austin leaned his head against the tree and studied the sky. Could he learn to be a father? Did he want to? Was his desire to have Rebecca walk away and take the baby with her just a way for him to cover his feelings of inadequacy?

He shook his head. He was right not to get involved. Look at how he'd hurt David today. This was just one event in a child's life. There were thousands, and he had the potential to screw up every single one of them. He couldn't risk it. It wasn't fair to any kid.

David's sobs faded to sniffles. "Austin, are you mad at me?"

"No, why?"

"'Cause you didn't come to my party before. Did I mess up the airplane bad?"

"No. You did a wonderful job. I'm proud of you."

David sighed and leaned against him. "So you're not mad?"

Austin swallowed hard. Even though Rebecca had told him what David was feeling, he hadn't wanted to believe her. Now he knew the truth. He could walk away from this boy, leaving him with the same type of wounds his mother had inflicted on him, or he could speak the words and start the healing. The former was all he knew how to do. The latter left *him* open to pain.

But David was only a little boy.

"I was never mad," Austin said slowly, staring out into the night. "Sometimes I don't want to know that people care about me. It's hard for me to let people like me. When they do it makes me uncomfortable."

"'Cause you don't like 'em back," David said, his voice very small.

"No!" Austin looked down and cupped the boy's chin in one of his hands. "No. Because I *do* like you back. It scares me."

"Why?"

It sounded too dumb for words, yet of anyone, David would understand. "I'm always afraid if I care about people too much, they'll go away."

David nodded. "Like my mom and dad."

"Yes. But if you don't care, no one ever loves you. You don't get to love anyone back. You spend your life alone. It's safe, but it's not right."

"You're not alone, Austin," David said with the confidence of youth. "You've got Rebecca."

He wasn't so sure anymore. But that wasn't for the boy to worry about. "I'm sorry I missed your party. I didn't mean to hurt you."

David smiled up at him. "I understand. I'm glad you came now." He thought for a minute. "Oh, thanks for the ponies."

Austin remembered the package he'd brought over with him. He reached around the tree and held it out. "This is for you. Happy birthday."

David grinned and tore at the wrappings. When he raised the lid on the box, he stared at the rows of woodworking tools. "Golly, look at this."

"They're scaled down so they'll be easier to work with," Austin said, absorbing the boy's wide smile and the light in his eyes. "You'll have to be careful, though, and only use them with supervision. We never did finish that birdhouse. I thought you might want to bring them over tomorrow and we'll get to work."

David reached up and flung his arms around Austin's neck. He squeezed hard. "I love you," he whispered. "I knew you'd remember me. I knew you wouldn't forget."

"I'll never forget," Austin promised.

"When I'm gone, will you write me?"

Austin pulled him back and stared at him. "What are you talking about?"

David shrugged and stared at his new tools. "I was in the hallway the other night and I heard Mary tellin' someone that my family is going to send me to a boarding school. I don't know where." He looked up hopefully. "Will you write?"

"Yes," Austin promised. He touched the boy's face, his hair, then finally pulled him against his chest and held on. "I'll write."

David chattered about his party and all the presents he'd received. His voice got slower and slower, until he fell asleep. Austin continued to hold him, to listen to his soft breathing. It was happening again. The family would send David to a school and forget about him. They would abandon him until it came time to move him somewhere else. He would never be wanted, never have a home, never know what it was like to be loved.

It was already starting. David had so easily resigned himself to his fate. Austin raised his gaze to the heavens and silently screamed at a world that would allow this tragedy to occur again.

It was close to midnight when he made his way back to the barn. He'd delivered David to bed, then spent an hour with

Kyle setting up the train set. If the other man had noticed his lack of conversation, he had never let on.

Austin climbed the stairs quietly, thinking Rebecca might be asleep. When he reached the loft, he saw her sitting in the living room. A lamp shone from the corner, but other than that it was dark.

"You were gone when I got back," she said.

"I went to see David." He sat across from her in the wing chair. She was curled up in a corner of the sofa. The large cushions looked as if they could swallow her whole. "We talked about my missing his party. I guess we made up."

"I'm glad."

He leaned forward and rested his elbows on his knees, lacing his fingers together. "He said that his family wants to send him to a boarding school."

"I know."

"Is that why you want to adopt him?"

"I wanted *us* to adopt him," she said, "because I thought we could give him a warm and loving home. I knew about their plans. Given the choice between being shuffled between unwilling relatives and the stable environment of a boarding school, the school comes out ahead in my book."

"I agree."

"Finally. We're in accord about something."

He hated the bitterness in her voice. "I'm sorry, Rebecca."

She pulled her knees closer to her chest. "Are you? About what?"

"About everything."

"That's nice and general. It's clean, tidy, covers everything without your having to admit to any wrong. I'm impressed."

"Don't be sarcastic," he said, staring at her.

"Why? I'm trying to speak to you on your level. I thought you'd appreciate it."

"Don't be like me."

"Be careful, Austin," she said, tossing her head. Her hair settled around her shoulders. "Someone might make the mistake of believing you actually cared. You wouldn't want that to happen. It would be a calamity. The earth might have to open up and swallow us whole."

He rose to his feet. "Stop it."

"Why? Aren't I being the perfect, loving little wife anymore? Do you miss her? I have news for you, pal. This is what it's like living with you. Nothing matters, not feelings or people. It's all just a game. You hide, then try to destroy anyone who is stupid enough to go looking for you." She sighed and dropped her forehead to her knees. "You win. I'm done playing."

He flinched as if she'd slapped him. "You're leaving." It wasn't a question.

"I don't know." She raised her head and met his gaze. He saw the pain in her beautiful eyes, the hurt and disillusionment he'd put there. "I want to believe it's going to be okay. I want to trust that I can win you over, but I don't know anymore." She shook her head. "I assumed loving you was enough, but it isn't, is it?"

"No," he said hoarsely.

"I thought as much. You have to love me back. You're not going to."

He didn't say anything. He couldn't. Love her back. Oh, God, and then what? Trust her? Trust that it was going to last? Trust that she could know the darkest, ugliest part of him and still be there every day? No, it wasn't possible.

He walked over to the window and stared out into the darkness.

"What do you see there?" she asked. "What do you stare at? The past? Do you relive those lonely times over and over again? Do you ever see me? Hear my voice? Do you ever allow yourself to believe?"

"I try," he whispered, fighting the emptiness clawing at him.

"But you don't yet."

"No."

He heard her sigh. The reflection from the lamp allowed him to watch her stand up and walk close to him. When she was directly behind him, he felt her hands on his back.

"I had this dream of a fairy-tale wedding," she said. "I wanted to wear a beautiful white dress and be surrounded by all my friends and family. I wanted to be in a church filled with roses and sunlight, and ringing with the sounds of laughter and happiness. I wanted to marry my prince there, ride off on a white horse and live happily ever after."

His chest tightened, making it hard to breathe. "Then Wayne died and you lost your dream."

"Wayne? No, Austin. You were the prince in that dream of mine." She leaned against his back and wrapped her arms around his waist. He stiffened at the contact, but she didn't pull away. "It was always you. From the very beginning. Despite everything, I love you. I'll always love you. Even knowing the secret you try to hide."

"No." He turned quickly and grabbed her wrists, setting her away from him. "You don't know anything." Her gaze held his. Love and light radiated from her face, hurting his eyes, but he couldn't look away.

"You're wrong," she said. "I figured it out. I thought it was about the way you watched me with the children. I thought you needed me to touch you and hold you, but that was only a symptom. The problem isn't that you're not worth the trouble. The problem is you believe you're not worth loving. But you are. You're kind and gentle. Generous. You treat me like I'm the most precious thing you've seen. You hold me in the darkness, you fight for me, you believe in me and what I want. The only part of me you won't accept is the part that loves you. Watch out, Austin. That's all of me. Every cell of my being is filled with love for you. You can't yell it out of me. You can't make me stop loving you."

She pulled her wrists free of his grasp and touched his face. He jerked back as if burned. She smiled sadly. "Be careful, though. You can't make me not love you, but you can drive me away."

With that she turned and headed for the stairs. He watched her go, wanting to call her back, but unable to form the words. He felt as if his world had shifted on its axis. Nothing was as he'd thought it should be.

Rebecca knew. Somehow she'd figured out the truth. That he wasn't worth loving. That he had a flaw so horrible even his own mother had recoiled from him. And yet Rebecca claimed to love him. It wasn't possible. He wouldn't let it be. He couldn't.

If he believed she loved him now, he would have to admit how much he needed that love. He would have to stare into the face of his empty life and know the suffering he'd endured. Better to turn his back on it all. Better to be alone than to risk it all.

He watched from the window, but she didn't appear. At least she hadn't gone for one of the cars. He closed his eyes and steadied his breathing. The silence surrounded him, pressing against his body. It deafened him.

There was a time when he'd enjoyed the silence. That was before his life had been filled with the sounds of Rebecca. Now the quiet tormented him. He would get used to it again, he told himself. He would have to if he was to survive without her.

Outside the circle. Alone. He'd been happy there. Outside the circle, where David now stood. But the boy wasn't happy. He hadn't learned how to pretend it didn't matter that he didn't fit in. How to pretend he wasn't in agony with every breath, knowing he would live out his days in mind-destroying silence.

"Rebecca," he whispered. Oh, God, what if it was too late?

He raced across the room and tore down the stairs. When he reached the foyer, he ripped open the door and stared out into the night, searching for her.

"Rebecca," he called.

"Austin? I'm right here." She sat on the steps, looking up at him. "What's wrong?"

"I thought you were gone." He was panting, barely able to get the words out.

"I was going to take a walk, but I'm too tired."

He leaned down and brought her to her feet. Tightly holding both of her hands, he said, "Don't leave me."

She sighed. "I was being melodramatic. I'm sorry. I won't leave you, despite your lack of belief in us. I love you, Austin. I'm going to keep saying it until you believe me."

He released her hands and cupped her face. He'd been given another chance. A last chance. It wasn't too late. "You are so beautiful," he whispered. "I love you, Rebecca Lucas. I love you with my heart and soul, such as they are. Don't leave me. Please. I would never survive the silence."

"Austin?"

He bent down and kissed her. Softly, tenderly, his lips pressing against hers. She trembled in his embrace.

"Austin, you're not kidding, are you?"

He smiled. "No. I've been frightened of caring, but I'm more frightened of losing you forever. Of not seeing our child. I don't know what kind of husband and father I'm going to be, but I'll do my best."

"You're a damn fine husband," she said, holding him close. "The best."

"Rebecca?"

"Hmm?"

He kissed the top of her head, then her nose. "You're far too innocent to swear."

"I was trying to relate to you on your level." In the moonlight, he saw her smile.

"I love you," he said again.

Her smile broadened. "I'll never get tired of hearing those words. The way you've fought me on this, you'd think I was asking for blood. It's not so hard, is it?"

"No," he answered, lowering his mouth to hers. Now that he believed, loving her, being loved by her, was going to be the easiest thing he'd ever done.

Epilogue

The church was filled with white roses and sunlight. The sounds of laughter and happiness stretched up to the arched ceiling of the old building.

Rebecca stood at the altar, with her husband at her side. Her two sisters, her parents and Elizabeth stood on her left. Travis and his brothers stood on Austin's right. In front of them, the minister cradled their newborn son.

As the Reverend Johnson touched the holy water to the baby's forehead and proclaimed him to be christened Austin Jason Lucas—Austin after his father, Jason after his mother's father—Rebecca had to fight back her tears. She sniffed softly. Austin reached for her hand and squeezed it. She smiled at him and wondered what she'd done to deserve such happiness.

Everything was working out wonderfully, she thought as her eyes grew misty. The new home had been built for the children. She and Austin had remodeled his big house and were moving in this weekend. Their son had been born healthy and perfect, with his father's gray eyes and his mother's smile.

The reverend handed her back her son, then bowed his head for the final blessing.

The audience of well-wishers crowded around them. Austin accepted the attention easily. In the past few months he'd grown more comfortable with the people in town, more willing to be a part of the community.

"That was wonderful, dear," her mother said, giving Rebecca a hug. "Little Jason was perfect. Weren't you, sweetie?" She touched the baby's cheek.

Elizabeth congratulated her next. Julia observed the celebration solemnly from her mother's arms. "At least they're close enough in age to play together," Elizabeth said.

"Just eight months apart." Rebecca smiled. "Maybe they'll grow up and get married."

Travis came through the crowd to find his wife. "Matchmaking already? Don't you think they're a little young?"

"No," the two women said together, then laughed.

Rebecca looked around for Austin, but he was lost in the crowd. She raised herself on tiptoe trying to see him. Kyle came up to her.

"I just wanted to say congratulations," he said. "I can't come to the house for lunch."

"Why?" Rebecca asked, narrowing her gaze. Kyle had the oddest expression on his face.

"I have to help a friend move."

"*Friend?* Why do I know this friend is a female?"

Instead of teasing her about his prowess with women, Kyle simply looked uncomfortable. "It's not like that," he said. "Sandy is a friend of the family. All my brothers know her. I thought she'd left Glenwood for good, but she's moving back. I just want to help."

There was an earnestness about him she'd never seen before. "She sounds like a special lady."

Kyle bent down and kissed her cheek. "Yeah, she is. Or at least she used to be. I haven't seen her since I was sixteen. Take care of little Jason here and yourself. I'm glad you're happy."

She smiled at him. "You be happy, too."

"I am." But his dark eyes were tinged with sadness, the way Travis's had been before he'd had the good sense to fall in love with Elizabeth. What was it about these Haynes men?

Rebecca watched Kyle leave, then turned to search for her husband again. She saw him on the outside of the crowd. He didn't notice her. He was looking around at all the people. She waited, knowing he wouldn't stay outside the circle. In the past few months, he'd allowed himself to love and be loved by her. He'd become the warm, tender man she'd always dreamed of. He'd changed.

Austin stared into the crowd, then ducked low. When he straightened, he had David in his arms. He stepped into the throng and began working his way toward her. She met his gaze and smiled, then focused on the eight-year-old boy who was talking animatedly. The adoption had been finalized earlier that week. She glanced at the baby in her arms and knew they really were a family.

Austin stepped around a young couple, then moved next to her. She held out her free arm and embraced him.

"I love you," he said quietly.

"For how long?" she teased, glancing up at him. His gray eyes held her own. "Just for today?"

"For always," he promised. "You and David and Jason. Forever."

He lowered his mouth to hers and kissed her. She clung to him, savoring the sweetness, trusting in the future. Austin had stepped inside the circle of their love to stay.

* * * * *

Get Ready to be Swept Away by
Silhouette's Spring Collection

Abduction
& Seduction

These passion-filled stories explore both the dangerous
desires of men and the seductive powers of women.
Written by three of our most celebrated authors, they are
sure to capture your hearts.

Diana Palmer
Brings us a spin-off of her Long, Tall Texans series

Joan Johnston
Crafts a beguiling Western romance

Rebecca Brandewyne
New York Times bestselling author
makes a smashing contemporary debut

Available in March at your favorite retail outlet.

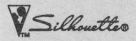

WHAT EVER HAPPENED TO...?

Have you been wondering when much-loved characters will finally get their own stories? Well, have we got a lineup for you! Silhouette Special Edition is proud to present a *Spin-off Spectacular!* Be sure to catch these exciting titles from some of your favorite authors:

HUSBAND: SOME ASSEMBLY REQUIRED (SE #931 January) Shawna Saunders has finally found Mr. Right in the dashing Murphy Pendleton, last seen in *Marie Ferrarella*'s BABY IN THE MIDDLE (SE #892).

SAME TIME, NEXT YEAR (SE #937 February) In this tie-in to *Debbie Macomber*'s popular series THOSE MANNING MEN and THOSE MANNING SISTERS, a yearly reunion between friends suddenly has them in the marrying mood!

A FAMILY HOME (SE #938 February) Adam Cutler discovers the best reason for staying home is the love he's found with sweet-natured and sexy Lainey Bates in *Celeste Hamilton*'s follow-up to WHICH WAY IS HOME? (SE #897).

JAKE'S MOUNTAIN (SE #945 March) Jake Harris never met anyone as stubborn—or as alluring—as Dr. Maggie Matthews in *Christine Flynn*'s latest, a spin-off to WHEN MORNING COMES (SE #922).

Don't miss these wonderful titles, only for our readers—only from Silhouette Special Edition!

A ROSE AND A WEDDING VOW (SE #944)
by Andrea Edwards

Matt Michaelson returned home to face Liz—his brother's widow…a woman he'd never forgotten. Could falling in love with *this* Michaelson man heal the wounds of Liz's lonely past?

A ROSE AND A WEDDING VOW, SE #944 (3/95), is the next story in this stirring trilogy by Andrea Edwards. THIS TIME, FOREVER—sometimes a love is so strong, nothing can stand in its way, not even time. Look for the last installment, A SECRET AND A BRIDAL PLEDGE, in May 1995.

THE SULTAN'S WIVES
Tracy Sinclair
(SE #943, March)

When a story in an exotic locale beckoned, nothing could
keep Pippa Bennington from scooping the
competition. But this time, her eager journalist's heart landed
her squarely in, of all things, a harem!
Pippa was falling for the seductive charms of
Mikolar al-Rasheed—but what exactly *were* the
sultan's true intentions?

Don't miss
THE SULTAN'S WIVES,
by Tracy Sinclair,
available in March!

She's friend, wife, mother—she's you! And beside each
Special Woman stands a wonderfully
special man. It's a celebration of our heroines—
and the men who become part of their lives.

SILHOUETTE... Where Passion Lives

Don't miss these Silhouette favorites by some of our most distinguished authors! And now you can receive a discount by ordering two or more titles!